Tempus Fugitive

The Tamar Black Saga - Book Three

I0666666

By Nicola Rhodes

IBSN: 978-0-9561495-2-7

In the same series
Djinnx'd
Reality Bites
Tempus Fugitive
The Day Before Tomorrow
Faerie Tale
Anything But Ordinary
Rise of the Nephilim
Pantheon

And I saw another mighty angel come down from heaven, clothed with a cloud: and a rainbow was upon his head, and his face was as if it were the sun, and his feet were as pillars of fire: and he had in his hand a little book open: and he set his right foot upon the sea, and his left foot on the earth, and cried with a loud voice, as when a lion roareth: and when he had cried, seven thunders uttered their voices. And when the seven thunders had uttered their voices, I was about to write: and I heard a voice from heaven saying unto me, 'Seal up those things which the seven thunders uttered, and write them not.'

And the angel which I saw stand upon the sea and upon the earth lifted his hand to heaven, and sware by him that liveth for ever and ever, who created heaven, and the things that therein are, and the earth, and the things that therein are, and the sea, and the things which are therein, that there should be time no longer.

REVELATION. X. 1-6.

The nature of man is evil; his goodness is acquired.

Xun Zi, Warring States Period.

~ Author's Preface ~

It is not recommended that you read this story without having read the preceding novels, (for which I can honestly claim world-wide readership – since a copy of 'Djinnx'd' was once carried, with the title clearly visible, in the back pocket of chap who went all the way round the world on a folding motor scooter.) However, if you have bought this book because you liked the cover or just picked up this copy on a train, then the next few pages might make what follows slightly less confusing.

The story so far ...

Many years ago (around five thousand give or take, but who's counting?) young Tamar lived in Ancient Greece (Or "Greece", as it was known then) she found a bottle and released a Djinn (a type of demon, known these days as Genies) who played on her foolish greed and tricked her into taking his place. She wishes for Djinn like powers and gets them, at a price – becoming a Djinn herself and being trapped in the bottle as a slave.

Fast forward five thousand years and Tamar becomes the slave of Denny, who, despite appearances, is a hero. Denny decides to help Tamar free herself, and they embark on a quest together, to find the Djinn who trapped her in the first place.

During the quest Tamar and Denny become close – but not as close as they would have liked, due to the strength of Tamar's powers, which can kill at a touch.

The quest is ultimately successful. (If you want to know the details, buy the flaming book) and Askphrit (the Djinn) becomes trapped in the bottle again. Tamar retains her Djinn like powers in deference to the laws of wishcraft. Unfortunately, this means that, even though she is now technically human, she and Denny are still unable to be together.

With Tamar's powers and Denny's heroic tendencies, they naturally become heroic vigilantes, and together she and Denny embark on a scheme to free all Djinn and make them mortal. But when Tamar decides to free Askphrit in this same manner, without telling Denny what she is doing, the results are catastrophic.

*

It is one year later, and Denny begins to have a recurring nightmare, is someone trying to tell him something? In the dream, the world is covered in darkness and people are dying. At the same time, both he and Tamar become aware that they are being distracted from something big that is going on.

When a hostage situation goes wrong, Tamar meets a strange pale man who frightens her, she does not tell Denny why.

Detective Inspector Jack Stiles is being followed by a mysterious hooded stranger, whom a Cabal of unknown origin has sent after him. When a team of marauding vampires captures him, the mysterious stranger rescues him and is revealed to be a girl with extraordinary powers. They are pretty much in the middle of nowhere and have to make their way back on foot through a snowy and mountainous region.

Denny is alone, Tamar having gone away on a mission. He is worried about her; she should have been back by now.

He sets off to try to find her and has an adventure of his own. He is captured by vampires and taken to an old house in the middle of the countryside, which is mysteriously shrouded in darkness for about a mile around. Here he finds a great treasure; a demon-forged dagger called an Athame, which he uses to escape. This Athame gives him demonic powers, similar to Tamar's but not as strong – Tamar's powers are also technically demonic. He uses the Athame to get back home.

Meanwhile Tamar has revealed to Stiles who she really is, and they have discovered from a captured vampire that Stiles is under sentence of death by the vampire god Ran-Kur. She has also worked out that they are trapped somehow in an alternate reality, with no way to get out. Nevertheless, she teleports them to Denny's London flat to prove her point.

Denny, sensing their presence because of the Athame uses his new gift to release them, but he does not tell them that it was he who did it. Nor does he mention the Athame to them at all.

Denny then starts exhibiting some uncharacteristic behaviour, when it becomes apparent to him that Stiles has a crush on Tamar, for example, the usually laid back and gentle Denny threatens to kill him. He does, however, find the prophecy relating to Stiles, which implicates him in the destruction of all vampires. This would tend to explain why they want him dead. He also discovers a way to kill a god, after they decide that with Ran-Kur gone the threat to Stiles will be lifted, since the vampires are under his control.

At this point, the pale man who worried Tamar reappears and reveals that he is a vampire called Peirce. He tells them that he does not believe in the prophecy and that he thinks it is just a method of control that someone is using. He does not believe in Ran-Kur either; he wants to help, he says. They do not trust him and trap him in a bottle when he dematerialises into smoke.

In order to kill Ran-Kur they have to find a mythological creature known as the "Purple Hart". Denny comes across this information in another mysterious dream.

Thus, using information found on the magical Internet, they set off on a quest. On the way, they pick up a witch, Cindy, whom they found earlier, in case they needed a witch to summon Hecaté the goddess of witches to help them kill Ran-Kur. They summoned her without Cindy's help. But Hecaté refused to help.

They need Cindy now, as the quest begins with the search for the old witch of the caves, and only a witch knows how to find her.

In the caves, the old witch sends Tamar, Stiles and Cindy on the quest but refuses Denny. After they have gone, Denny uses the Athame to kill the witch and take her power. He then goes back to the world, which is by now plunged into darkness, just like in his dream. Vampires are roaming the streets at will and Denny divides his time between hunting them down and killing them, and gathering ingredients for another summoning spell to use on Ran-Kur when the others return.

While on the quest they meet an assortment of weird beings including a shape shifter called Eugene, who they take along with them.

The quest completed, Tamar summons Ran-Kur and dispatches him, almost losing her own life in the process.

They then realise that something is wrong. The darkness has not lifted; the power behind it is still out there.

They decide that the power must reside in the house that Denny was taken to, and they release Peirce so that he can lead them there.

He leads them through an invisible portal that vampires use to travel, and they break into the house, with Cindy's help. She calls upon Hecaté to break the darkness and scatter the vampires, who, obviously, do not do well in sunlight. The others are impressed, but Cindy admits that it was not her own power that did it.

Once inside, they find some grisly dungeons populated by humans. It is, according to Peirce, a sort of larder. In one of the cells, they find, to their surprise, that Hecaté is imprisoned. The, chains forged by Hephaestus, hold her and even the Athame cannot break them. Stiles offers to stay with her.

Hecaté tells them that it was not she who answered their summons and that she has been chained up by the one the vampires call "The Master" for many months.

Tamar and Denny realise that they have been duped.

Following Peirce they enter the great hall and confront "The Master" who Tamar recognises as none other than Askphrit himself.

Denny then turns on Tamar, plunging the Athame into her heart and draining her power. He ranges himself by Askphrit who imprisons Tamar in a magical cage before beginning his dénouement.

He explains how, after 30 years as a miserable mortal, brooding on his wrongs, he found a sorcerer to send him back in time. This sorcerer had obtained the codes to mainframe, the core of the universal matrix. Askphrit took the codes and killed the sorcerer. He then went back to find his former self and cut a deal to regain his powers. This action caused a major split in reality. In one, vampires flourished under the leadership of Askphrit posing as Ran-Kur, while in the other, they dwindled away. While in the past, Askphrit wrote the prophecy relating to Stiles in order to lure Tamar into killing the real Ran-Kur, thus transferring his god like status to Askphrit. The Athame he had obtained in order to give to Denny in order to corrupt him. It had to be him, as the only person Tamar trusted enough to let him get near enough to destroy her. Askphrit knew he did not have the power to do this himself.

At this point, Denny turns on Askphrit and plunges the Athame into his heart. The cage around Tamar vanishes and she is, rather confusingly, revealed to be Denny. Denny turns into Tamar; they had glamoured into each other, Tamar explains.

Firstly, the Athame had not corrupted Denny for long, because Tamar had discovered it and had taken it away to be blessed.

They had become each other in order to lure Askphrit into a false sense of security, leaving Tamar free to deal with him, while he believed his plan had worked.

At this point, the thwarted and enraged Askphrit makes a break for it. He escapes into the past, using his knowledge of the codes to mainframe. Without the codes, Tamar and Denny are helpless to go after him.

Although he has now lost his Djinn powers, he is still a god, and capable of causing a lot of trouble in the past.

Tamar and Denny decide to stay on in the house instead of returning to London. Part of the reason for this is to see if they cannot find the codes to mainframe and go after him.

I told you, you should have read the other books.

Now, if you can be bothered, read on…

For Jen, who can always be bothered to read on.

~ Prologue ~

To call the room badly lit was like saying that the past is behind us – pretty obvious really. But it all depends on your point of view.

The shady characters around the table did not think the room badly lit. As far as they were concerned, it was just the right amount of lit. They were aware, also, that the past is not necessarily behind us – not if you have the codes to the archives of history in the mainframe of the universal matrix. And somebody did. A dangerous lunatic, who would cause no end of trouble if he were not stopped, and there was only one person who could do it.'

'We have no choice,' said the tall thin man, who was clearly leading the meeting. (You could tell by his authoritative manner – and his funny hat.)

'We have to give her the codes so that she can go after him.'

There was a chorus of dissent; these were cautious men – if they *were* men

'We cannot.'

'We *must* not.'

'It is not for us to interfere.'

The thin man waved a hand for silence. 'We have *already* interfered,' he said, 'now we must help to put things right. Think! Imagine the damage he will do. Why, he might destroy the world. Do you think he would care? All he cares about is his revenge on she who took away his powers as a Djinn and destroyed his plans. He will do anything to achieve his objective, and *we* are to blame. We are the ones who let this thing get out of hand. Had we not played his game for him, he would never have got this far.'

There were some murmurs of agreement.

'We sent her after him. Because of us, she killed the vampire's god, the one they called Ran-Kur, and transferred his power to the lunatic. We allowed him to fool her because we allowed him to fool us – *us*!' he thundered. 'And by God, we *are* going to help her to stop him. Tamar Black is our only hope now.'

One figure tentatively raised a hand. 'Um ...?'

'Yes Sligo, what is it?'

'Well sir, it's just that ... er – well the thing is, we were wondering, you see, do we really think that she is the best person for the job? She's so impulsive, you see,' he paused nervously and looked around for backup. He got none. The leader looked at him in thunderous silence. He gulped and plunged on. 'All I meant was that, well, last time she made so many mistakes ...'

'The mistakes were ours also, Sligo, as I believe I have already pointed out.'

'Yes sir, quite! But then she got mortals involved, sir, rather irresponsible we, er – I thought,'

'You thought so, did you?' the leader frowned. Sligo cowered. The others tried to look as if they had nothing to do with anything at all, in any way whatsoever and had never seen the unfortunate Sligo in their lives before.

'All right, all right,' said the leader, 'now listen to me, if you are referring to the involvement of the policeman, Stiles. He was *already* involved, if you remember? She rescued him from the vampires that our lunatic friend had sent after him. He wrote the prophecy himself. A fact that even we did not pick up on until it was too late. If you are referring to the unfortunate involvement of the witch – well we all make mistakes. Besides, it turned out well enough. In any event, I do not intend to justify my decision to you. Indeed no other choice is before us. She is the only one who can do it, and, more importantly, she is the only one who *will*.'

'But, how do we *know* she will go after him?'

'She will. She will have no choice. If she does not, he will take his revenge. It has already begun.'

PART ONE: TIME HOPPING

~ **Chapter One** ~

BOMBS WERE WHISTLING down from the sky. The streets were deserted. 'Very prudent,' the stranger thought. However, it would not be difficult to make it seem like an accident.

This suited his sense of style; a murder was such an untidy thing, so completely without finesse. In any case, the people who counted would see his hand in what had happened.

Yes, this was much better, so much more elegant and satisfactory. Now he just had to find his man.

He was probably in a bomb shelter somewhere; he was a cowardly type, hadn't he avoided the draft? Very different from his descendant – that cursed nuisance.

Now the only question was: was it a communal bomb shelter or a private one? He headed out to the man's address to find out.

* * *

'I think that's about it,' said Denny with satisfaction.

'The house looks beautiful,' agreed Tamar. 'You wouldn't think it was the same place.'

'Well, letting some sunlight in didn't hurt.'

'It *should* look good; it took long enough. I don't know why you insisted on doing it all manually, though, even the garden.'

'What else did we have to do? Besides it's more satisfying to do it yourself, it gives you a sense of accomplishment.'

'Don't preach, admit it, you were just bored.'

'We should have a housewarming party,' he said, changing the subject.

'For our *vast* number of friends?' she said, sarcastically.

'Well, there's Jack and Hecaté, and Cindy and Eugene, and we should invite the neighbours, from the village down there. After all, we did rid the place of all the vampires – they should be *pleased* to welcome us. Besides, that's what a housewarming is for, to meet your new neighbours.'

'You're really enjoying this aren't you?'

'What?'

'Having a home of your own.'

'Yeah, why not, aren't you?'

Tamar smiled sheepishly. 'Yes, I am I suppose,' she admitted. 'Okay, a party. But I'm not doing the catering without using magic, I'm sick of doing everything the mortal way, it's so *slow*.'

They wandered out into their new garden. You could tell that Tamar had cheated a bit out here; the cypresses were too perfect, and anyway, they had not been there a week ago. Neither had the weeping willows or the pond. The truth was Tamar had used a good deal of magic to make the house and garden both look better, in much the same way as she made herself look like a supermodel. Her own face, the one she had been born with, had not seen the light of day for many thousands of years, and she liked it that way. Vanity was definitely her favourite besetting sin, that and a love of comfort and a strong belief in her own good taste. Their former abode, Denny's grotty London flat had been a work of art by the time she had finished wiggling her perfect nose. Denny was inclined to be indulgent; he had been a slacker since before there had been a word for it, and he could not have cared less about the state of the bathroom, or his own appearance. But if she wanted a designer life, he was not bothered about that either, as long as he did not have to do anything, and just so long as she did not try to tidy *him* up too much.

Strangely enough she didn't. She liked him pretty much the way he was. A foil to her beauty, she felt, was better than a rival. Men were not meant to be pretty. Not that Denny was ugly exactly, just pale and thin and scruffy. The only thing she might possibly have changed about him was his propensity for picking out awful tunes on his battered and beloved guitar, a habit of his which nearly drove her to distraction. 'You sound like an ape tuning up a broken fiddle with its toes,' she told him, but to no avail. If only he would stick to singing in the shower – he was *good* at that. In fact, his singing voice was truly remarkable, unlike the songs he occasionally wrote, which were only remarkable for how truly awful they were.

They had decided to get a car, for the sake of appearances. Tamar had had her heart set on a Jaguar XL, but Denny turned up one afternoon with a perfectly ordinary, although brand new and gleaming, Citroën.

Tamar was scathing. 'Honestly Denny, you might make an effort to have a *bit* of style,' she said. 'I mean, anybody who's nobody drives one of those.'

'Well?'

'Well.'

'Look, I'm sorry, but this is who I am. I *am* nobody and I like it. If you don't like it then ... oh I give up.'

Tamar had settled it by turning the Citroën into the car of her dreams, just by looking sternly at it. A method which worked on most things – even inanimate objects were intimidated by her stare – but which, unfortunately, had no effect whatsoever on Denny, unlike most men, who will at least change their socks after enough evil looks.

In the end, most of their new home, like their old one, was the result of imagination. A fact of which Denny was actually well aware, but he did not really care.

The house, however, unlike the flat, had been fairly magnificent to begin with. It now resembled, externally at least, due to Tamar's extensive renovations and wild imagination, nothing so much as a small castle situated in the middle of several acres of land, surrounded by rolling countryside peppered with quaint villages. Denny hated it, a confirmed urbanite he was distinctly uncomfortable around nature, and the sound of silence was one that he found profoundly unnerving. But the house itself, he had to admit, was pretty impressive. It had two large wings, several reception rooms, a huge kitchen, with a range oven large enough to roast a whole ox and enough bedrooms to house several cricket teams – if you included the ones in the attic. It had taken Tamar and himself several months to get the place to their liking (without magic, it would have undoubtedly taken several years) or rather to *her* liking. Her only concession being the conversion of one of the smaller reception rooms into a game room. The main hall, they had divided into smaller areas with room dividers to make a cosy living space, as recommended in the various copies of "Home Drivel" that littered the place since Tamar had begun renovations – Denny was thinking it was about time to cut off her supply. Of all the things he had never expected from her, an over-weaning interest in curtain fabric would have been top of the list.

Since the main room was at the back of the house, they had ripped down the heavy curtains and made French windows that opened out onto the garden. The all-important computer, which Askphrit had used to access mainframe and disappear into the past, was in this room, cleverly concealed in the panelling, and available at the touch of a lever. Behind this room was the weapons training area, which Denny had insisted on, in case he ever needed it again, if he lost his Athame which gave him extraordinary powers. In any case, he still trained for three hours every day, just in case. Tamar loved the house and all the trappings of luxury. Denny quite liked the house, although, unlike Askphrit, its previous owner, Denny had no great desire to play Lord of the manor. He did like having a proper garden, though, even if most of it *was* created by magic.

The sunshine was real enough, and it felt good, after many months of darkness, to feel it on their faces, and the backs of their necks. It was early spring, but it felt hot.

'Mmm,' said Tamar, 'it's nice isn't it? Warm.'

Denny shivered.

'What's the matter?' asked Tamar.

"I dunno. It felt like somebody walked over my grave, and I just had this really strong memory of my mother telling me how my granddad died in the war. He was bombed out, in his house, before he could get to the shelter. Mum said they found bits of him all over the garden – horrible. That story always made me shudder as a kid. I had nightmares about it; I suppose that's why it seemed like I actually saw it, just now, like a dream.'

'Why now, all of a sudden? Were you thinking about him?'

'No, why would I? I never met him.'

Tamar narrowed her eyes. 'Does your mother remember him?' She asked this as if it was of vital importance.

'Denny frowned. 'No, I just said, he died in the war, before she was born.'

'I wouldn't be too sure about that,' said Tamar, and she snapped her fingers. 'Tempus Suspendré,' she said. Time froze. Denny stood before her like a statue.

Tamar breathed a sigh of relief. She touched Denny's face. 'Still here,' she said.

Despite the seriousness of the situation, she could not help but smile, a little guiltily, at the memory this action conjured up. She had never told him, but she had, on occasion frozen Denny like this, just so that she could touch him and kiss him without having him die on her. Until the power of the Athame, a ceremonial knife used by demons to steal magic powers, had come into Denny's possession, only the briefest of contact had been possible due to Tamar's own inner power, which was so overwhelming, that she could kill a mortal with a touch. But with Denny frozen, she could touch him for as long as she wanted to, since technically it was still only for a second of his time. This was no longer a problem since Denny now had almost as much power as her – as long as he had the Athame. It had not been nearly the same.

She unfroze him, being careful not to unfreeze time anywhere else. That could be disastrous.

Denny blinked. 'W – what happened? You sort of – jumped, like a bad recording.'

Tamar squinted at him; he was getting more observant, he had never noticed before. 'I had to stop time,' she told him.

Denny looked up; there were birds frozen in the sky. 'Why?'

She ran her fingers through her hair. 'Well,' she said, uncertainly. 'I don't quite know how to explain it. You know that Askphrit has gone into the past somewhere?'

'Yes.'

'Well, what I think may have happened is: he's killed your grandfather to make sure that you never get born, but he got the timing just a little bit wrong, your mother had obviously already been conceived – lucky for us.'

'No, no – I told you my granddad died in the war, my mother told me.'

'He did *now*, but that's only because Askphrit went back in time to make sure of it. That's why you remember it that way.'

'Oh! I see – I think. So, maybe in – what, another timeline, I *did* know him?'

'Quite possibly.'

'*Bastard*!'

'Yes, that's what I've always said,' said Tamar calmly.

'Mind you,' Denny added, 'if he was anything like the rest of my family, it's probably no loss.' He mused for a moment on this then asked, 'So, why did you freeze time?'

'Because he *will* realise his mistake, and that means that you could vanish from existence at any second.'

Denny was startled. 'Any second?'

'Yes, he's in the past, remember? It doesn't matter how long it actually takes him, it'll still happen instantly. It'll be as if you've never existed.'

Denny thought about this. 'That means that you'd be trapped back in your bottle. If I never existed, then I couldn't have set you free.'

'That's his plan no doubt.'

'So, why doesn't he just go after *you*? Kill you in the past?'

'He can't do that, *I'm* the one who set *him* free. No, the part of history he wants to change is when you and I met. That's when all his problems started. I expected something like this.'

'You could have *told* me.'

'Sorry, I was hoping I wouldn't have to.'

Denny suddenly panicked and patted his pockets; he drew out a weird looking dagger. This was the Athame, the magic dagger that gave him certain special powers; he had picked it up fairly recently. Askphrit had led him to it, in fact, in the hope that its evil influence would lead him to destruction and ultimately the destruction of Tamar, but she had taken it from him and had it blessed to remove the evil. Now it was just a useful tool.

Denny breathed a sigh of relief. 'Still got this, anyway,' he said. 'I thought maybe he might have gone back and stopped me from finding it; after all, he knows exactly when I got it. He gave it to me.'

Tamar shook her head. 'No, if he'd done that, you wouldn't remember anything about it, as far as you'd be concerned, it never would have happened. Try to keep up.'

'I wonder what else he's changed?' said Denny ruminatively. 'I mean if our memories change, how would we know?'

'We wouldn't.'

'Christ!'

Denny looked up at the sky again; it was weird to see the birds static in the sky, and the trees and clouds undisturbed by the breeze.

He shook himself. 'So, what are we going to do? You can't leave time frozen forever.'

'No,' she admitted, 'we have to go after him. You'll be safer in the past at any rate, as long as it's before you were born anyway.'

'Why?'

'Because you didn't exist then, so the "you" that's in the past, will be the "you" from *now* – from this moment in time – and for now, at least, you still exist.'

'How do you know all this? – You know what, never mind. It's all academic anyway, surely? We *can't* get into the past; we don't have the codes to the archives. He didn't leave them on his computer, after all – we looked.'

'Well maybe they're somewhere in the house, it *was* his house after all.'

'Oh yes, Lord Askphrit, Lord of the manor – in a house full of treacherous vampires, do you really think he would have just left them lying about?'

'No, of course not, but those vampires were under his control. He was their god, or at least that's what he told them, until I made it the truth. He might have put them in a safe somewhere.'

'And if he didn't? If we can't find them?'

'We'll just have to improvise.'

~ Chapter Two ~

SHE WAS ONE classy dame, a real cool drink of water, but she was trouble with a Capital T. She said her name was Hecaté. Maybe it was, and maybe it wasn't. Maybe it was just "Problem", with a capital P.

'Mind if I smoke?' she asked.

Jack Stiles, Private Detective, leaned back in his chair and tipped his stylish trilby forward over his eyes. Behind him, the pink neon sign from across the street flickered intermittently through the half closed blinds. It had taken him months to find an office with this peculiarity. He felt it added the right ambience. In addition to this, he had a large battered looking desk with an old metal fan whirring constantly, even in the coldest weather, which riffled the edges of a stack of papers, held down by a large paperweight in the shape of a nude lady. Beside this was a large black telephone. On the edge of the desk was a whisky bottle, again for ambience, it was actually filled with cold tea. Stiles, a reformed alcoholic, did not wish to put temptation in his way. The office was dark and gloomy; the only light coming through the glass fronted door on which could be read the legend

JACK STILES

P.I.

The *piece de resistance* as far as Stiles was concerned was a genuine newspaper clipping attached to a notice board, with the headline: "Detective Chief Inspector Fired from Scotland Yard!" With a grainy picture of himself underneath it, being manhandled drunkenly by two junior officers out of the prestigious offices and on to the street. Talk about ambience. It was only a shame that his name was not Sam.

'Go ahead,' he said, lighting up a cigar and handing her the lighter.

'I do not need that,' she said, as the smoke rose from her feet.

She perched herself on the edge of his desk and leaned seductively over it toward him, and pouted when this did not elicit the response she had been hoping for, or indeed any response at all. She waved a hand in front of his face. He was frozen. She glanced at the clock – stopped. There was only one person on the whole planet that Hecaté knew of, who was capable of stopping time. 'Tamar!' she thought. 'So it has begun.'

Hecaté, being a goddess – the goddess of witches, in fact, was not affected by the spell, and she was capable of breaking it, at least on a small scale, that is she could free Stiles. She thought that she probably should, but he would, she knew, want to go and help Tamar, it was the policeman in him. Stiles had been a D.C.I in Scotland Yard until his recent adventures with Tamar when he had gone missing for four months with no word, and had come back to find that he no longer had a job. He could scarcely explain that he had been kidnapped by vampires, because he was indicated in a prophecy about the end of vampire-kind, and had ended up on a quest to kill a god.

Hecaté was also part of the prophecy – probably, and that was how they had met. Now she just wanted him to herself, at least for a while. She did not want him going off on some mad adventure and probably getting himself killed.

She unfroze him anyway. She tugged on his arm.

'What just happened?' he said, his confusion mirroring Denny's and occurring at much the same moment.

Hecaté told him what she thought must have happened, and what she thought was behind it.

'Well, we should go and see if we can help,' said Stiles, predictably.

Hecaté sighed. 'I thought you would say that,' she said.

* * *

'What do you mean, improvise?' said Denny.

'Well, we already have *one* archive code.'

'That's only to a deleted file. It doesn't lead anywhere. How's that going to help?'

'We can hit "escape" see where it takes us. Maybe, it'll get us into the mainframe, and ...'

'*Maybe*?' Denny was outraged.

'And, if we get into the mainframe, we're halfway there,' she continued stubbornly. 'We should be able to access the history files. It'll be a bit hit and miss, we could end up anywhere, they're numbered I think, not named.'

'I am not liking this plan,' said Denny, obstinately.

'Well, come up with a better one,' she challenged.

'I don't even understand *this* one.'

'Look it's this or nothing,' she said. 'In or out?'

'I don't suppose I've got any choice,' he sighed. 'Okay, I'll get on it.' He sat at the computer and began typing. 'I hate doing this,' he said, 'it always leads to trouble.'

'We're already *in* trouble,' said Tamar dryly.

'That's what I heard,' said a voice behind her, she spun round.

'Jack!' she squealed in delight. 'What are you doing here?'

'Hecaté,' he indicated her. 'Your little time freeze didn't affect her, so she unfroze me and we thought you might need some help.' He shrugged.

He nodded to Denny. 'All right mate?'

Denny shrugged. 'Okay,' he said, 'considering. I guess it's my turn to have a mad god trying to kill me.'

'Uh, huh, well, anything we can do ... What are you up to?'

'Hacking,' said Denny, laconically.

Tamar explained.

'Sounds – confusing,' Stiles said, non-committally.

'It sounds extremely dangerous and foolish,' said Hecaté. 'Jack, I do not wish for you to go.'

'I don't think you should either,' said Tamar unexpectedly. She had a great respect for Stiles.

'Why not?' Stiles was hurt.

'Because I think you might be more use here. We might need somebody to sort of co-ordinate from here. If we get in, that is.'

'Explain?'

'Oh, yes, yes, I see,' said Hecaté before Tamar could open her mouth. 'That *would* make it safer.'

'Would it now?' said Denny. 'And what would we have done if Jack hadn't turned up?'

'Risked it,' said Tamar.

'I still don't know what you expect me to do,' said Stiles.

'I do,' said Hecaté. 'It is probably better if I do it. You go with them if you want to,' she added unexpectedly. 'I know that you do.'

'And what are you going to do?'

Hecaté rolled her eyes. 'Always with the questions,' she said. 'I will track historical anomalies, so that I always know where you are, and I can pull you out if you get into trouble.'

'Pull us out how?'

'I would have to enter the file to retrieve you.'

'But how would you find us?'

'I will *know* where you are,' she said impatiently. '*You* will be the anomaly.'

Stiles nodded, satisfied 'That's if I'm going,' he looked at Tamar and Denny questioningly.

Tamar nodded. 'It's okay, with me,' she said.

'And it's okay with him,' said Denny.

'I found it,' said Denny. 'One deleted file ready and waiting, what now?'

Tamar looked at the screen. 'I'm not sure, I think we go in, like before.'

'You think! What if you're wrong?'

'Okay, hit "escape" and see what happens.'

They lost the file.

'Damn! Damn, damn, damn, damn, DAMN!' Tamar was making the most of her favourite word.

'Calm down,' admonished Denny. 'I'll get it back, just as soon as the screen clears.'

'What's it doing?' asked Stiles, interestedly. He was trying to keep the relief out of his voice.

'I don't know, I think maybe I crashed it.'

The screen was sort of – fizzing, not like a snowy TV screen, but more like a carbonated drink, it looked like the actual screen was bubbling, and if there was an image there, then it was badly distorted. It was kind of worrying.

Tamar was pacing the room furiously, and it was a large room. She was moving so fast she was practically a blur. Denny tried to catch her by the arms; it was like trying to catch a psychotic windmill.

'Tamar! *Tamar*! Stop it! If it crashes then we go and get another one, and try again. The screen bleeped, and they stopped and turned – Tamar stopped so suddenly that her feet created scorch marks on the floor. The screen had cleared, and there, clear as a crystal ball, were the words.

< WELCOME TO MAINFRAME >

Tamar whooped. 'YES! We did it, oh we did it, we – did it. Well, okay *you* did it. You're a genius. A genius!' She flung her arms around him and gave him a huge kiss.

She noticed that he was not really sharing her enthusiasm. 'You don't seem very excited,' she said.

'Well, no, I am, it's just that ... well, we're not quite there yet, are we?'

He pointed at the screen. What file do we want?' he asked. They both stared at the screen. Neither of them had ever seen anything like it.

It was the most densely packed list of files and sub-files that was ever seen. The type was so small, that human eyes could never have made it out. And this was evidently only the menu.

'Oh my God,' said Tamar, 'try pressing "help"

Denny did so. The screen changed. It was now a representation of what was presumably the entire universe. 'Oh, shit,' he said, 'now what?'

'Try "help" again' said Tamar, unable to think of anything else.

This time the screen cleared and a message appeared WHICH GALAXY DO YOU WISH TO ACCESS?

Denny rubbed his hands together in satisfaction. 'Ah, now we're getting somewhere,' he said. 'Er, does anyone know what galaxy we're in?'

No one did. Denny sat there for so long that a rather disturbing screensaver came up. A relic of Askphrit no doubt, as it depicted Tamar being brutally and rather messily chopped up into tiny bits.

'Well, *that'll* have to go,' Denny observed, glancing warily at Tamar, who was laughing. 'Oh I don't know,' she said, 'I rather like it. It's good to be reminded of our own mortality now and again.'

'I'd rather be reminded of Askphrit's mortality,' grunted Denny.

'Good idea,' responded Tamar. 'We'll change it to a picture of *him* being hacked to bits.'

'Later,' said Denny, getting rid of the picture and asking the computer for a list of galaxies to choose from. The idea having just occurred to him.

The list proved to be alarmingly long.

'We'll just have to go through them one by one and hope Earth's galaxy is near the beginning,' said Denny

'It won't be,' said Tamar gloomily.

'Oh, don't be so negative,'

'I'm not being negative, I'm being realistic.'

'No you're not, you always ...'

'Always what? No, you know what just shut up, and I ...'

'M32,' announced Stiles triumphantly, from behind a huge encyclopaedia.

Denny and Tamar stopped fighting. 'What?' they said together.

'The name of our galaxy,' Stiles told them. 'M32. Says so right here.'

'Oh,' Tamar was momentarily staggered.

Denny grinned. 'Thanks mate,' he said, 'glad one of us is thinking anyway.'

He went back to the previous menu and typed it in. 'I just hope that's what *they* call it too,'

Tamar opened her mouth and then shut it again. Denny was right, there was no point in being negative.

Denny had found it. He scrolled through the solar system and was fascinated to discover that there had indeed, never been life on Mars. 'So much for that theory then.'

'Oh do get on with it,' said Tamar impatiently.

'Here it is. Earth,' he announced, 'what now?' he added, as he brought up the files relating to humanity.

The list of files included: -

Deleted files.

Archives – historical – all.

Archives – prehistorical.

Personal files – historical.

Personal files – current.

Mythical files – historical.

Mythical files – current.

Mythical files – personal – historical/current.

Miscellaneous.

There were of course a lot more than these, but this is what it narrowed down to.

'So, what do we want?' asked Denny. 'Historical – all, or personal – historical?

'That's people I guess,' she replied, can you imagine how many of them there'll be? Everybody who ever lived, and if they're numbered, not named ...' she left the sentence hanging.

'Okay, so historical – all?'

She nodded. 'And that'll be bad enough.'

Denny selected the appropriate file and hit "enter" the screen popped up.

PLEASE ENTER PASSWORD

'Oh,' said Tamar.

'Don't worry,' said Denny, rubbing his hands together. 'I can break in I think, I expected this; you didn't think the files would be unprotected did you?'

'We should never have been able to get this far,' she said. 'Not without the codes to mainframe, I never thought ... you're sure you can do it?'

'I *should* be able to, but before I do, are we sure this is the file we want? I mean if we can access the personal files, might we not be able to go straight to him? My granddad I mean, Askphrit's bound to be there.'

'Not without the codes to the files. We won't know which file is his.'

'So, how will we know which file to go to in the historical files?'

'We won't, but there won't be as many to choose from.'

'What about, mythical – personal?' said Stiles. 'To find Askphrit, would that work?'

'It might, but there are at least three of him floating about out there now, and two of Ran-Kur, because of what we did. Historically speaking, it's a whole big mess. If we access the historical files, we can search different periods of history for him, I hope. Look I know it's not a perfect plan, even with the codes, we wouldn't know where to start looking, but we have to start somewhere.' She looked at them imploringly. 'Just getting into the past at all is a huge accomplishment. And once we're there, we'll have all the time in the world, literally. We *will* find him.'

Denny cracked his knuckles. 'Okay, this shouldn't take long.'

* * *

It was not really three hours later, because time had stopped, but it sure felt like it to those waiting, when Denny finally said. 'Okay, I can't do it.'

Tamar was surprisingly calm at this news. 'Never mind,' she said, 'there might be another way to break in.'

'What?' asked Stiles.

She turned to Denny. 'Do you need a rest?'

'No,' he said, surprised. 'I'm fine, it's like I only just sat down.'

'That'll be because time's stopped,' said Tamar. 'I keep forgetting, I suppose it's because we're all moving about like normal.'

'Normal?'

'Well … normal for us anyway.'

'What's this other way to break in?' reiterated Stiles.

'Well, we just break in, in a more literal sense, from the deleted file. We can get into that – we know we can.'

'But we don't know that we can get *out*,' Denny pointed out. 'Last time it was Clive who helped us out.'

'Who's Clive?' asked Stiles.

'A clerk, who looks after the files,' said Tamar. 'And we didn't know he would be there when we went in, that didn't stop us.'

'I don't propose that it should stop us now,' said Denny. 'I just want Jack to know what he's getting himself in to.'

'I thought you said that Hecaté could pull us out, if things got hairy,' said Stiles.

Tamar looked awkward. 'That idea rather depended on us getting in to the historical files from here,' she admitted. 'The problem with this way is: we might not get into the mainframe at all. We could end up stuck in the deleted file. And even if we do get in, Hecaté won't have access to the files from here.'

'I will work on it,' offered Hecaté. 'Maybe I will have luck.'

'Well, I'm going,' said Tamar. 'Bring up the file.'

'How come the deleted files don't have passwords?' asked Denny. 'I never thought of it before.'

'I guess they don't bother, because there's nothing in them. Besides, we got given the "back door" way in, and that's how we'll get into mainframe.'

'We?' said Stiles.

'Yes,' said Denny. We, at least, I'm going.'

'Then I guess I am too,' said Stiles.

Hecaté sighed.

~Chapter Three ~

THE FILE HAD BEEN emptied since Askphrit's time there, when he had been hiding out there as Kelon – a sorceress. This incarnation, as a woman, he had explained away as a ruse to prevent Tamar from finding him, as she had good reason to want to do, since he was responsible for her slavery as a Djinn. But, since then, they had reason to wonder about this – there was definitely something camp about him.

The file was now just empty space; it felt strange to be standing on a surface that, to all intents and purposes, was not there. Even Tamar could not claim to be used to this sort of thing.

'So,' said Stiles, 'this is the middle of nowhere, is it? I like it, I might build a holiday home here. A real get away from it all.'

'That's an entirely feasible plan,' Tamar told him. 'Maybe we'll come back to it, but for now, we have to – EXIT FILE,' she finished loudly.

A gap appeared in the nothing (if you can imagine that) but they all saw it quite clearly. As they approached it, a door slammed in the gap. It bore the legend, "FIRE ESCAPE DOOR", and it had the proper bar to push and everything. It was painted red.

Tamar pushed the bar; beyond the door was a wall of fire.

'Firewall,' said Denny laconically, and somewhat pointlessly. 'It's not *real* fire I guess, but then again, we're only data ourselves, I don't know if we should risk it.'

'We won't have to,' said Tamar. She was busy with a piece of chalk. On the "wall" she had drawn a crude facsimile of a fire extinguisher.

Chalk is not, perhaps, the most obvious of supplies to bring on an adventure, but it all depends on where you are going, in this case, it was invaluable.

'Software,' she said, as the fire extinguisher became solid in her hands.

Denny nodded and grinned. 'You think of everything.'

* * *

Once the "fire" was out, they walked through the door into a long corridor with doors all along it; each door was labelled much as the file list had read except they were all deleted files. At the end of the corridor was a door marked "MAINFRAME". They went through it, into another corridor lined with doors.

'Mainframe,' gasped Tamar in awe.

'It's huge,' said Denny complainingly and not at all in awe at all.

It was indeed vast; the corridor in front of them stretched on into infinity and possibly further. The human brain is not designed to register this, which might explain why Stiles said, 'It's not as impressive as I thought it would be, somehow,'

He had a point in a way. If you disregarded the immense size and complexity of the place, with its labyrinth of corridors and its multi-layered dimensional effects, which some Maori painters have tried to represent with their dream paths, which, of course is, what Stiles did – his brain just short circuited what it could not handle – then the place had a flat utilitarian look about it, like the world's biggest tax office.

'We won't find it any easier to get into those files from here, not without the passwords,' said Denny, discouragingly.

'Oh God, you're such an old woman sometimes,' said Tamar. 'Do you have any idea where we are? It's amazing.

We're actually *in* mainframe. All the universe is controlled from here, no mortal, or anything else has ever been here before.'

'Except Askphrit,' said Denny.

This comment brought Tamar back down to earth. 'Right, right, except Askphrit – the bastard. We have to find the historical files.'

'Shouldn't be too hard, just look at the doors,' said Stiles pragmatically.

'But it's so big,' said Denny again.

It took them fourteen hours of searching to find the right file. It had taken them nine hours to even find the department of Earth.

The door, when they finally found it, was not even locked. They opened it, and a guard appeared out of nowhere. 'Password?' it demanded. (I say "it", because gender and even species was indeterminate under all the armour. It looked more than anything like an oversized chess piece.)

'Told you,' said Denny.

'Um,' said Tamar. It was a mistake.

The guard started up a wailing cry. 'UNAUTHORISED USER!' over and over again.

'Shit!' said Tamar.

Denny had an inspiration. 'Password?' he snapped.

The guard stopped wailing. 'What?' it said.

'I wish to be assigned a new password,' said Denny.

'That'll never work,' Stiles hissed to Tamar.

'Hmm, I don't know,' said Tamar. 'This is a closed network, the security's laughable. They don't expect anyone to get this far.'

'Assign new password – working,' said the guard. 'New password is XXC241D.'

'XXC241D,' Denny repeated. The guard vanished.

'Brilliant,' said Tamar.

'No,' said Denny. 'I should have thought of it before, back at home, if I had, then Hecaté would have it too, she'd be able to monitor us.'

'She could look for Askphrit too,' said Tamar.

'Is there any way we can get it to her?' asked Stiles.

'Only if one of us goes back,' said Tamar.

'Goes back, how?'

Denny grinned. 'You click your heels together three times, and repeat after me – there's no place like home,' he said.

'I'll punch you in a minute,' said Stiles.

'Actually,' said Tamar. 'He's not kidding. Well he is about the heel clicking, but you *can* go back if you want to.'

'You're assuming *I'll* be the one to go back. – Okay, okay, I'll go, it has to be me, doesn't it? What do I have to do?'

'Go back to the deleted file and well – just make a wish.'

'You're kidding?'

'No, wish really hard that the file is still open at our end and then say "close file" you should find yourself back at home.'

'Should?'

'Hey give me a break. I've never done this before.'

'Okay, I'll give it a try. Better write down that password for me.'

Denny did so. 'Know which file you're going to?'

'Um, better write that down too. And er, got a map?'

*

'Which one?' asked Denny, as they surveyed the vast array of small doors, each about the size of a serving hatch, and numbered, as Tamar had predicted, not named. 'There's millions of them.'

'More,' said Tamar, gloomily.

'So, let's start by looking in a few, see where they lead, maybe there's a pattern in the codes. I mean, what are we looking for, 1944?'

'Presumably. If Askphrit's even still there. I mean he might have gone anywhere. You do have other ancestors.'

'Okay, well we have to start somewhere, I suppose. This is going to take forever.'

'Longer.'

'So, pick a door – any door.'

She opened the nearest one; behind it was a black hole, so no clues there. They would have to wait until they reached the other side, before they knew where they were.

'Great!' said Tamar, meaning anything but.

'Wait a minute,' said Denny. 'How do we get out again? I mean we could end up anywhere, dinosaurs – the middle ages – the *seventies*!'

Tamar smiled and patted him on the shoulder. 'Don't worry,' she said. She stepped to one side and pulled open the door. 'File open,' she said, and closed the door, 'file closed. As long as we leave the door open we just have to say "close file" to get back here. I think.'

'You *think*? Oh never mind, we could do this all day, let's just get on with it.'

* * *

Stiles re-materialised in almost exactly the same spot he had left from. Which was unfortunate since Hecaté was occupying that spot at the time, seated at the computer, trying to hack her way into the files. But the universe compensates and Stiles was shifted out of her way, just in time, giving him an uneasy feeling of disorientation.

She was shocked, but pleased to see him. He had, she informed him, only been gone for a few minutes. And why, she felt compelled to ask, was he all charred looking? He explained and had a few questions of his own.

Time, it transpired, is relative after all, and the time spent in the deleted file, Hecaté surmised, did not count as time at all, all this, further confused, by the fact that time in the present was frozen.

Stiles did not know whether he was coming or going. 'Am I getting any older at the moment?' he asked. The idea of retarding the ageing process was extraordinarily alluring to a man somewhere past forty.

'Mortals,' snorted Hecaté. 'Of course you are! Although no one else is – being frozen, as they are.'

'Oh,' Stiles was disappointed. 'Oh well, never mind. What are you doing there?'

'I have, thanks to this very useful password, reached the mainframe, historical files, if I am correct, this anachronism here – ' she indicated a highlighted report, 'Would seem to indicate that our friends are in Mediaeval Europe. Why, do you think?'

'Lost, probably. Are they all right?'

'Hard to say.'

* * *

'Well, that's a lot of peasants – with pitchforks,' commented Denny. 'What's going on, do you think?'

'Who cares? They probably have some grudge against whoever lives in the castle over there. It's none of our business.'

'Where – sorry – *when* are we?'

'Dark ages, I can't be more specific, but judging from the accents and the scenery – it's familiar – I think we're in Aquitaine.'

'France?'

'No, Aquitaine, Texas.'

'Very funny. Let's go. He's not going to be here, is he?'

But it was too late; they had been seen.

They were advanced upon, and, before they could disappear into the undergrowth, they were surrounded.

It transpired that they had turned up in the middle of a siege. One of many that occurred during the run up to the hundred years war. (Which actually went on for one hundred and sixteen years in total, and stopped occasionally for no apparent reason.) Tamar remembered bits of it. She estimated that they were around the end of the twelfth century. Quite some time before the hundred years war began in 1337. She based this on frequent references from the serfs and soldiers to *Coeur de Lion* – Lionheart.

Denny was excited when he heard this, but Tamar was scornful. 'We won't actually get to *see* him,' she said. 'Depending on the year, he's either the Duke of Aquitaine or the King of England and Duke of Normandy – too important for the likes of *us*! Anyway, he spent most of his reign in the Holy Land, either that or in prison in Germany.

They had been taken prisoner, their strange clothes and sudden appearance marking them out as possible enemy spies. This, by the way, was the anachronism that Hecaté had spotted. They were both, unfortunately, wearing jeans and Tamar was sporting a T-shirt emblazoned with the legend "Cool Chick".

'Next time, we change clothes before anyone spots us,' said Denny.

'Well, duh! Look, we'll get out of here as soon as they chuck us in a dungeon. We'll be alone then.'

But they were not taken to a dungeon; they were brought before the King.

The Lionheart himself, back in France to defend his dominions from his bother Prince John.

Tamar now revised her estimate, it must be around 1188, she said. After Richard's triumphant return and near to the end of his reign.

They were standing in a great hall, surrounded by knights and minstrels and of course, on the dais, behind a long table, was the King himself in all his splendour. They both felt extremely conspicuous, not to mention underdressed.

'I feel like a Yankee in King Arthur's Court,' said Denny. 'Hey, you would know, was he real?'

'Not now!' hissed Tamar.

They were forced to their knees.

'Who are you?' asked the King. 'Are you spies? You serve my treacherous brother John who some call "soft sword", who has tried to wrest my kingdom from me while I languished in the Emperor's prison?' He spoke in French of course, and old French at that, but Tamar could understand him, and so, to his surprise, could Denny. It must be the power of the Athame, he thought.

'No, my liege,' said Tamar. Subservience came easily to her, after so many years of servitude.

'I say you are!' thundered Richard. He was an impressive figure, every inch the archetypal king, tall and fair, and regal, and a right chump. He stepped down from the dais and drew his sword. He thrust it at Tamar, as the one who had spoken. 'You will tell the truth,' he said. 'You will tell me everything.' He stepped back. 'In time,' he added.

'Can't you, you know, bat your eyes at him or something?' hissed Denny.

'I don't think it would do any good,' she hissed back. 'I think *you'd* have more luck than I would, at that.'

'What? Richard the Lionheart, really?' he shook his head. 'That wasn't in any of the history books.'

'He never made a secret of it,' she told him. 'Well I mean, look at him, who's going to mess with him?' Of course he didn't advertise it either, but mostly people knew. – Except his wife,' she added as an afterthought.

'SILENCE!' thundered the King. He waved a hand, and a minstrel began to play.

'Now *that's* torture,' said Denny. 'If he keeps that up, I'll tell him anything he wants to hear.'

'That's how torture usually works,' agreed Tamar.

The King looked hard at Denny and leaned over to say something to one of his courtiers.

'What do you think he's saying?' hissed Denny.

Tamar shrugged. 'Have that boy washed, and brought to my tent?' she suggested.

'That's not funny.'

'Take them away,' said the King, impatiently. They were hustled out of the hall, and chained up outside, unfortunately in plain sight of far too many curious eyes.

'And where is Sir Antoine?' they heard the King demand as they were shoved out the door.

* * *

It is called displacement. When something is full, then adding more only makes it overflow.

Hecate and Stiles were dealing with the overflow.

As represented, in this case, by the intolerably belligerent Sir Antoine D'Arcy. A man who would easily make up the total mass of Denny and Tamar combined – and perhaps a small dog too.

He had arrived in much the same manner as Stiles had on his return from the deleted file. That is to say – unexpectedly.

He had then, on perceiving his surroundings, let out a bellow of protest – as you might expect – and charged Stiles like a maddened buffalo, sword drawn and screaming defiance.

Hecate sighed; she had no idea who this maniac was or why he had suddenly appeared,   but explanations could wait. The first thing to do was to prevent him from skewering Stiles on the end of his sword.

* * *

'Well, this is great,' said Denny.   'The latest thing in manacles.'

'I know. Whatever happened to an old fashioned dungeon? Nice and cosy – and *private*.   It's funny; this just isn't Richards's style.'

'Well, you have to admit, we *are* a couple of shady characters – what do you mean, not his style? How the hell would *you* know?'

'I just mean he never did things this way – from what I heard at the time.'

'Well, look, why don't we just get out of here? People believed in magic in these days, didn't they? What could it hurt?'

'I think two people just vanishing into thin air, might be too much for them. The most they would have encountered before this would have been the odd witch, and they were *very* careful. We've caused enough trouble just by getting caught, who knows what the repercussions will be from that.'

'I bet Askphrit's not worrying about that. I bet he'd just ...'

'Well, I'm not Askphrit, and I'm not changing history any more than I can help.'

'I didn't mean ... Look, what's the worst that could happen? So a few people see us vanish, so what? In a hundred years, who's going to care?'

'You of all people should know better. Look what Askphrit's time travelling antics nearly did to *you*.'

'But that was deliberate. He's trying to kill me.'

'Okay, suppose one of those people is an ancestor of yours. They see us vanish and end up in a lunatic asylum, never get married and have children, *ergo* you never exist.'

'Oh, I see.'

'And that could happen to anyone. It doesn't matter whether or not it's your ancestor. That's just an example. All these people are the ancestors of *somebody*. We don't have the right. One of these people could be the ancestor of De Gaulle for all we know. But anyway, it doesn't matter, even if you never have an impact on history, that doesn't make it all right for someone to mess around with your life.'

'Okay, okay, I agree, I just hadn't thought it through.'

There was a silence.

'The thing is,' said Denny, eventually, 'what *are* we going to do? If everything you just said is right, then we can't leave Askphrit running around in history doing God knows what!'

'I know, I know, I'll think of something, we've been in worse jams than this. But I'm not going to do what *he* would do. Two wrongs don't make a right.'

'Don't spout cliché's at me. I'll think you've lost your edge. When they come for us, we'll just have to fight, and make sure we don't kill anyone.'

'Agreed.'

'Or, if they leave us here, maybe we could escape at night.'

'They won't leave us, without a guard.'

'I suppose not.'

A burly guard smacked Denny across the head. 'Shut up,' he was told. 'You'll have your chance to talk later, at the trial.'

'Trial?' Denny hissed at Tamar.

'Coals of fire,' said Tamar, 'coals of fire.'

'Gulp.'

'No, we'll be fine. We have a magic assist, remember? Besides, it'll never get that far.'

'So, you have a plan?'

'Yeah, just leave it to me.'

'Why am I not surprised to hear you say that?'

* * *

'Thanks!' breathed Stiles, 'I'm not ready to be made into kebabs just yet,' He tried to grin.

'Hmm,' Hecate was gazing thoughtfully at the stranger, now sleeping peacefully on the floor, having been hurriedly picked up and slammed heavily against the wall, thus bumping his head a little in the process. 'Where do you suppose he came from?'

Stiles shrugged. 'History by the looks of him. Why isn't he frozen like everyone else?'

Hecate shook her head. 'The historical files ...' she mused. 'This man has been thrown clear of the file that Tamar and Denny have entered – that is clear enough, but why...?'

'Well, if *you* don't know...' Stiles left this sentence hanging.

'We must find a way to send him back,' said Hecate effectively resolving all redundant speculation into one easy problem. Well one very difficult problem actually, but at least it was one they could get to grips with. Theoretically anyway.

* * *

They were left chained up all night. Around midnight, they had hoped that the man guarding them was about to fall asleep, he was definitely nodding, but then another guard, who was as fresh as a daisy, relieved him.

'I've been thinking,' said Denny. 'How will we know when we've found Askphrit? I mean he could be here, for all we know.'

'He isn't.'

'How do you know?'

'I just know.'

'Like you knew how to get in and out of the files? How do you know all this stuff all of a sudden?'

'I don't know, I just do.' She thought about it. 'It's weird, now you come to mention it, it's like I'm being told, and then it's as if I always knew, but I know I didn't. I think we're being – helped.'

'Helped? By who?'

'Or what. Maybe it's ...'

'What?'

'Nothing – I don't know.'

'Well, if there *is* someone who has that kind of power, why don't they just go after Askphrit themselves?'

'I don't know, maybe they can't.'

'Well, why couldn't they give us a bit more to go on, like the codes? Or if they can tell you where he *isn't*, why can't they tell you where he *is*? It's like Clive all over again. Everything's a bloody mystery. Everything's a bloody great slog.'

Tamar did not answer, so he carried on. 'So, you're sure, that saying "close ...".'

'Shhh.'

'Sorry, but you're sure it'll work?'

'Yes.'

Denny fell silent. There did not seem to be much else to say.

At dawn, three guards came for them, one each to unlock them and a spare, presumably to look menacing. When they were unlocked from the posts, Denny waited until the manacles were put back on his wrists; in other words, he had two pieces of very heavy metal attached to the end of his arms. Or to put it yet another way, his arms were like a hammer. He brought his arms down on the nearest guard's sword arm; the guard dropped the sword, cursing, and he bent down automatically to retrieve it. Denny swung his arms down onto the man's head, knocking him out, despite the helmet. Tamar followed suit. As Denny flipped the sword from the ground with his foot and caught it, the third and last guard fled, screaming 'Demons! Demons!'

Tamar and Denny ran; a phalanx of soldiers had appeared with creditable alacrity.

'Jump!' yelled Tamar, indicating the outer wall, which was at least thirty feet high. 'We might as well. We're demons now, apparently.'

They leaped the wall, Tamar somersaulting like "Wonder Woman"; she had a wicked urge to give out an ululating war cry – so she did. Denny landed on top of the wall and waved mischievously before jumping off. There were gasps of wonder and fear. 'See, see, demons – they're demons, leave them alone.'

They ran into a nearby copse. 'So much for not scaring anyone, with our freaky powers,' said Denny. 'Demons indeed!'

'It could have gone better,' admitted Tamar. 'But demons they can handle, there's a large section of the public here who believe that the Plantagenets are the spawn of the Devil himself and that King Henry, Richard's father, was a demon.'

'Oh, well in that case ... *are* they?'

'It's a possibility I suppose.'

'Are you making fun of me?'

'It's a possibility.'

Tamar held up her wrists. 'I hate wearing these things,' she said. 'Bad memories.'

'Yes, well, you can get these ones off,' Denny pointed out, removing his own. With a flick of the wrist, they fell apart.

'We're alone,' she said. 'Let's get out of here.'

They looked at each other 'How?' Denny asked.

'Catch hands,' she instructed him. 'Now, "close file",' she said, and the world disappeared.

They landed back in the file room in the same inelegant manner that they had left. Denny looked resignedly at the rows and rows of little file doors stretching on into infinity. 'How do you think it works?' he asked. 'I mean is there a file for every day or is it every hour or what? And we ended up in France, but what about the rest of the world at that particular time or day or whatever?'

'I don't know, do I?' Tamar hated making this admission at any time, and the more so now, because she knew he had a point. The possibilities were indeed quite literally, endless. And, without any sort of system or key, how in the hell were they going to find Askphrit in the vast annals of the past?

'We were in that last one for several days,' she said thoughtfully. 'Perhaps these are sort of main files with sub files in each if you only know how to access them. 'I mean, once in the file, you can cross distances as well as continuing to move through time. These files aren't infinite, not really. Perhaps each file could be viewed as just an access point. I mean its history right? So it all joins up in the end it's really just one massive, big file when you think about it.'

Denny laughed.

'What's so funny about that?'

'Oh, it's just you, that's all. You don't know, any more than I do, how it all works. But you still managed to make the nothing that you know, up into an explanation.'

'Well, it's a theory isn't it? We'd know better if we had the proper codes.'

'Well, we don't, we're just data in the machine, not the operators.'

'Nicely put, that's exactly how it is.'

'So, what makes you think we have *any* chance here? We're lost.'

'We knew that already. We just have to hope. Besides, I get the feeling we're not as alone in this as we seem to be.'

'An operator?'

'Could be.' She nodded uncertainly. 'Any way, don't forget we literally have all the time in the world, we *will* run him to earth in the end. Now pick a file it's your turn.'

* * *

'Well, it would help if we knew the file he came from,' said Stiles. 'Assuming he really did ... hey where did he go?'

Hecate raised an eyebrow. 'Interesting,' she said. 'He has returned to whence he came.'

'Apparently,' said Stiles slightly sceptically. It couldn't be that easy, surely?

Hecate dusted her hands together. 'Well,' she said, 'that appears to have solved that little problem for us anyway. A strange anomaly no doubt.'

'Yeah?' said Stiles. 'Then who's that then?'

~ Chapter Four ~

'*IN NOMINE PATRIS, et Filii, et Spiritus Sancti. Amen,*' intoned the priest. They had crashed a wedding. And once again, they had been spotted.

'Don't get any ideas,' said Denny.

'Like what?' said Tamar, "innocent face" replacing the dreamy eyed expression that she had been wearing.

'I saw that look.'

Tamar gave him a look that was anything but dreamy.

'Okay, so, where are we now? You're the expert, aren't you?' said Denny.

'In a lot of trouble,' she said, as the church was stormed by soldiers.

'Not again?' groaned Denny.

But the soldiers were not interested in them; they seized the priest and the happy couple and arrested them, in the name of Queen Elizabeth, for idolatry (which Tamar explained as meaning because they were Catholic) and treason. They were in the sixteenth century. They took the opportunity, while everyone's attention was distracted, to match their clothes to the period.

'What'll happen to them?' hissed Denny.

'They'll be hanged,' she told him, 'and we can't interfere, as much as we might want to.'

There was worse to come. The soldiers barred the doors of the church, trapping the few people who had braved the wedding, inside, and set fire to it.

'Okay,' said Tamar, 'that does it! To hell with the rules, let's get them out of here.'

'You won't get any argument from me,' said Denny.

It was an old building even for the time; the door was solid oak and the only windows were tiny slits through which a child could not have passed. The door was blocked by a crush of people trying to knock it down. The few children in the church were sensibly leaning as far through the windows as they could, trying to breathe as much fresh air as they could.

Denny cleared the door as best he could, as a burning beam fell from the ceiling. Tamar leaped and caught it one handed, to gasps of wonder, interspersed with coughing fits. She pole vaulted with the beam, which was still smouldering, and aimed a flying kick at the door, which crashed off its hinges.

More than one person had lost consciousness by this time, so Tamar and Denny ended up carrying them out.

Tamar found herself the subject of much pointing and whispering.

'Such strength, in a woman, it's not natural.'

'And she wasn't afraid of the fire at all.'

'Did you see? She *flew* on that beam.'

'She's a witch.'

'Where did she come from? She's not one of us.'

'But – she saved us.'

'With her supernatural powers, she's in league with Lucifer.'

'And who is he? Her familiar, in his human form.'

And the inevitable – 'Get them.'

The townspeople were advancing on them; there were suddenly a lot more of them, and their faces were lit up with cruelty – born of fear, but also a desire for entertainment.

'Witch – witch – witch.'

'Put her to the test, fetch the pricker, he'll find the mark.'

'Aye, the mark of Satan, she'll have it, mark my words.'

'Well, that's gratitude for you,' said Denny. 'What do we do now?'

'Give 'em what they want,' said Tamar grimly. 'It won't be my first ducking. You get out of here.' To his horror, she turned him into a cat; his clothes, along with the Athame, fell in a heap on the ground; he crawled out from among them and scampered away as the roar of the crowd escalated. 'Witch – witch – witch – witch!'

A man in a tall black hat, with an air of authority, obviously the witch pricker, appeared. Tamar was surrounded and dragged away.

Denny crept forward to his discarded clothes and found the Athame among them; he tried to use it to turn himself back, but it would not work; apparently, only Tamar could turn him back. He watched in horror as she was stripped; the mob was searching, so he gathered for a mark on her body. The Witch Pricker would then stick a pin in it, if it did not bleed, that meant she was a witch. The mark was not found, but the pricker said that this was inconclusive; the evidence against her was such that she would have to face the ducking test. Hadn't they all witnessed her familiar turn from a human to a cat? And she had been seen to fly on a piece of burning wood.

The ducking test apparently meant that she would be weighted down and thrown into the river. A witch would float, protected by her lord, Lucifer, an innocent woman would drown. If a woman should survive the ducking, thus proving that she was a witch, she would be hanged. Heads I win, tails you lose.

Tamar was bound hand and foot, and weighted down with a bag of stones around her neck, and she was thrown into the river – she sank immediately.

Denny shot forward with a cry, well, it came out as more of a yowl. He felt the indignity of his position as a burly man grabbed him by the scruff of his neck.

'It's the witches familiar,' shouted a woman.

'Drown it,' called another.

Denny squirmed and twisted frantically, scratching up the face of the man as best he could.

'Look at it,' said someone. 'Such venom, that's no ordinary cat. Throw it in after the witch.'

Denny was stuffed into a sack, which was also weighted down with stones. Without the Athame, he was completely helpless. He suddenly felt weary and stopped struggling; he was thrown into the water. He felt a strange sense of calm; he even saw the funny side. Here he was – a cat in a sack, sinking to the bottom of a lake. Of all the ways to go ...

* * *

'Who's that then?' said Stiles pointing at a tall robed man with an ascetic look about him 'A Christian priest,' Hecaté told him.

The priest gazed calmly at them and then spoke. 'The Lord be praised, for Heaven is more wondrous and beautiful than ever I could have dreamed.'

Hecaté and Stiles looked at each other in disbelief. It was clear the man believed himself dead for some reason, but ... Heaven? Here?

'The mind is a powerful deceiver,' said Hecaté. 'His faith has led him to see angels in the faces of the clouds.'

'What?' said Stiles uncomprehendingly.

'He is seeing what he expected to see when he died, rather that what is really here,' she translated.

'But he isn't dead,' said Stiles. 'Is he?' he looked worried. It was bad enough that he was here at all without him being a ghost too.

'He believes he is,' said Hecaté.

'From the fire and sword wielding hands of the infidel, I was delivered unto the sanctuary of the kingdom of Heaven,' confirmed the priest in lugubrious tones.

'Great!' said Stiles. 'So, what are we supposed to do with him then?'

'And his dog,' he added, suddenly noticing a Great Dane sniffing around the back of the chair.

'I doubt it is his own dog,' said Hecaté, as if this was relevant.

'Who cares? How do we get rid of them?'

'I imagine they will go on their own like the other,' she said.

Stiles laughed. 'Oh boy is he in for a shock,' he said. 'World's first "near death experience". He won't be too happy to find out he's not in Heaven after all will he?'

Hecaté frowned. 'That is true,' she said. 'It could cause problems.'

'Changing history and all that?' asked Stiles.

'Precisely,' Hecaté affirmed.

'Well, there's not really a lot we can do about it is there?' he asked. 'It's not as if we can keep him here... no ... no, no, no!'

* * *

Tamar floated along the riverbed, waiting for the townspeople to disperse; it was calm down here, cool and refreshing. She had, of course, given herself a handy set of gills. She could vaguely hear shouting, but, through the water, could not make out the words. 'Celebrating no doubt,' she thought, scornfully. 'No wonder I never liked mortals much – until Denny. I hope he's all right.'

After a while she got bored, the scenery under water palls quickly, fish and weeds, and more fish, with some more weeds. Deadly dull, so, she decided to swim upstream and climb out, somewhere away from public view. She dragged herself, inelegantly on to the shore – just in case anyone was around, and lay gasping on the bank. Just in time, she remembered to get rid of the gills.

She sat up and looked around. She could not see anyone, so she manifested herself some clothes, and dried her hair. Ah – magic – so much more efficient than a hairdryer.

Now, blonde or redhead? She had to go back and find Denny, but turning up, back in the town, looking like herself was definitely a bad idea. Blonde, she decided, the more contrast with her usual appearance, the better – and blue eyes, for that Nordic look.

She made her way back to the town. Now that she was no longer either in a burning church, or being harassed by a bloodthirsty mob, she had leisure to look around a bit; she thought she might be in Plymouth. Any minute now, the Spanish Armada might be sighted. 'Oh, well,' she thought. 'I've already seen it.'

There was no sign of Denny, not a black cat in sight, in fact. 'Why did I *do* that? What a stupid thing to do.' But she did find his clothes; the Athame, however, was gone.

* * *

From inside the bag, slightly muffled, Denny heard an authoritative and cultured voice demanding loudly to know just what these people thought they were up to. The bag was swung through the air, and daylight appeared as the bag was opened. Denny saw a pale faced man looking curiously at him.

'You people were about to drown this cat.' It was not a question.

'My lord, it is no ordinary cat, it is a witches familiar, sir.'

'What nonsense,' said the man contemptuously. He sighed. 'When will you peasants learn to do without all this ridiculous superstition?'

'We saw it change from a man into a cat, sir. The witch did it.'

'And where is this witch?'

There was a silence.

'I asked you a question,' snapped the man. 'Where is this supposed witch?'

A small boy came forward. 'At the bottom of the river sir,' he said, before he was hustled away by what was presumably his mother. Denny had a first class view of their discomfiture, from his rescuer's arms.

'I see,' said the man coldly. 'There will be no more of this, do you understand? I forbid it.'

The men in the crowd touched their caps; the women curtseyed clumsily, as they all said. 'Yes sir.'

The man stalked away, holding Denny in his arms; abruptly he stopped and turned round. 'If I understand your superstitions correctly,' he said, 'If the alleged witch has drowned, then, even according your stupid beliefs, she was not a witch, isn't that correct? So, why would you drown what is clearly, even by your standards a perfectly ordinary cat? You might want to think about that.'

The man talked to Denny as he walked, although, of course, really he thought he was just talking to himself. 'Fools!' he was saying, 'when will they learn? Poor kitty, you had a narrow escape, there. What a pity I did not arrive earlier, and save that poor woman's life. Your owner, I suppose. Well you can come home with me, you'll be safe there. I hope you're a good mouser. Witches indeed! What nonsense! Well, they will not do it again; they would not dare to disobey me.'

He took Denny, now renamed Tinker by the cook, to the kitchens of his vast home. The cook went into transports of delight, at the "pretty kitty" that she seemed to assume was female. Denny, naturally, took umbrage at this, and went into a corner to sulk, there being no escape possible at the moment. Denny had never owned a cat, or any pet, not after he killed the class hamster, by accidentally vacuuming it up, so he was not certain, but he thought he might be let out at night. People did that he was sure. Unless those noises outside at three a.m. really were children screaming. And even in Denny's old neighbourhood, he doubted it – not *every* night.

He was frantic to get away; he had to get back and find out what had happened to Tamar, get the Athame back and get the hell out of here. Two young kitchen maids appeared, and made a fuss of him, which was not an altogether unpleasant experience, 'if only they knew,' he thought, amusedly. But he had to focus, look for an open window – how could there not be an open window? It was like a furnace in here.

'Actually, it's kind of comfortable,' he thought. He was getting sleepy; he moved a little closer to the stove, 'Ah, that's it.' He settled down with his nose on his paws and fell asleep.

* * *

Tamar was wandering through the town. Asking for her cat did not seem like a smart move; neither did asking for her "ceremonial knife", which, since it had undoubtedly been found by someone in Denny's discarded clothes, would put her back in the river *tout de suite.*

'Where the hell is he?' she muttered under her breath.

She wandered through the streets until a red-faced man stopped her. 'There you are wench,' he snapped. 'Where have you been? You're late.' And before she could stop him, he had dragged her into a tavern. 'Get to work, you lazy slut,' he growled. Obviously, he had mistaken her for someone else. Apparently she had inadvertently made herself look exactly like a girl called Sally. This was confirmed when the other barmaid, Lucy, called her by that name. Since she did not want to draw undue attention to herself, she decided to go along with it, and hope that the real Sally did not suddenly turn up.

She had been balancing trays and schlepping backwards and forwards for six hours, putting up with insults, innuendoes, and inappropriate fondling, before she finally snapped.

A large bearded man with a face like a boar and breath like a direct line from a sewer grabbed her and pulled her onto his knee, he slurred something at her with a gust of beery breath, and tried to kiss her. She had had enough; with a well-practised move, she stood up, and flipped him over her head.

'Pig! – Keep your filthy hands off me, privy breath,' she snarled. The whole tavern was staring at her in silence. *Uh oh.*

'Witch!' shouted a man, pointing at her. Others took up the cry.

Here we go again.

She was hustled outside. Since it was dark, they lighted torches and marched her toward the town square, others joining the procession, bringing along pitchforks to prod her along with. The witch pricker was awakened, and hurried along after them in his night-shirt.

'Twice in one day,' she thought, 'that's got to be some kind of record.'

They tore her bodice from her shoulders, and a loud voice was heard over the top of the crowd's chanting. 'STOP!' The crowd parted and Tamar saw a thin, pale, well-dressed man, 'Let that woman go,' he ordered.

'But she's a witch,' protested the fat man, whom she had attacked.

'Do you dare to defy me? I said let her go.'

Reluctantly they stood away from her. The man came forward. 'Come with me,' he said, it did not sound like a suggestion.

'Thank you sir,' said Tamar, 'but ...'

'Come along now,' reiterated the man. 'Do you want to be strung up?'

Tamar shrugged; she followed the man.

* * *

The man told her that his name was William Tracey and that he was the Squire in these parts; that is – he owned the land and most of the local people. He asked Tamar her name – she told him it was Sally – and offered to put her in the kitchens.

Since she had had enough of drudgery and had things to do, she considered declining, but it would seem ungrateful to a man of this type, not to mention, suspicious. She would have a certain amount of freedom to search while being under William's protection, and, as soon as she had found Denny, she could leave.

He took her to meet the cook. While listening, or rather pretending to listen, to the interminable list of rules and instructions, her attention wandered, and she saw the cat, asleep by the fire. The cook followed her gaze. 'Oh that's Tinker, he's a nice pussens – yes he is.'

'Tinker?' snorted Tamar, before she could stop herself. 'Poor Denny,' she thought. 'What a come down.'

The cook bristled. 'What's wrong with that?' she demanded.

'Oh, oh, no, nothing. It's just, I think that may be *my* cat, his name is D – Dodge.

'*Your* cat?' said William, interestedly. 'So, you are the witch that was ducked earlier today? And you survived I take it, so they tried to duck you again. Am I correct?'

'In a manner of speaking – sir,' she said.

'Witch?' exclaimed the cook. 'Sir I mean no disrespect, but I cannot have a witch in my kitchen sir, the girls ...'

'*Whose* kitchen?' asked William, mildly enough.

The cook bobbed a curtsey, 'Sir I ...'

He interrupted her. 'Mrs. Trott, you know I do not approve of all this superstitious nonsense. There are no such things as witches; this girl is no more a witch than I am. I take it, you do not accuse *me*?'

'Oh sir, you will have your little joke.'

'I assure you, Mrs. Trott, I see nothing amusing in the murder of innocent women, in the name of religious intolerance, for that is what it is as I have tried to tell you. These so-called witches are merely followers of the ancient religion of this country, although they themselves have forgotten it. They are Pagans Mrs. Trott, nothing more. No matter what they, or you, believe, they no more have magic powers that that kettle. Am I making myself clear?'

'Yes sir.'

William looked at Tamar, 'I do not believe I have convinced her,' he said. 'Perhaps it would be better if you came with me for now. There will be gossip no doubt, but nothing can prevent that anyway. I sense that if I leave you here, you will have a hard time of it.' He stalked away. Before she followed him, Tamar grabbed Denny, stifling the cook's protest with the hardest look anyone had ever received.

* * *

Denny was asleep by the fire; William was questioning Tamar, and lecturing her on the folly of believing in witchcraft, which she found amusing at first, but then, increasingly tedious. She was getting restless; she wished to be off, and the longer Denny was a cat, the harder he would find it to adjust to two-leggedness again.

He told her that the people believed that their ancient religion was witchcraft because their lives were so dull and oppressed it gave them something to live for, some excitement, some rebellion. Tamar yawned; she already knew all this, and she hoped he would take the hint and suggest they retire. When he did not, but continued to go on and on about ridiculous superstition, she was tempted to turn Denny back into a man, right there. That ought to shut him up. Not that she disliked him, she agreed with most of what he said, and the world would be a better place, if there were more men who believed in tolerance, as he did. But still ... so dull, so oblivious, and so intensely stuck-up. For all his admirable qualities, he was a typical, upper class twit, only not so stupid.

Eventually he decided to retire for the night and he showed her upstairs to a guest-room. She took Denny with her, and turned him back the moment they were alone. Then she sorted him out some clothes.

'What's with the new look?' he asked.

She explained. He was not surprised.

'I lost the Athame,' he told her, it was in my clothes.'

'I know, it isn't now, somebody must have gone through them and picked it up.'

'You're kidding! What are we going to do?'

Tamar hung her head. 'I don't know, I'm sorry, this is all my fault. I don't know what came over me. How did you end up here?'

He told her. She hung her head, again. 'You were almost drowned? I'm so, so...'

'Sorry, I know. Look it doesn't matter now, we have to find the Athame – even if I didn't want it, which I do, we can't leave that kind of power in some peasant's hands; it'll change history in the worst way.'

'Tell me about it,' she agreed. 'I can sense when magic is being used, usually, but that means, we won't know where it is, until after someone has used it. And we'll still have to search.'

'I think we should both be in disguise,' he said.

*

Tamar decided to leave a note. The next morning, William was to read, in some bemusement, the following copperplate production:-

Dear Mr. Tracey.

I must apologise for taking my leave of you in so abrupt a manner. No doubt you will think it strange, but I am as you will now realise, an educated woman and not a kitchen maid and I have, moreover friends and family who await me. I am sorry for not revealing this to you, there are reasons but it is not my secret to reveal. Many thanks for your service to me and for looking after my cat also, a small thing you may think, but you may believe me when I say, it meant a great deal to me.

If there shall ever come a time when my debt can be repaid, you can look to me to honour it, and in this I pledge my word.

Think not too hardly of me
Your Servant
Sally Evans.

* * *

Tamar and Denny returned to the town under cover of darkness, and began their search. But they found no sign, anywhere, that anyone had been using magic of any kind.

'Doesn't mean anything,' said Tamar. 'I mean, how long was it before you learned to use it?'

'Not long,' he replied. 'But then, I was in the middle of nowhere with no food, no water, no way home, and being chased by vampires. If I'd been safe and sound at home, I might never have worked it out. Whoever's got it, probably just stuck it in a drawer somewhere.'

'They'll probably try to sell it, in that case. Its solid silver, it'd probably fetch enough to feed a family for a year in these parts.'

'They'd have to be careful, though, it might look to some people like stolen goods – which I suppose it is.'

'Good point. So, some kind of Black Market?'

'Did they have those, in those – I mean these – days?' asked Denny, surprised.

'Of course, smuggling, especially round here, was – is, the main criminal activity. How do you think they got rid of all that stuff, waved a magic wand?'

'So, are you saying that *my* Athame could end up in the hands of some pirate?'

'Good idea, let's go down to the cove.'

'What idea? What cove?' But Tamar was off.

* * *

Denny caught up with her in a rocky inlet. 'What are we doing here?'

'Smugglers,' she told him, enigmatically as far as he was concerned. But he was used to her clipped explanations. Usually, though, they were backed up with a certain amount of access to her thoughts, but for some reason she was shutting him out.

'What do you mean – smugglers? Don't be so cryptic.'

'These are smugglers caves. See over there? That's where they light the signal fires.' She pointed to a jut in the cliff face, which was still smouldering. 'What you said, about pirates – I just think whoever's got the Athame, will probably try to sell it here, where the smugglers trade. Who else would want a fine silver knife with a dodgy provenance? Well, who else who could afford it? Smugglers and pirates, that's who. So I thought, maybe whoever's got it might bring it here, to trade.'

Denny was doubtful. 'Hmm, bit of a long shot.'

'Makes sense, trust me, Besides – look, if they don't come tonight, they probably won't come at all. Anyway, this is our only chance to find out. If nobody comes with it, then we'll have to try something else.'

'But there's nobody here.'

'Wait.'

* * *

It was almost dawn before anything happened. Tamar shook Denny awake; she had let him sleep for a while. Since he had lost the Athame, his human weaknesses, such as needing to sleep and eat, had returned – the sleepiness might also have been a residual trait of his "cattiness".

He resented this thraldom to his body, missed the freedom of not needing sleep and food to survive. How had he ever survived 25 whole years like that?

In the half-light, he could just make out around five shadowy figures stealthily approaching the cave.

'Pirates?' he whispered.

'Or smugglers, what's the difference?' She glanced at his excited face. 'You know, you should forget whatever you read about smugglers in story books, these men are brutal thugs, killers, the gangland criminals of their day. Don't think that drug-dealers are a modern invention, these guys were up to it a long time before this.'

Denny gulped. 'That's encouraging,' he said. 'So, if one of these guys should get hold of the Athame ...?'

'Badness would ensure, on a massive scale.'

'Gulp.'

'Shhh now, I want to listen.'

Another man had appeared from over a rise, hobbling with a staff and bowed down, he gave the impression of being an elderly man. He had the Athame; Denny could sense it. He nudged Tamar and nodded, she nodded back.

They could not hear what the old man replied when one ruffian demanded in a loud voice. 'What do you want old man?' But they both saw the glint of the blade, and the ensuing conversation, which took place *sotto voce*, was not hard to imagine.

After only a few minutes, the big ruffian took his own knife from his belt, stabbed the old man, and took the Athame out of his hand. Three of them carried the old man's body to the sea and threw him in.

'Damn!' said Tamar. 'I didn't see that coming, I should have prevented it. He must have insulted them.'

'What could you have done, without, you know, giving away the fact that you're you know – *special*?'

'I don't know.'

'Can't you just, freeze time again, and get it back?' Denny was frantic by now, he wanted his prize. It was so close.

'Um, well, no I can't. You see, time is already frozen where we left it, I can't do it again in another time; it won't work.'

'Oh hell, I forgot. So what are we going to do?'

'Get captured.'

'What kind of a plan is that?'

'It's not.'

The smugglers or pirates or whatever they were, were advancing on them. They had been seen – again.

'We're really bad at this covert stuff,' observed Denny.

* * *

They were hustled aboard a tiny boat and rowed out to sea, where the ship was waiting.

The pirates were uproariously delighted with their capture; laughing and drinking and making sinister remarks about the fate that awaited their captives once they were handed over to the Captain.

'Can't you just grab it and we'll get out of here? We could jump overboard.'

Tamar ignored this, no more risks, he would just have to wait, 'Who is your Captain?' she asked them.

'Aha,' smirked one, 'Have you ever heard of the Dread Pirate Hogarth?'

Tamar choked.

Denny looked curiously at her. 'Dread Pirate Hogarth?' he said, 'Sounds like something *you'd* come up with.'

'You know me too well,' she managed through gritted teeth.

'What's the matter? Do you know this guy? You look like you've seen a ghost.'

'In a manner of speaking.' She was silent for a moment, thoughtful. 'Look,' she said, 'there's a chance that you'll recognise this Captain, just promise me something – don't react.'

'That *I'll* recognise him? How's that? Oh is it – him? Have we found him? Do you know something?'

'Something,' she said, cagily. 'Shhh, now.' The pirates were giving them funny looks.'

* * *

They were hustled on board and prodded forward with the ends of the pirates' swords; the other pirates crowded forward to get a look at them, most were drunk, and all were leering and spitting on the deck.

'Tremble before the Dread Pirate Hogarth!' They were told as they were forced to their knees. 'Scourge of the seven seas, terror of the Barbary Coast, on your knees dogs!'

The Dread Pirate Hogarth was indeed an imposing figure, tall and dashing, flamboyantly dressed, and, strangely enough, masked. He stood, hands on hips like a pantomime villain

'Any minute now,' thought Denny, 'he'll slap his thigh and break into a song about the high seas.'

Naturally, this did not happen. Captain Hogarth looked the prisoners over; he took a long, intense look at Denny, and then said. 'Take them to my cabin.' As he spoke, Denny felt a strange quiver, a feeling of familiarity. They were manhandled into the cabin; Tamar was strangely silent and restless. The cabin was lavish, in the way that only magic can create, as Denny realised.

'Who is this guy?' he asked. 'Why should I know him? What ...?'

'I'm not sure,' she said. 'It was a long time ago. I just have this feeling. Now shut up.'

Denny recognised that tone; he shut up, just as the Captain entered the cabin. He held up the Athame. 'Now, do I take it that this fine dagger belongs to one of you?'

'It's mine,' said Denny, before Tamar could stop him.

'Yours is it? How peculiar, you are not a Demon. You're much too sweet.' He laughed at Denny's stunned face. 'Yes I know what *this* is.' He took Denny's chin in a silk gloved hand. 'But who are *you*?' he said, stroking Denny's face and hair, almost seductively. 'You're pretty! I think I might keep you.'

Not again! Denny was silent.

'You think that an impertinent question from a man in a mask?' He said. 'Very well, you shall see my face.' He took the mask off, in a dramatic gesture. Denny's reaction was all that the Captain could have hoped for; he gasped in amazement. Then he looked at Tamar. 'You devil,' he said.

* * *

'We aren't keeping him here,' said Stiles, referring to the preist. 'Won't that just make things worse anyway?'

Hecaté shrugged helplessly. 'What else is there to do?' she asked. 'If we can work out how to ...'

'How to what?'

'How to insert this man back into history without affecting the timeline,' she said firmly.

Stiles groaned. It's always something, isn't it?'

'How are we supposed to keep him here anyway?' he added. 'Won't he just vanish like the other one?'

'Ah, of course,' said Hecaté as a light dawned on her. 'When Tamar and Denny exit the file'

'Huh?'

'This is obviously where he has come from,' she said. 'The file our friends are currently searching – he has been moved out of the way to make room for them. Temporal displacement.'

'Okay, so ... how were you planning on keeping him here then?'

'By the strength of my will of course,' she said as if this should have been obvious. 'I *am* a goddess you know.'

Stiles did not like this plan for reasons he could not quite put his finger on. But surely messing about with the files any more than necessary was a bad idea – things were bad enough as they were. However, she was right; she *was* a goddess and ought to know better than he did about these matters.

Hecaté saw his face. 'Anyway,' she said, 'we also have a job to do here.'

'And what about him?'

'He seems happy enough,' she said. 'We must not neglect Tamar and Denny because of this interruption.'

'*Interruption*?' Stiles sighed. 'Where are they now?'

'In trouble,' said Hecaté shortly.

'Par for the course,' said Stiles dryly. 'Do they need help?'

'Not yet,' said Hecaté. 'In fact, I am not at all sure *what* they are doing, I just know that they have been in this region of history for far too long now if they have not found the monster.'

'Maybe they have.'

'No, he is not here, I see no signs'

Stiles sighed. 'You know this could take months – so to speak.'

'Years,' she corrected him.

'Cripes, have we got enough food?'

Hecaté smiled.

'You know, there's something funny about all this,' said Stiles – the perennially suspicious. 'I mean, why would Askphrit miss? Miss Denny's granddad I mean. It's almost as if …' he trailed off.

'As if what?'

'Nothing, it doesn't matter. There's nothing we can do about it now anyway.'

* * *

'It was during one of my periods of freedom,' explained Tamar, 'I was bored; I just wanted to know what it would be like.'

'So, you took up piracy for a lark?'

'What are you two talking about?' asked the "other" Tamar, the one dressed up as Captain Hook.

Tamar (our Tamar) and Denny looked at each other and shrugged. Tamar put on her usual face. The other Tamar gasped. 'By Allah that's *my* face! – Take it off at once, you don't know who you're dealing with.'

Tamar said. 'I think I do,' and the other peered at her, then stepped back in shock. She had seen it.

She sat down, as if she was winded. 'How is this possible?' she managed, eventually.

'You know better than that,' said Tamar. 'You know we can't tell you, you of all people understand, and especially since it deals with your own future.'

Yes, I understand,' she glanced at Denny. 'Who's he?' she whispered. 'He's – well he's very um –.'

'He is, isn't he?' Tamar smiled. 'He's – no I can't tell you, just try to forget you ever saw him.'

'I don't think I can.'

'Try, it's important.'

'You could wish for it.'

'Good idea.'

There was a loud banging on the cabin door. 'Go away!' snapped Captain Tamar, angrily.

'But Captain ...'

'Oh for god's sake!' she rose and wrenched open the door. 'What is it?'

'Spaniards Captain.'

'Oh hell!' She turned to her guests; at least I know I'll survive it.'

'Of course you will,' said Tamar. 'You *are* immortal.'

'Oh yes of course I am. Well here's your Athame, you'd better get going.' As she handed it over, she took hold of Denny's hand and would not let go.

'Um,'

'Oh let him go,' said Tamar. 'You can't keep him, not yet.'

Captain Tamar let go of him reluctantly. 'I suppose so,' she let her gaze linger on him, longingly. 'See you soon?' she asked hopefully.

'Stop fishing,' said Tamar. 'Close file.'

The cabin vanished and they were back in the file room, the last thing they heard was 'Goodbye.'

'I just didn't have the heart to tell her that she's about to be captured by the Spaniards and end up back in the bottle again,' said Tamar.

~ Chapter Five ~

IT WAS A BRIGHT, sunny day, which made a pleasant change. They were quite obviously in a small town or suburb in the mid to late twentieth century. The streets were quiet, and there were few cars about. The street they stood on was mostly taken up by a large comprehensive school. And it was evidently late afternoon, probably midweek.

With few people or vehicles as clues, it was surprising how difficult it was to judge the decade. Houses and streets changed so little in reality. Not at all how science fiction writers once foresaw the march of progress. There was a red telephone box on the corner. This only meant that it could be any time between the fifties and the eighties. Denny narrowed it down further when he spotted a turquoise mini parked in a driveway. It had to be the sixties or later he said. Even the few people they could see afforded little in the way of data. Fashions in the twentieth century changed far less than those same science fiction writers could ever have conceived. As Denny pointed out. 'Have you ever seen anybody wearing a tinfoil jumpsuit, in real life?'

And Tamar, doyenne of style, agreed that the girl in the miniskirt could be from either the late sixties, early seventies or any time after the early eighties. Or she could just be from the mid-seventies and be behind the fashion; it was impossible to tell. An elderly lady in a headscarf could as easily be from the forties or last week.

If they could only see into the inside of the houses, they might have a better idea, technology being a far better guide than the people themselves.

I do not undertake to explain their fascination with this conundrum, except to say that it is possible that it would strike anyone else in the same way, were they to find themselves in this position. In every other file they had entered they had found it relatively easy to identify the time period within a few years. Only the modern world, it seemed, was so uniform and unchanging. Denny and Tamar felt quite determined to find out when they were before they left. It was strange when you think about it. Here, they had no reason to hang around, nobody had seen them (and it would probably not have mattered much if they had) Tamar could not sense Askphrit, and nothing peculiar was going on, and yet they did not want to leave.

'I reckon it's the 'eighties,' said Denny.

''Sixties,' countered Tamar. 'It's so quiet; that's because, all the men are at work and the women are at home. They didn't have two car families in the sixties; that's why most of the driveways are empty.'

'In the 'eighties the women would be at work too,' argued Denny. 'That's why they aren't out in the street talking or gardening or whatever.'

'Could even be the nineties then,' mused Tamar, 'by that reckoning.'

'No,' said Denny, positively. 'They didn't have those red telephone boxes by that time, they'd all gone.'

'You do notice some funny things,' observed Tamar. 'Let's look at the sign on outside the school, see what year it was built; that might narrow it down a bit.'

They wandered over. The sign read Mill Lane Comprehensive. Built 1968. This then was inconclusive.

'Well, we can't ask anyone,' said Tamar. 'Not unless we want to be taken for wandering lunatics.'

'Why do we care so much?' wondered Denny.

'Let's go and find a newspaper stand,' said Tamar, ignoring this, since she had no answer for it.

'Where's the fun in that?' asked Denny, thereby answering his own question if he had but realised it. 'If we do that, we might as well ask somebody. I thought we were trying to work it out. It's a pretty poor show, if we can't figure it out between us, don't you think?'

'Oh, who cares?' said Tamar suddenly tired of the whole thing. 'That bastard isn't here anyway, let's just go.'

At that moment, the clock across the street struck the half-hour, causing them to automatically look at it.

'Well, at least we know what time it is,' observed Denny. 'And it's 1985,' he added.

Tamar thought this was a gambit to draw her back into the guessing game, and she was not to be drawn. She shrugged. 'If you say so,' she said, 'let's go.'

'No, it really is. I saw ...' the rest of his words were drowned out by a clamorous ringing which echoed over the street.

'School's out,' said Denny dryly. 'Who would have thought the bell would sound so loud out here? We'd better go,' he added, 'or else we'll be drowned in a sea of hormones. And I wouldn't like to answer for the effect you might have on a hormonal sixteen year old boy –specially looking like *that*.'

'Like what?'

'Like what.' snorted Denny. 'You know very well, like what.'

'I just look like I always do,' she protested.

'That's what I mean. Look out they're coming.'

There was indeed a steady stream of scrofulous sweaty humanity headed their way making a noise like a flock of seagulls, and some of them had hairstyles to match.

There was no time to get away. Tamar, referring to age old instincts of blending in with her surroundings, instantly and without stopping to think, manufactured uniforms to match the ones the kids were wearing, just as they were caught up with the tide.

Denny was surprised to suddenly find himself chewing something, and, before he knew what he was doing, he blew a large pink bubble which popped all over his face.

He gave Tamar a baleful look, especially as she was, quite naturally, choking on a laugh that had bubbled to the surface.

'Whoops,' she giggled.

Denny was so intent on giving Tamar a dirty look that he ran into a group of large boys, almost knocking one of them over. He apologised, but he knew it was a waste of time, these were rough boys, and Denny looked even less impressive than usual at the moment, what with the bubblegum and the school uniform. Tamar had not even bothered to make it scruffy like it should be.

The boys rounded on him; Denny sighed internally. He had no desire to hurt children, which, despite their size, was what they were. He would have to let the boy beat him up – a little anyway. At least he knew it would not really hurt. Not like it used to.

A smaller boy with what looked suspiciously like make-up on, suddenly called out 'Phillpot!' mysteriously enough to Tamar, although Denny got the point immediately. Evidently some fearsome, ogrerish member of the faculty was on the warpath. Denny understood it to be a reprieve, and was proved right when all the boys ran including himself. Tamar shrugged and followed. It should be pointed out here, that the inevitability of an ensuing fight had been completely lost on her, so that, when the boy in question Mark –somebody caught up with them in the park that Denny had headed for – for privacy in order to close the file, she was surprised by his vehement attitude and also his bad language.

'All right puke breath,' was this savant's opening line. 'Now you're going to get it.'

'I thought as much,' said Denny resignedly. 'Come on then, I haven't got all day.'

'Are you trying to be funny?' snarled Mark – somebody.

'Not really.'

Tamar interrupted. 'What the hell is going on here?' She was nonplussed. Apart from anything, if they were going to fight, it ought to be about her, that was the usual way of it in her experience. But it seemed that, on the contrary, Mark – somebody was not even aware of her presence. An unheard of thing. And why fight at all, Denny had apologised hadn't he? Then what was the problem?

Denny cleared it up for her in one succinct word. 'Bullying.'

Tamer knew about this from Denny's stories of his adolescence, but had never had occasion to witness it before. People who own a Djinn tend not to suffer from bullying much.

Her own inexperience betrayed her now as she remarked. 'How ridiculous.'

However unlikely, this comment had an effect on Mark – somebody, who now turned to look properly at Tamar for the first time, and was embarrassed.

He looked at the ground and was heard to mutter. 'This your girlfriend?'

Denny wisely answered in the negative, and threw Tamar a warning glance not to contradict him. He could see where this was going.

'Sister?'

Denny hesitated; this was tricky. Brothers, in his experience, were despised creatures, and, therefore, quite acceptable beating up fodder. A friend on the other hand …

He, therefore, shook his head. 'Just a friend,' he decided.

Mark – something's attitude changed slightly. He became friendlier, although still somewhat truculent. 'Oh, right,' he said.

They were about to part on reasonably good terms when it happened.

Three large men who had pulled up in a black unmarked van, unnoticed by the three of them, had been ambling around apparently aimlessly until as if with one mind they made a grab for what they thought were three school-kids. Mark –

somebody panicked and struggled until his captor hit him on the head with a large cudgel of some kind and he went as limp as a boneless fish. Denny and Tamar were taken by surprise, but did not bother to offer any resistance as their heads were covered over with black hoods and they were bundled into the van along with Mark – somebody. They were too used to this sort of thing by now to be overly concerned about their own welfare. Habit had made them far more concerned about an untimely display of their powers; thus they submitted docilely. In time, they would just vanish from whatever prison they ended up in, and their captors would never know what had happened to them. Mark – somebody might be more of a problem, after all, they could not leave him behind. But they could cross that bridge when they came to it.

* * *

The two men guarding them in the van – the third one was driving – were engaged in an argument about their prisoners. It appeared that they only wanted to keep Tamar, as she had the most market value. From this, they understood that these men were white slave traders. Tamar rolled her eyes, although in her black hood, no one saw her. 'Honestly,' she thought, 'we can't go *anywhere*.'

One man argued that they had had to take the boys, since they couldn't leave them behind to talk. And besides, they would get something for them. The other man was all for throwing them out of the van further down the road. 'By the time they get home, we'll be long gone,' he asserted. He also maintained that they would cost more to feed and transport than they were worth. Denny was not at all insulted by this attitude; he was used to it. But he hoped that this plan would be abandoned, since it would mean that he would have to take some drastic action after all, which was to be avoided if possible. Mark – somebody was still unconscious, so he did not have an opinion at this point.

* * *

'Get me that report,' shouted the thin man across the room.

'Yes sir,' a young lackey came scurrying across with a small disc in his hand.

'What have they been doing all this time?' he muttered.

'They certainly have been in that file a long time,' agreed the lackey. 'Getting absolutely nowhere,' was his private thought.

The thin man inserted his report into his personal disc reader and frowned for a few moments.

'I hate these jobs,' he said suddenly. Then his face cleared. 'However, we seem to be on schedule, more or less,' he added mysteriously enough. 'Not that it matters much in the end. It's not as if we'll be getting any credit for this one even if it turns out all right.' He sighed.

The lackey was puzzled. But then again, this whole assignment was confusing and apparently pointless. They had been monitoring the progress of the pursuit which made some sort of sense as far as it went, but, on the other hand, he knew full well that they were not logging any information officially.

And they were interfering in the pursuit too, and that was definitely "unofficial". But only, apparently, to the extent of small clues and tiny pieces of knowledge that were being given to the pursuers, however, it was enough to give the lackey the opinion that his superior knew enough to end this at any time. So why didn't he? Why keep giving out little dribs and drabs of information in such small amounts as to be almost completely useless?

And then again, the behaviour of the pursuers themselves was odd. Why, for instance, when they knew that their quarry was not in the file they had entered, did they consistently stay there for far longer than was necessary? They appeared to be wasting an awful lot of time on side issues in the lackey's opinion.

So what did the boss mean, "On schedule?"

* * *

The man who had wanted to hold on to all the captives had won the argument, and they had, all three of them (Mark – somebody, having regained consciousness) been bundled out of the van, hoods over their faces, and taken into some sort of large warehouse, where their hoods had been removed, and ropes around their wrists and ankles had been added.

Here they waited for about an hour, Mark – somebody, white faced and trembling, and Denny and Tamar remarkably at ease; guarded at all times by a hulking, chain smoking kidnapper. The three men all looked decidedly similar. Dark, brooding types with monobrows and stubborn chins, they might have been brothers, particularly when one considered the way they continually argued.

Denny and Tamar exchanged thoughts 'Can't we stage something?' asked Denny. 'Something believable? There's only one of them. I don't think Mark – whatever his name is, can take much more of this,'

'We're bound and gagged, what do you suggest? We're supposed to be school-kids, what could we do, *realistically*?' It is not easy to use italics in telepathy, but somehow Tamar managed it.

Denny shook his head.

'Well?' thought Tamar after a pause.

'Oh, sorry, I don't know what to do, but I think we're at a private airfield. If we don't do something soon they're going to whisk us off to God only knows where. And Mark – thingy too,' he added, in case she had forgotten.

'I know, I know,' she replied testily. 'But ...' and here she was interrupted by the arrival of the other two men who hauled them roughly to their feet and propelled them outside to the waiting plane.

* * *

'AAAAGH!' bellowed Stiles in aggravation. Remind me never to have kids!' he added. He had been tried beyond the limits of his patience by the sudden advent of Lucy and Samuel aged 13 or thereabouts. Lucy had immediately burst into noisy sobs, which showed no signs of abating, and Samuel, after hitting Lucy on the head a few times (apparently to calm her down), was now amusing himself by kicking a football at the wood panelling (having given up Lucy as a bad job).

They had been here a total of about three minutes, and Stiles was already seriously contemplating committing his first double homicide.

Bump – BANG, bump – BANG, bump, bump, BANG.... the noise stopped abruptly and Stiles managed half a sigh of relief before Samuel apparently turned into an aeroplane 'Nnnneeeeeaaaaaaaww!'

The good news was that this sudden divergence caused Lucy to look up in surprise and stop crying in order to start laughing. This was marginally better Stiles supposed. But there was still the problem of Samuel, now jumping from one piece of furniture to another.

The problem for Stiles was that he had not had the gentle lead up to this – the years of babyhood and toddlerhood and early schooldays. He had been dropped in at the deep end as it were.

'STOP IT!' he bellowed. This had no discernible effect on Samuel at all, and Lucy started crying again. He looked at Hecaté in desperation.

'Food,' she told him. 'Give them biscuits and crisps,'

'We haven't got any,' objected Stiles.

'Oh ye of little faith,' said Hecaté with a faint smile. 'I am a goddess you know?'

* * *

They had succeeded in calming Mark – something down a little, mostly by example. And all of them were aware, by now, that the fate that awaited Tamar at the end of this journey was by far the worst of them. She was to be sold into a Harem in the Far East the men had told them. She had been picked out especially for a customer, being just what he had ordered. Much like car thieves steal cars to order for favoured customers. Mark – something was so horrified by this idea, that it did much to take his mind off his own fate. Tamar was not too pleased by the idea either, since she could see no way, at the moment, to get out of it. 'I bet he's fat,' she complained, 'and old – and smelly.'

'It won't come to that,' said Denny grimly. The man guarding them laughed derisively. 'Worry about yourself,' he advised Denny before stomping off to the cockpit.

There was no way to tell how time was going in the stuffy windowless interior of the small plane, but after what seemed an interminable journey, the plane seemed to be coming in to land. 'Probably only to refuel,' suggested Denny. 'There's no way a plane this size could make the trip to the Far East in one go.'

'Maybe this is our chance to escape,' said Tamar. There were no guards at this time, probably, as Denny suggested, because they had only stopped to refuel.

'But we don't know where we are,' said Mark – somebody (who I think, from now on, should be referred to only by his given name, to save time)

'Does it matter?' asked Denny impatiently. 'Think of Tam, we have to get away if we can. And we don't know what they might do to *us* either,' he added as an afterthought.

Mark, whose attitude to Denny had changed to a sort of grovelling respect, immediately capitulated. 'Okay, so what shall we do?' He transferred his gaze to Tamar with a mute apology in his eyes as well as a kind of yearning that Tamar knew only too well.

She shook her head briskly as if to dismiss all silly sentiment. 'Not now,' she told him. 'We haven't got time for all that.' And she crawled on her hands and knees to the cockpit. 'It's empty,' she informed them, 'Come on, we'll get out this way.'

'Where are the men?' asked Mark, as if she would know. She shook her head and shrugged. 'Not here.'

'Fair enough,' said Denny, 'let's go. He led the way.

They climbed out of the cockpit and ran silently behind the plane, going cautiously for they did not know where the men might be. They seemed to be in a large hangar which could have been anywhere. They never got to find out where they were. As they reached the rear of the plane Denny was met by a gun which was almost pushed up his nose, he skidded to a halt and sighed.

'I thought you might try something like this,' said the man roughly amused. 'Especially *you*,' he shoved Denny backwards by the shoulders. 'I must say, you don't look like much, but you've got balls, I'll say that for you. Okay back inside.' He herded them back onto the plane and locked it up. They could see him through the cockpit standing outside, watching.

'What do we do now?' asked Mark.

The second part of the journey did not go as smoothly as the first.

It never does as you may have noticed. A journey, once begun again after a break for lunch or whatever, never continues as before. The traffic is worse, for example. The driver/pilot is in a bad mood and the passengers feel sick and tired and fed up. In this case, they were hit by turbulence. The little plane rocked and rolled alarmingly as it was buffeted about the sky.

An argument ensued between two of the men about Tamar. One of them wanted to have a little fun with her, a test run as he rather gracelessly put it. The other man was against this, and Denny was relieved to notice that the man who was against it, was the same man who had earlier won the argument in the van. She wasn't a toy he claimed, but merchandise. So it was hands off, *nitsky, comprendré?* She was to be sold "as new" not second hand.

All this was rather distasteful, to say the least, although to Tamar it held an element of amusement. 'If only they knew,' she thought. She was not, of course, in the least bit concerned for herself. If the "customer" tried to lay even one fat greasy finger on her, she would have no compunction in scattering him into his component atoms. But she did feel a tearing pity for the other girls who had found themselves in this position. The same pity that Mark was currently feeling for her.

Denny was merely furious. So furious, in fact, that the man in question never knew how close he came to being thrown bodily through the carcass of the plane and out into the void. It was his good luck (although he did not know enough of his peril to feel it) that the other man won the argument, and he sloped off rather sulkily to the cockpit.

They flew on in silence.

It occurred to Tamar that quite soon they would be separated, having had, she deemed, no chance of escape. Once they landed, all three of them would face a drastically different situation. She had the best of it, she knew. At least she knew what she was headed for. Although she had no fear for Denny, or Mark either with Denny to look after him, she was still uneasy. Mark was the real problem here. She could think, and she was sure that Denny too could think, of a million ways to get themselves out of this mess if it was just them, but nothing that would work without giving themselves away to Mark.

She cast the man into a charmed sleep and Mark too, so that they could talk. Telepathy was wearing after a while.

'We have to make a plan about what to do after we escape,' she said.

Denny nodded. He was certain, as she was, that they *would* escape at some point once they were on the ground, but they would have to meet up somewhere if they had been separated.

The problem was geography. 'We don't know the lay of the land,' he said.

'And we probably won't have time to make plans after we land, before they separate us,' she said gloomily, referring to some earlier conversations that the men had not troubled to conceal.

Tamar was suddenly overcome with a strange feeling. She snuggled closer to Denny and laid her head on his shoulder. 'I have a horrible feeling about this,' she said. 'I feel like I'm not going to see you again for a long time.'

Denny didn't feel as if he could dissent. He put his arms around her.

'I think I need a nice memory,' she hinted, 'something to hang onto you know.'

Denny did know, and he was nothing loth. And when the man and Mark woke up, it was to find Tamar and Denny asleep in each other's arms with smiles on their faces.

Mark sighed to himself; he was not really surprised. Disappointed, but not surprised.

It was as they had surmised; when they landed they were herded off in different directions. Tamar to a car that appeared to be waiting for them and Denny and Mark to a large open van, which was already heaving with bodies – young men, like themselves. Denny just had time to whisper to Tamar 'I'll find you,' before they were dragged apart.

* * *

It was like a slumber party, the most opulent slumber party ever. Tamar enjoyed the luxury but not the feelings of unease that she sensed in the others as well as herself. She was largely ignored by the other "wives" as she supposed they must be called. She decided that she would rather be a concubine than a wife. There was something so permanent about the term "wife" not to mention the dowdy associations that the word conjured up. Not that you could imagine any of these women pushing a hoover. They were glamorous and languid; overdressed in jewels and underdressed in every other way. Tamar despised them. They looked like Houris. Tamar hated Houris. And there was something else about them that she found chillingly familiar. They moved, spoke, behaved, and even *looked* almost exactly the same as each other. There was a mechanical sameness about their movements, and they looked like so many Dutch dolls. She wondered idly if they were actually robots. "The Stepford Concubines". She was speculating on this, when a largish older woman approached her, and laid a plump be-ringed hand on her shoulder. She spoke in Arabic, but, of course, Tamar understood her. 'Poor, poor girl,' she said, 'you must not be afraid.' Without being asked, this oddly motherly type sat down beside Tamar and began to talk to her.

She was the king's first wife, and the mother of his heir. She too had been taken from her family when only a young girl, Ah, she had been beautiful then. This was the law in the small kingdom that they lived in, but not in the land that Tamar came from. Her son, who was a fine man, had been educated in the west, and he would be appalled by this transgression. Indeed he deplored what he called these barbaric customs and was planning to reform them when he came to the throne. But would he? wondered Tamar. Men talked like this, but rarely followed through, when it was easier not to.

A fine man, such a warrior, she was told. As becomes a Kings son, a born leader of men.

'Not like the old king, ah I talk treason, but I am old now, I am past fear, and I no longer feel the need to repeat lies and nonsense and the talk of fools and cravens. I will say what I mean.'

Tamar found herself warming to this woman.

'Do not worry about meeting the king tonight little one, for he is old now, if you know what I mean. He no longer has the strength to match the will. You will see. He will pet you and make much of you, but he will demand nothing from you.' She giggled. 'He is past it,' she whispered.

Tamar realised that the woman was trying to comfort her, and she appreciated it. She could only admire this woman who had obviously been forced to marry beneath her, to a man so pathetic that he felt the need to pretend a desire for young wives that he evidently no longer had.

If this son of hers, that she was so proud of, was indeed the fine man she spoke of, then it was clear to Tamar, at least, whom he took after.

This cosy discussion was broken up when the eunuchs appeared, to take Tamar away to be "prepared" for the king.

As they led her away, a young, richly dressed man entered the room. Tamar was surprised – this was no eunuch. He went straight to the old woman. 'Mother,' he said.

The eunuchs hovered nervously, obviously wanting to turn him out, but not daring to. Even if he had not been the prince, his was such a commanding presence that it is debatable whether they would have done anything anyway. He followed his mother's gaze and caught Tamar's eye for a moment. As she was hustled away, she saw the fury in his face before he turned his back on her.

His voice was raised some of his conversation reached Tamar in her bath in the next room. Isolated words and phrases: 'kidnap' ... 'westerner' ...'barbarism'... 'must be stopped.' ... 'old bastard.' ... 'doesn't he realise?' ... 'twentieth century.'

Tamar smiled, but he could not help her, however vehement his emotions. However, it appeared that his mother was right about him; he was all right.

He was gone by the time Tamar emerged from her bath, then she was dressed and made up. Two guards appeared. It was time to meet the king.

* * *

Crack! The whip fell mercilessly on Denny's shoulders and back. He winced and bit his lip, but he would not cry out, he would not give them that satisfaction.

Crack! Denny sagged forward, his back was bleeding freely now. The men had taken the Athame from him when they had stripped him, but he was made of sterner stuff than he looked in any case – even without it.

He was aware that he was being "broken in". That the purpose of this treatment was to soften him up and break his spirit. This and the rotten food – which was quite literally rotten and crawling with weevils, the only protein that it contained, and the noisome dungeon that they were locked in, menaced by guards with pungent body odour and stagnant breath, who would pick up on the slightest thing as an excuse for a handing out a beating. Which brings us quite neatly back to the whip, whistling though the air and landing on Denny's tender, bleeding back. The "softening up" might have worked on Denny under other circumstances, but, as it happened, all he could think of was that he must get the Athame back somehow.

If he had but known it, the guards were a little afraid of him, it was not natural to be so indifferent to such punishments as they could hand out. And the other prisoners were in awe of him. He had not cried out once. The guards were aware of these feelings which only increased their hatred of him. He was clearly dangerous, and it would probably be safer to kill him, in front of the other prisoners, of course. As a lesson.

Denny, wrapped up in his own thoughts, was unaware of any of this, he did not realise his own danger. Because, of course, without the Athame he could be killed as easily as the next man.

He was thrown into a corner roughly by the infuriated and frustrated guard who had completely failed to raise so much as a whimper. Hopefully he would die on his own from his suppurating wounds. It had happened before.

But Denny was far from dying. He and Mark were in a common prison among thieves and murderers as well as other slaves, who had been placed there by the traders to be held by the guards for a sensible gratuity, and softened up until the traders were ready for them. This was illegal, but apparently common practice and the guards were well paid to turn a blind eye. As he fell into a pile of filth in the corner, Denny noticed something that made him sit up.

Most of the other prisoners were thieves, and one of them, a malignant rat-like man with only one hand left, showing that he had been caught stealing before, evidently had not lost the habit just because he was in prison. Out of the corner of his eye, Denny saw that he had stolen the Athame from the guard. He was sat in a dark corner looking at the hypnotic patterns on the blade – turning it over and over again, unable to tear his gaze away. Denny understood; he had been the same way with it when he had first acquired it. But all the same, it was a fool thing to do in a place like this; he could be spotted at any moment. Denny knew he had to get it away from the man as soon as he could, before the guards did.

He inched forward on his knees, and only then did he become aware of the pain in his back and limbs, it was agonizing. Denny winced in a fashion that the guard, had he been watching, would have found highly gratifying. The man who had his Athame was about his own height and build, but Denny was so damaged by the recent assault, that he was not certain that he was a match for him in this condition. His only comfort was that the man did not know what he held in his remaining hand. If he had, it would have been pointless to even try to take it from him. The man would simply use the Athame to kill him. He might do that anyway, after all it *was* a blade. Denny shrugged; a painful operation in his current state. He had to have it back. And not just because he needed it. Denny might be in a deplorable state, and the thief in comparatively good health – he had not been whipped yet – but he did not despair. Thanks to Tamar and his recent adventures, Denny had been trained for a fight in ways that this man could surely never have conceived of. He did not bother to dupe himself with reassuring drivel about his being on the side of right and how right would win out in the end. This was down to cunning.

He could not risk a noisy confrontation which might attract the attention of the guards. And he knew also, that, in his weakened state that would be the least of his difficulties. No, there was no way out of it; he would have to kill the man. It was the only way to do this silently. It went against everything that he believed in and yet he continued to edge forward slowly. He was so intent on his goal, that he was almost unaware of the rage that was possessing him. It was his Athame, his own, his precious, if you will. What right did this greasy little man have to steal it from him? He would have it back if he swung for it. All the same, he was cautious. He stopped and glanced around warily and caught the eye of Mark, who was watching him with undisguised astonishment. *Damn him, he would give the game away.* Denny stopped short and frowned. Mark looked from Denny to the man, saw the knife and winked at him, to show that he could see what he was up to. Then – a miracle!

Mark, showing more courage than sense, created a distraction by the simple expedient of making a lot of noise.

Denny took his opportunity; he grabbed the thief from behind, one hand over his mouth, the other making a vice like grip on the thief's wrist, twisting his arm up his back and forcing him to drop the Athame. Summoning the last of his strength, he kicked the man aside and grasped his prize, and as his fingers closed over the hilt he felt his strength return although his pain did not lessen. He looked around; the distraction had worked; no one had noticed anything. It had happened so fast that the thief had not had time to react, but now he was getting to his feet with such a look of maddened outrage in his eyes that Denny made haste to thump his head and knock him out cold, before his protestations should alert the guards.

So far so good. He had the Athame back, and his rage had subsided the moment he had hold of it again, so much so that he wondered where it had come from – how much did he rely on this thing, really? However, he did not have time to ponder that right now, for their next problem was looming up fast. Mark was being dragged forward by two burly guards, who were clearly only too pleased to have an excuse to hand out a beating.

Without missing a beat, Denny used the Athame to slice through the manacles on his legs and stood up, retrieved the sheath from the recumbent thief and put the Athame away, he would not need it to fight, he thought. He used the manacles on his wrists in the same way as he had on the guards of King Richard, that is, he knocked the nearest guard on the head with them. Not even pausing to think 'this is becoming a habit,' he swung round and hit the other guard, who went down like a sack of coal. He grabbed the keys from the guard's belt and threw them to Mark, then he groaned. The pain in his back was burning now. He felt faint with it. Apparently, although the Athame could protect the bearer from injury, it could not heal injuries previously sustained. Denny knew from experience that the Athame had no power to heal or mend, only to destroy. It was the way it had been made. Having it blessed to remove its evil, had not changed its basic nature.

However, he did not have time to worry about that now. Problem number three was now looming on the horizon. The guards were out of action, and it had been done so swiftly and silently that there was no reason to suppose that anyone would come to investigate, for a while at least. There was, therefore, time to release all the prisoners; the question was, should they? Mark had freed his own bonds and was now looking questioningly at Denny with the keys in his hands, obviously wondering the same thing. Denny considered. On the one hand, many of these guys were innocent slaves, to leave them here would be indefensible surely? On the other hand, what would they do with them if they freed them? Mark was going to be problem enough in all conscience. Then again, most of the prisoners were thieves and murderers, Denny did not want to release them, desperate as they would now be, to ravage the local population. And how would they know which was which anyway? They all looked the same, thin, filthy and ragged. Then again, there was the problem of the hue and cry they would raise if Denny and Mark escaped without helping them. Mind you, that needn't be a problem. If necessary he could make himself and Mark invisible – Mark would never even realise. What finally decided him was the realisation that this was the past he was in, he should not change it more than he could help – who knew what the repercussions would be?

Reluctantly, and feeling incredibly guilty, he shook his head at Mark and took the keys from him to unlock his wrists. 'Come on,' he said, 'let's get out of here, while we still can.'

Mark looked back at the huddled prisoners 'But ...' he gestured.

'I know,' said Denny impatiently, 'but we really can't. I can't explain it. We're not supposed to *be* here.'

Mark was baffled by this explanation as you might expect. But he was after all only a boy, and although he believed Denny to be no older than himself, Denny did not act that way and Mark had had a bad time of it recently. So he did not argue, but fell in behind Denny, who turned back, just before they climbed out into the sunshine, to quell the noise of the disappointed prisoners by casting them into charmed sleep. A very easy trick which even an inexperienced witch can perform easily.

* * *

'A charmed sleep,' Hecaté, told Stiles, 'very easy magic, and it will not hurt them until we decide what to do with them.'

'That's fine,' said Stiles, but what about the other problem? Those kids must've turned up after Denny and Tamar went into another file. Which means that the Priest should have been returned to his file by now. Won't it leave a sort of a ... gap or something?' Stiles was struggling to express concepts that he really did not understand.

'It does not matter,' said Hecaté.

'I'm sure it *does*,' muttered Stiles mutinously.

'It will be as if they never existed,' she said, 'until they are returned to their proper place.

'But they aren't supposed be *here* are they?' he persisted. 'Aren't they sort of ...

'Nowhere,' she told him. 'They are nowhere.'

They're *here*,' insisted Stiles. 'I can *see* them. Look I can see how one takes the place of another. Denny and Tamar are gone, and the priest and the dog filled the space they left. But now we have two more, if this goes on there won't be any room for them.'

'The universe compensates,'

'Well how come it didn't compensate when Denny and Tamar entered the first file?'

'It did,' she told him.

'Oh yes,' said Stiles, remembering, 'by sending Lord Whatsisface here, fair enough, but how is it "compensating" for this lot?' His face turned white. 'Oh Lord,' he said.

~ Chapter Six ~

THE KING WAS not exactly what Tamar had expected. Tall and thin, he was bent with age and very lined. Yet he had a noble looking face that must have once been remarkable for its beauty. Tamar, however, was not ready yet to revise her opinion of him. And yet, perhaps he was just old and proud and not willing to give up a thousand years of tradition in favour of a way of life that he could not be expected to understand. Still, just let him try anything …

The king made a gesture to her. She shrugged, not comprehending. The king made the gesture again rather impatiently, and a courtier came forward and whispered to her. 'The king would like to know if you would dance for him?'

'No.'

The courtier looked worried; as well he might, it being his task to repeat this unwelcome news to the king.

Tamar relieved him; she addressed the king herself, in perfect Arabic. 'I do not dance,' she said. 'Not for you, not for anybody. You needn't think *you're* anything special. And I'm not doing anything else either, so there!' In retrospect she thought that the "so there" might be taken for childish defiance, and immediately wished she had not added it. It seemed, she felt, to weaken her position – for when has childish defiance ever been of the slightest effect?

The king seemed to feel the same way. Instead of becoming angry, as one might have expected (and Tamar certainly did) he gave her an indulgent smile, such as one might give to a favoured child, whose unruly behaviour is constantly overlooked and indulged as a source of amusement to nobody but the doting parent.

'Okay,' she thought, 'I'll dance for the old bastard. I'll dance him into a heart attack.'

She was perfectly capable of doing this, and at that moment perfectly without compassion, so furious was she. So, she nodded to the courtier who signalled the musicians, and struck a pose, removing her veil with a flourish as she did so. In a county where this was tantamount to taking off all your clothes, and, in view of the face that she revealed, this was a particularly merciless beginning. The old king actually gasped and clutched his chest. Tamar smiled cruelly, at that moment the beauty of her countenance was only matched by the blackness of her heart.

At that very moment, Denny was being whipped to within an inch of his life – as the saying goes – in this man's name. And Tamar, with that subtle connection that she had with him, could feel every stroke. So she moved with sinuous grace to the throbbing beat that filled the room, every beat seemed to stab the old man to the heart, in time to the lash of the whipfall on Denny's back.

The courtiers were sweating; the old king was going purple in the face, fighting for breath and still she danced. 'It's nothing but what my darling is suffering at this very moment,' she thought, 'and he is a better man than you could ever be if you lived a thousand years.'

The room seemed to grow dim and through her own pain, the old king's face swam through a mist, growing larger and larger and with an almost imploring look. Although, whether imploring her to stop or not to stop, was more than she could tell.

Abruptly the pain ceased, and Tamar faltered in her dance, the impetus suddenly withdrawn. And the music followed her to a halting close.

In the ensuing silence, the courtiers drew a deep breath of relief and the king fell forward with his head on his knees. Tamar was horrified. All the hate that had welled up inside her had drained away as suddenly as it had come. *What had she done?* She turned and ran from the room. She was stopped by two guards outside the door who, at a signal from a courtier, took hold of her by the elbows and courteously, but firmly, escorted her back to the harem. She was too distraught to feel the humiliation of her position or to take advantage of it either. They were stopped by a tall personage whom Tamar quite failed to recognize, at first, as the prince. He was on his way to the king it appeared. A war with a neighbouring fiefdom was likely to escalate, it seemed. And to make matters worse, two prisoners had escaped from the dungeons. At this Tamar raised her head (which had been bowed in shame) to listen. The prisoners had evidently had outside assistance. The guards and all the other prisoners had apparently been drugged, and the escapees were nowhere to be found, surely an impossibility unless somebody was hiding them. Tamar caught a strange look on the prince's face as these facts were related to him. A slight smile was playing about his lips, and he was watching Tamar's face closely, as if to gauge her reaction. He nodded, as if he was satisfied about something. Then he turned to the guards and gave some rapid orders about the search for the prisoners and the gathering of troops for the impending skirmish. Then he turned on his heel abruptly and left.

* * *

The oddest thing about the man who was sheltering them, Denny decided, was that he was apparently not at all afraid of the consequences, which, Denny assumed, would be dire if he was caught. He had heard their story with equanimity and without surprise. Denny had not seen any harm in telling him. What could he do, after all?

Now that Denny had the Athame back in his possession, he felt invulnerable. (Which he was not of course – only comparatively so. Compared to you, for example – or me. Compared to Tamar, he may as well have been wearing a sign reading "Beat me, bite me, whip me, kill me". Compared to Tamar he was as vulnerable as a snail out of its shell. Everything is relative.)

In any case, the man seemed trustworthy enough, and it was a convenient place to hide until he came up with a plan to find Tamar. Much better than using magic in front of Mark, who had probably had as much as he could take anyway.

They had almost run straight into this man as soon as they had left the prison. He had looked at them curiously for a second and then, just as Denny was about to reach for the Athame, had put his finger on his lip to indicate silence and beckoned them to follow him. It was all the more unlikely, when one considered that they were obvious westerners; even covered in grime, their skin was far lighter than his. Why would he risk so much for the sake of two grubby foreigners? It made no sense, and Denny was initially suspicious. This feeling was much relieved by the food and wine and soft beds and the fact that the man spoke good English. Much better, in fact, than Denny's own. He heard their story, as I have said, without comment, and then he left them abruptly saying he would be back soon and cautioning them not to stir outside on pain of death. For in the daytime, there would be guards looking for them, he said, and at night there would be bandits.

Nevertheless, Denny followed him.

* * *

Tamar had been dumped, unceremoniously back in the harem, and the guards had scurried away in a great hurry.

Shortly after this, the harem were informed that they were to be moved. War was imminent, and their lord intended to ride out, therefore his wives and concubines must join him. Tamar had never heard anything so ridiculous. Everything about it was ludicrous. That a man with one and a half feet in his grave should ride out to war, when he had a young son who was perfectly capable. That this old man should expose his women to danger for no good reason. The man did not have the strength to lift a paper knife, let alone raise a sword – or anything else.

* * *

On the third day, the women had been living in a tent behind enemy lines, the prince called on his mother. He had come from the battlefield he said, and he looked it. He strode in resplendent in scarlet, his cloak flying out behind him. No longer did he seem even remotely civilised, he had thrown off the veneer of a western education and looked like what he was, a savage, a tiger among men, a King. He reminded Tamar of his father.

He stayed only a short time, talking urgently with his mother, and then he left, casting a dark look at Tamar as he passed her.

A few minutes later the king's first wife and Tamar's only friend in the harem (for the other women were not past jealousy) sauntered casually over to her. There was nothing unusual in this, for she often came to talk to Tamar, being the only one who did. The other women did not even raise their eyes, and Tamar assumed that she wanted to talk proudly of her son, as she often did. She was, therefore, surprised, when the woman whispered to her. 'I have a message for you, from my son.'

Tamar raised her eyebrows.

'You are to meet him tonight, at midnight. I will show you where.' She would say no more, and shuffled quickly away. Tamar was not altogether surprised at this assignation; she believed she understood. Well, she would go. She would just have to quickly disabuse him of any notions that he had formed in regard to her. But it might just turn out to be just what she had been waiting for. An opportunity.

* * *

The king's wife led her to the appointed spot and left her there, under the shade of a tree, the name of which, not being a botanist, Tamar did not know. It was hot, not the faintest breath of a wind disturbed the branches above her, yet she felt a chill, she thought she was observed. And then she saw him. He was sat on horseback just about twenty yards away, looking straight at her. He was bathed in moonlight, and she could see him clearly, but she realised that he could not see her, as she was in shadow.

She took the opportunity to study him. He was dressed in a long scarlet robe, and she could just make out from here, the hawk like curve of his nose. He sat the horse with such stillness that she wondered for a moment if he were a statue. The animal was clearly under his complete control.

There was a power in him that she could sense from here. It was not arrogance though, nor just simple physical strength. It was something else, something less definable –something that had nothing to do with his rank. He was a man that men would always follow, that rarest of things, a born leader.

Suddenly he seemed to make up his mind. He kicked the horse and turned it toward her and began to gallop straight for her. He had seen her after all. It was such a magnificent sight, that Tamar felt her heart give a treacherous flutter as he bore down on her, robes flying out behind him. Such a flutter as her heart had never given before for anybody but … Denny? As he swerved the horse around slowing to scoop her up behind him, she looked into his face. Surely those were Denny's eyes, looking out of that dark, handsome face.

* * *

They had planned it between them, Denny explained. Although the Prince, could not have known just how complete Denny's disguise would be. Denny laughed when he thought of it. He told her most of what had happened, glossing over his ordeal in the prison hastily, and neglecting to mention that his wounds from the beating, that she seemed, to his surprise, to be aware of, had not yet healed. He had become himself again, before they went to pick up the waiting Mark. And Tamar was glad of it. It had been unnerving to hear Denny's voice coming from the unfamiliar face of the prince.

'He had already seen you,' Denny told her, sat around a campfire after some hours riding. 'And when he heard our story, he knew who you must be. I have to admit, we probably couldn't have done it without him. We only had the vaguest idea of where you might be, but *he* knew. He got us into the army, and it was funny to think of all those guards looking for us, when we were right under their noses. And you know the rest.'

'How much does he know?' She indicated the sleeping Mark. He was an awkward rider, being new to it, and their progress had been slow, and he had found it tiring, as most new riders did. He would ache in the morning.

'Only as much as is good for him,' Denny assured her.

'What are we going to do about him?'

Denny shrugged and the robe slipped off his shoulders revealing the angry welts on his back and shoulders.

Tamar gasped. 'Oh my God! Denny, why didn't you tell me?'

'Oh, I'm okay,' said Denny, hastily covering up again. 'The Athame doesn't heal, you know. But it's not so bad now.'

'But I can heal you, even if the Athame can't. You really should have told me you were still hurt.'

'Don't fuss.'

She gave him a look.

'Okay, okay,' he gave in and bared his back. 'Leave the black eye for now,' he said. 'We don't want Mark Whatisname wondering.'

'Which brings us back to my original question,' said Tamar. 'What are we going to do about him? How are we going to get him home?'

'Would …? No never mind.'

'What?'

'Would leaving him in his bed, and letting him think it was all a nightmare, work? Silly I know, but …'

'And the fact that he's been missing from home for a fortnight? You don't think that somebody might bring it up? His mum, for instance.'

'Are you saying you *can* do it? Alter his memory I mean?'

'Technically, no. But I can wipe away the pain of the last weeks, and without that, the memories would fade on their own. It's our emotions that keep our experiences alive in our memory'

'So, he *could* believe it was all a dream?'

'But, Denny. What about the time?'

'I know, I know,' Denny shook his head sagely. 'What a pity we can't go back in time.'*

---

* Mark– somebody was deposited back in his own bed thirteen days before this conversation was to take place, by person or persons unknown. And aside from a severe telling off for staying out all night, suffered no ill effects from his adventure. Tamar and Denny never did find out his full name. The file, once closed, naturally, re-opened at the same entry point as before. Thus proving Tamar's theory of how the files worked to be the correct one

~ Chapter Seven ~

'*VIKINGS*?' SNORTED Denny in disgust. 'What is this, a school trip?'

'Shhh, they'll hear you,' Tamar pulled him behind a bush. 'We don't want to get tangled up with these bozos, believe me.'

'Dangerous are they?'

'Well, I suppose so, not to us though. No, what I mean is they're idiots. Imagine Bart Simpson, grown up and crossed with a Mill-Wall supporter and you're getting close.'

'Oh.'

'And talk about sexist! They make Australians look PC.'

'Ah,' Denny nodded, sagely. 'Gave you a hard time, did they?'

Vikings they were – about 30 of them, give or take, but making enough noise for 100 at least. Most of them were drunk, and all of them were fighting. Even Denny was unnerved at the casual way they were knocking seven kinds of shit out of each other. The fact that they were doing this with broadswords instead of their fists just made it bloodier, and not any less like a drunken brawl, which it clearly was. They did not even seem particularly angry. Apparently this was just a typical Saturday night.

'Did they always act like this?' asked Denny, watching in fascinated horror as a bloody head rolled within two feet of him.

'Oh no, only when they'd been drinking, they stopped when they went to sleep.'

'You know, I read that the Vikings were like this, but I always thought it was, you know, popular prejudice, exaggeration, that sort of thing.'

'Oh they're not so bad when they're sober. I mean you're right in a way, all the accounts you've ever read were written by the people they plundered. Naturally they were prejudiced. They usually only get drunk *after* a raid, not during it. Add to that, the fact that the only people who could write in these times were the clergy and what you get are grossly inflated accounts of their vicious barbarism.'

'Grossly inflated? *Look* at them! That one's just chopped off that guy's arm!'

'Like I said, they're drunk. Besides, they didn't do that to villagers, there's no sport in it, if they're not fighting back.'

'C'mon, let's get out of here,' she added.

'I'm glad you said that, I had a horrible feeling you were going to suggest we try to break it up.'

Tamar shuddered. 'Not this time. I hate these guys. I hope they all kill each oth …'

Denny and Tamar looked at each other in shock. What had interrupted her was the unmistakable sound of a gunshot.

Or it could have been a car backfiring, but in either case …

'Isn't it a bit too early for firearms?' asked Denny, king of the obvious.

'Oh, only about four hundred years or so, nothing really.'

'Tamar, is this the time for sarcasm? What the hell does it *mean*?' is Askphrit here?'

'I can't sense him, but he may have been here. Have you got any Nordic ancestors that you know of? You are very blond.'

'Not that I know of.'

'It probably doesn't matter. He's not here now anyway, and maybe he never was. This anachronism is just an example of what can happen when you get unauthorised people running around in history, changing God knows what. We'll probably get back to discover that the flintlock was invented in the Stone Age.'

'But it wasn't.'

'Not when we left,' she agreed. 'But now – who knows? We're going to have to expect to see this kind of thing, and sometimes it'll probably be our fault. No matter how careful we try to be.'

'But we haven't been to the Stone Age,' Denny pointed out.

'Not yet,' said Tamar darkly.

Denny tried to figure this one out and gave up. 'So what do we do?' he said.

'There's nothing we *can* do, not here. We just have to keep looking for Askphrit. That's what we're here for.'

A horrible thought struck Denny. 'What if we're too late?' he asked. 'I mean, what if he's already ... I mean, what if we get back, after we catch him, and I'm, you know, erased. You can't keep the world frozen forever, just in case.'

'Hmmm.' Tamar frowned as she tried to work out this temporal conundrum. 'I hadn't thought of that. I don't know, let me work on it.'

'And what are you planning on doing when we catch him anyway?'

'Got to catch him first.'

Without warning, at least without specific warning – after all, with their luck, they were always only a step away from disaster at any given time. As Denny said later, 'we *should* have expected it.' A drunken Viking came hurtling toward them sword upraised making a noise like, according to Tamar, "a constipated dinosaur."

'How would *you* know?' Denny actually found time to ask. 'That was before even your time.' Tamar shook her head sadly. 'So innocent,' she said enigmatically. 'Mind his head,' she added absently as Denny stepped aside lightly allowing the Viking to crash headfirst into a tree.

Apparently unhurt, he resumed his attack; Denny rolled his eyes in a manner very reminiscent of Tamar's usual fashion.

'You'd better fight him,' Tamar told him, 'if you don't he'll just keep coming. Believe me, I know these idiots.'

'I don't want to hurt him.'

'You won't, just stick to hitting him on the head.'

Denny shrugged and squared up to the enraged Viking, who did not know it, but who was about to get the pummelling of a lifetime …

Or not.

Denny raised his hands gingerly and clasped them behind his head. From behind him, he heard the soft click of the safety catch. He turned around slowly.

* * *

'From this to Abba,' said Denny. 'I don't know which was worse. Hey Bjorn,' he yelled. 'Where are the rest of the "Masters of the Universe"?'

Tamar gave him a questioning look. She was tied to the mast, and most of her other looks had been considerably more eloquent – and vicious. Denny was trying to make her smile, and not so far succeeding. She blamed him for all this, he knew, but being shot in the head would have been an inconvenient development, he felt. Particularly trying to explain why he had not actually died from it.

'Well, doesn't he look like "He Man", to you?' he explained.

Tamar grinned. 'By the power of Greyskull,' she giggled.

Denny relaxed; Tamar did not often sulk, preferring to deal out mayhem on a democratic basis when she was crossed. But when she did, she was unbearable.

The Conan look-alike strode over to Denny. 'How do you know my name?' he demanded. Tamar stifled a laugh.

Denny shrugged. 'Wild guess,' he suggested.

Tamar snorted.

Bjorn gave him a sideways glance full of suspicion, 'Hmm,' he said, and added 'The Masters, by which I assume you mean the gods, are in Valhalla as ever. And, if you do not wish to go and meet them soon, you will keep your tongue behind your teeth – understand?'

Denny pulled a face to indicate that he did.

* * *

'Skol, Skol, Skol, Skol, Skol –   Skol, Skol, Skol, Skol, Skol.'

The Vikings were enjoying the new song that the skinny man had taught them, although Herger kept on forgetting the words, and Rethel kept on interrupting the second verse – 'Skol, Skol, Skol, Skol' – to belch loudly and disembowel the man next to him. But nobody really minded.

'He's big, he's pissed, when he shot he never missed, Beowulf, Beowulf'

'He killed, he died, his boots were all untied, his boots were all untied. All together now – 'Beowulf, Beowulf, Beowulf - Beowulf, Beowulf, Beo wu-ulf.'

Some old philosopher once said that mankind is only one meal away from the loss of civilisation – this is bollocks. Mankind, as personified here by Denny, is actually only a skin-full (of mead in this case) away from it, and he had not put up much of a fight either.

Womankind, on the other hand, is only one sexist pig away from the end of her tether – civilisation had nothing to do with it, she left that behind the first time he left the toilet seat up, and was now heading toward total meltdown – accelerating fast.

She was not sure how it had happened, one minute Denny had been acting perfectly normally – for him – and the next ...

Not that she had never seen him drunk before, but nothing on this scale. She had, she realised, underestimated the effects of mead on the uninitiated.

For an intelligent woman, Tamar could be surprisingly dense at times. Even now, she failed to take into account the effects of a large group of men, doing their man thing and letting off steam, on a young man who had been spending too much time in recent years in the sole company of a woman. Denny was drunk and rowdy because he *wanted* to be.

Also, he had never before experienced the feeling of being popular among other men; he was enjoying the experience immensely. These guys *liked* him.

Tamar was forgotten. She was, after all, in this context a mere woman. How could she understand the need to bond with his peers, get drunk and rowdy and generally act like a prat in order to prove and validate his role as a man? He was, for the first time in his life, "one of the lads", and it was great.

Of course, Tamar was not just *any* mere woman; neither did she appreciate being forgotten about. Perhaps Denny should have taken these facts into account.

There is nothing quite like seeing the man you love passed out on top of a heap of drunken Vikings with his pants on his head and drool encrusted on his chin, to cool the fires of passion – sometimes permanently.

'Odin!' she muttered crossly in reference to some earlier songs by the "boys" not all of which had been entirely reverential (downright dirty some of them had been.)

'I'll give them Odin.' She raised an eyebrow *a la* evil plotter. 'Hmm, not a bad idea …'

The fact that she had now moved into talking to herself mode shows just how bad the night had been. She was, in fact, in that state of mind people get into after the boys next door have been playing heavy rock all night long at a decibel level better suited to the alarm system of a nuclear power station. Dawn is breaking, silence has descended, you have to be at work in an hour and your brain has been reduced to a kind of irradiated porridge. So naturally, it seems like a good idea to turn up your own stereo to maximum with a plentiful selection of CD's programmed to play for at least six hours, open all the windows but not enough to allow entry   (some people have been known to take the speakers outside, but this allows tampering) and leave the house. (It is at this stage that many people start to refer to themselves in the third person – evil laughter has been known)

It was a variation on the "stereo at dawn" plan that Tamar had in mind.

'Oh I'll give them Odin all right, serve the bastards right. Tamar Black doesn't put up with this shit lying down.' (What did I tell you?)

'Tamar is nobody's doormat. Slave girl am I? Huh!'

Denny, unfortunately, had not corrected this assumption on the part of his new friends and would pay for it later – and for the rest of his life, probably.

She cracked her knuckles and settled down to summon Odin in her own inimitable style.

'Odin, you drunken scuzz -bucket get your omnipotent arse down here and deal out some retribution.'

She waited.

'Come ON! I know you can hear me, did you hear those songs? Are you just going to let them get away with that?'

'I'll tell Freya about your Valkyrie Acceleration Programme,' she added slyly.

'All right, all right, I heard you, and there's not a word of truth in those allegations, by the way.'

Tamar grinned. 'Does it matter?' she said. 'Mud sticks, I don't think you want that particular story in the Sagas, or do you?'

Odin's beard twitched. 'Damned reporters,' he snarled. 'They'll write anything. All that bollocks about Thor's appointment. Nepotism they said, they accused me –*me*! And all that guff about the Rheingold, never heard such a load of …'

'Well, they don't know any better do they?' Tamar said soothingly. 'Just look at it this way, in a hundred years, who's going to care?'

Odin stroked his beard. 'Hmm, I suppose you're right at that.'

Tamar kept a creditably straight face and moved smoothly into top gear.

'Freya will I suppose,' she said musingly.'

'What?'

'She'll still care, about the Valkyries, I mean.' She gave him a sly look. 'How long do you think it would take *her* to forgive and forget?'

'Odin shuddered. 'You've made your point. What do you want anyway?'

She gestured silently to the sleeping hordes, an evil grin on her face.

'How about a fate worse than death?'

Odin looked perplexed for a moment; then his face cleared. 'Marriage?' he said.

* * *

'Oh Lord,' said Stiles as he realised what must be happening. 'So ... people from *here* must be getting moved into the other files of history, to make space for *this* lot?'

'Of course they are not,' said Hecaté, but she looked uncertain.

'Uh huh,' said Stiles sceptically. 'Check the anomalies,' he suggested. 'See if it shows anything.'

'But surely ...'

'Please, just check it,' he begged. 'I really don't like this at all.'

'There are no anomalies in the first file,' said Hecaté in a relieved tone.

'Well there wouldn't be, would there?' said Stiles discouragingly. 'Lord Thingy got sent back there, so it's all back to normal now. What about the next one?'

Hecaté brought up the file. 'Well, it looks ... oh no!' she turned to Stiles with a distraught face.

'Hmmm,' said Stiles. 'I thought as much.' He looked at the sleeping Priest, dog, children and huge Viking who had recently joined them. 'You have to send them back,' he said. 'Whatever slight impact on history their little adventure here might have, it couldn't be worse than the files of history being filled up with random people who don't belong there surely?'

Hecaté bowed her head. 'You are right,' she said. 'I had not even considered ... How do you do that?' she said suddenly.

Stiles shrugged. 'Humans are just more used to thinking about the consequences I suppose,' he said.

Hecaté released the "captives" – for want of a better word, and they all vanished much like Sir Antoine had done.

Stiles breathed a sigh of relief. 'That's that sorted then,' he said. 'Now we can ...'

'Jack!' Hecaté tapped him nervously on the shoulder.

Stiles turned. 'Oh shit!' he swore. 'What the hell went wrong?'

~ Chapter Eight ~

'... SAID I WAS SORRY.' Denny had gone past the pleading thing and was now into the "aren't women unreasonable, what does she want – *blood*?" thing. The problem was of course, what it always is. He was *not* sorry; he would do it all again, and Tamar knew it. She pointed this out.

Denny held up his hands in defeat. A girlfriend who knows you too well is bad enough, but one who can read your mind, albeit on a limited basis, is a never ending argument in the making. Surely every man's nightmare.

'Okay, Okay,' he said. 'I admit it, I had fun; I've never been one of the lads before, I don't expect you to understand. It's like you said to me once, people *like* you, but I'm not used to I, and it … Anyway, the thing is, you're right, I'm *not* sorry for doing it. I reckon I needed it, it did me good. But, *but* – no hear me out. I *am* sorry that I upset you.' He opened his mind. 'Am I telling the truth?'

Tamar gazed at him intently and eventually pronounced reluctantly 'Yes, I guess you are. She still looked sulky.

Denny gave her a sideways grin that made her thaw a little. 'I suppose that's why girls aren't supposed to go on a lads night out,' he said. 'In case they never want to see you again.'

She grinned back, 'I guess Bjorn and the lads won't be having that problem anyway,' she said.

Denny shook his head. Divine retribution in his opinion was an overreaction, but he did not dare say so, he contented himself with. 'At least you didn't make me marry you.' Then he clapped a hand over his mouth. 'I m-mean ...' he stammered, back pedalling rapidly, as the look on her face threatened to scorch the flesh off his face. 'I just meant that if we did ... if we *were* to get married, I would want it to be for better reasons than that, um. I mean it's not very romantic is it? Er, ahem.' He gazed at his feet in apparent deep fascination. 'So, er where to next?' he backed into a door nervously and scrabbled at the handle. (Tamar's revenge should at this point be fairly obvious. Much more wondering just exactly what she *would* do to him and he would be a nervous wreck.)

* * *

It was dark and smoky; strange lights flashed overhead, and the room was filled with the rhythmic thumping of a drumbeat and pounding feet.

Through the murky atmosphere, a hundred or more bodies could just be seen swaying or jumping to the beat like so many zombies surrendering their will to some unseen power. Some moved their heads like pecking vultures, in time to the beat. One came near and stared briefly though unseeing eyes, then moved away as if drawn by some hidden force. Tamar involuntarily drew closer to Denny.

Then began a terrible wailing, which immediately sent the poor people into an appalling frenzy. 'Take me,' it shrieked, 'into insanity.' Tamar clutched at Denny.

'What is it?' she mouthed, her voice lost in the cacophony. Denny looked at her, his shoulders shaking.

'I'm frightened,' she admitted, but Denny was laughing out loud by now, and most disturbing of all, he was beginning to move like the rest of them, his head bobbing along to the beat. 'Dream tripper – tripping on my dreams,' he mouthed along with the wailing voice.

'Oh no, I've lost him,' she thought. 'I've got to get him out of here.'

She tried to drag him away from the dancers, as he tried to drag her toward them. She won, naturally.

'We *have* to go,' she mouthed at him. 'It's some kind of cult or demons or something.'

'No, it's not.' Denny looked surprised; 'it's just the nineties.'*

Tamar had spent most of the 1990s stuck in her bottle (As related in Djinnx'd) and had never been much of a night-clubber in any case due to her unusual circumstances. (She had attended a ball in 1873 – this was rather different). She was not one hundred percent convinced, that Denny was right, the nightclub still looked to her like a cavern of hell, and if these people were not under a powerful demonic influence then she did not know what. But if Denny was not worried … well, she *was*.

They were over by the bar; Denny was jigging along as they were slyly informed – in ear-splitting tones – that, in fact, "E's are good" – a euphemism completely lost on Tamar. She was just wondering why they could not simply leave – she was sure that these people would not notice if they grew elephant ears and flapped around the room with them. She was wrong about this, they would notice; they just would not be terribly surprised (E's are good, after all – the power of suggestion is a wonderful thing.) But Denny seemed to want to stay, she wondered why – it seemed like a terrible place to her, and he was drinking again.

One other thing was troubling her. If this *was* the 1990s, as Denny said, he was in danger of vanishing from existence. This was a period of time after his birth, and if he vanished, so would she, back into the bottle and Askphrit would win. She tried to explain this to him over the sound of a man telling everyone to take the "Last train to transcentral." (Q. Were

---

* We should not dismiss the possibility here that they were both right – remember in particular 1992

these subliminal messages?) but he did not seem to be able to hear her.

'Come and dance,' he mouthed to her as the song changed rather appositely to "Please don't go".

Tamar found this suspicious. She shook her head firmly and tried to hold him back, but he swigged back the last of his beer and was gone. Tamar leaned against the bar for a few minutes deliberating what to do next. Maybe there was nothing to worry about, Denny seemed okay, apart from his bizarre behaviour, and at least he was still here, that was comforting. And, she supposed things could be worse – at least thus far, there had been no hint of Britney Spears (maybe this was not hell after all.) Then to her horror and disbelief she found her feet tapping along to "Rhythm is a dancer". This would never do. She set her shoulders, downed the last of her Malibu and pineapple,* shuddered at the glass and set off toward the dance floor intending to drag Denny out of this evil place – by his shaggy hair if necessary.

This place could get into your head if you were not careful. She could feel the beat pulsing through her bones, the desire to dance was overwhelming (More evidence, she felt, that all was not what it seemed) and Denny was already enmeshed in its iniquitous clutches. (Tamar had a tendency toward unnecessary drama. – she was also spiralling into paranoia)

As for Denny, he was eighteen again. This is not a euphemism – at least not entirely. One problem that had not been foreseen by either of our errant time travellers, was that should Denny, being a mortal, find himself in a time period within his own lifetime, where he, in fact, already existed, he would become his former self from that period to avoid temporal anomalies, as two of one person cannot exist at the same time. (This rule does not apply to immortal beings and the supernatural in general – no one knows why, but it is probably a rule of narrative flow – the only exception being

---

* In the nineties all drinks ordered by women metamorphosed into a Malibu and pineapple – no one has ever been able to satisfactorily explain this. – Tamar, by the way, had not even ordered a drink

ghosts, have you ever heard of anyone being haunted by themselves?)

What had happened was this. The present Denny had been drawn into the aura of the past Denny. This explained why he was having feelings of Déjà vu. He had indeed been here before, except he had not because he was only eighteen, and this was the first time he had been here. Following me so far? Denny was his twenty six year old self living the life of his eighteen year old self. Put in a nutshell, it was a classic case of knowing then what you know now.

So far, his feelings of Déjà vu were vague at best, and he put it down to the fact that he had been in similar places in his past, maybe even this place, in other words, a coincidence. Things were about to get a lot more specific.

'I thought I told you never to come here again.' A large man, black greasy hair slicked back, hideous purple satin shirt stretched to straining point on overlarge shoulders was tapping Denny on the shoulder; Denny turned. Behind the bully was a selection of giggling jackals, all similarly dressed in cheap black suits and obviously pretty pleased with themselves.

One of them, with bleached spiky hair, and skinnier even than Denny himself, leaned over his mentor's shoulder, his Adam's apple bobbing excitedly. 'Yeah, we told you never to come here again,' he reiterated, somewhat unnecessarily in a high pitched voice.

Denny's head swam for a moment. The sense of Déjà vu overcame him so strongly that he could not focus for a moment.

Denny stared at this former tormentor his mind racing through the possibilities. This had not happened yet, but still he had a clear memory of it. This was Andy Clay, a monolith from Denny's teenage years and the author of an era of terror for Denny at secondary school. He experienced again (and also, conversely, for the first time) the feelings of injustice that had assailed him on this very occasion. He had thought he had left all this behind him, wasn't he a grown up now? Apparently not, because, even though this had not happened yet, he could clearly remember what was going to happen. He would be sent away with a face full of broken beer bottle and a severe inferiority complex. So, why wasn't he scared this time? 'This time? – Aha!' Denny did not really understand what had really happened here, but he did understand what he had now – A chance.

He stared coolly at his former tormentor. 'Hello Andy,' he said.

A breathless Tamar arrived behind him. 'Denny ...' she began, then she took in the scene 'Oh.'

Denny did not even look round. 'In a minute babe,' he murmured. Oh, this was too good to be true. Not only did he have the chance to clean Andy Clay's clocks once and for all. But also he, and all his cronies had now seen him with Tamar, the kind of woman they would never have a chance with even in their dreams. Brilliant!

Andy shifted his gormless gaze over Denny's shoulder and rather predictably said. 'Hello darling.'

Tamar, also rather predictably, bristled but said nothing. She had a weird feeling about this. 'What's going on?' she hissed.

'Unfinished business,' said Denny calmly.

Tamar got the point immediately. 'You can't' she told him frantically. 'You mustn't change the past.'

Denny ignored her; he was damned if he was going to get beaten up again – *again*? There was that confusion again, after all, if he did this he would not have been beaten up in the first place, would he? Whatever, it was his past and he would change it if he wanted to.

'It'll create a paradox,' Tamar said.

'I think it already has,' Denny told her. He could still remember the past as it had been, even though he had already decided to change it.

What Tamar knew instinctively but was not able to explain, was that since everything happens somewhere there would be a time line where Denny changed the outcome of this encounter and one where he did not – possibly because he never had the chance. If he did this now, there was a high probability that he would be shunted into an alternate reality, particularly in view of the unstable nature of their presence here. Actually, it was almost a certainty.

Andy had missed most of the actual words of this exchange and had, quite naturally misinterpreted Tamar's concern. He now pushed Denny aside and grabbed her round the shoulders. 'How about you and me have a little fun after I finish off this crap rat,' he suggested. 'Bet you'd rather be with a real man, eh?'

Denny, who knew Tamar rather well, looked enquiringly at her. Her face was a study in outrage. 'Okay,' she said, 'finish him.'

As an ironic touch, the words: "Peace in the valley – peace in the city – peace in your soul" were swelling in the background.

Andy cracked his knuckles. 'Right,' he said, 'this shouldn't take long.'

'It won't,' Tamar assured him.

'She wasn't talking to you,' said Denny.

Thirty seconds later Andy crawled away on his face. 'I never even touched him,' said Denny, disappointed. 'Well, hardly, anyway.'

Behind him Darren Barnes (known as Daz, if memory served) pulled out a flick knife and pointed it at Denny's neck.

There was a blur and Denny had Daz by the wrist. He looked at the knife contemptuously. 'That's not a knife,' he said and drew out the Athame with his free hand. '*This* is a knife.' (he had wanted to say this line ever since acquiring the Athame) and then it was all over. The gang vanished like, as Tamar pointed out later, 'gorillas in the mist.'

'I always wanted to say that,' said Denny happily, as the strains of "Dreams can come true" rose over the dance floor. 'Dance?'

Tamar nodded. 'This I can dance to,' she told him

* * *

When the lights came up shortly after this song had ended, it was a lot harder to simply vanish without people noticing. Suddenly, as if someone had hit a switch, the majority of the people in the place turned into rational beings, sitting about looking slightly unfocussed with dark rings under their eyes and untidy hair. The cavern of Hell became merely a slightly scuffed looking room, littered with empty bottles and dirty ashtrays. It had a tawdry, forsaken look about it, but it no longer looked in the least sinister. Tamar felt a little foolish – and a lot sticky.

There was nothing for it but to allow themselves to be herded outside with the others by the bouncers. They were met at the door by three police officers, one of whom seemed extremely familiar. From behind him, bobbed the excited head of Darren (Daz) Barnes. 'That's him, Sergeant,' he pointed at Denny from the safety of the Sergeant's broad shoulders. Actually they were not all that wide, the sergeant was about medium build, but they were positively hefty when compared to Daz's.

'He's got a weapon, a great big knife, I saw it, he threatened me. Go on. You search him.'

The sergeant gave Daz a look of contempt, with just a pinch of withering scorn.

And suddenly Tamar recognised him. She nudged Denny. 'Hey,' she whispered. 'look who it is.'

Denny focussed on the Sergeant's face. 'Well, I'll be damned,' he said quite loudly, he was still quite drunk.

Behind the Sergeant, Daz was dancing about excitedly. 'He attacked my friend too,' he said. 'Put him in hospital, well nearly.'

'Really?' said the Sergeant. 'What had he done to him?' he added almost absently.

'Nothing,' protested Daz indignantly. 'Unprovoked attack. Aren't you going to search him?'

The sergeant sighed. 'Yes, all right. Son,' he turned to Denny, who he really rather liked the look of. Denny looked to the sergeant like, what he would call in his rather old fashioned parlance, "a good sort", and the sergeant prided himself on being a good judge of character. 'I'm afraid we've received a complaint against you,' he continued. 'I'm going to have to search you.'

Denny grinned; he could not help himself. 'Okay Sarge,' he caught Stiles eye. '– ant,' he added and held his hands up, swaying slightly.

Tamar thought it was about time she stepped in here. She grabbed Denny and hissed fiercely in his ear. 'Sober up *now*.' Denny concentrated and his head cleared. He found himself staring into the perplexed eyes of a very young looking Jack Stiles. 'Oh,' he said.

'Okay,' said Tamar, 'I'll handle this, he used to fancy me when he was older.' She reviewed this sentence in her head. 'You know what I mean,' she added. 'But get rid of that knife, just in case.'

Stiles stepped forward now, 'I'm sorry about this, Miss,' he said, his eyes carefully blank. 'But I have received a complaint. I have to search your ...' he looked from Tamar to Denny. '... friend?'

Tamar suddenly felt intensely indignant on Denny's behalf. People always assumed that they were only friends. As if Denny could never find an attractive girlfriend. Denny, a man without any personal vanity of any kind, never seemed to take exception to this attitude, but Tamar was fed up with it. She grabbed Denny by the arm and said pointedly 'My *boyfriend*.' She fixed Stiles with an unfriendly eye. 'You know, as in my *lover*,' she added, just to make her meaning unequivocal.

'Nice flirting,' said Denny with a grin.

Tamar skidded in mid umbrage. 'Oh.'

'Never mind,' said Denny. 'He's wearing a wedding ring in any case.'

Tamar looked. 'Oh yes, of course.' She remembered now, Stiles had been married. He just never talked about it.

'Okay Sergeant,' said Denny raising his arms again. 'Go ahead, sorry about that.'

The search turned up no more than a few pounds in his wallet, a packet of chewing gum and a rather nice fountain pen, which had a strange, dull sheen in the dim light. There was no sign of a knife, large or otherwise.

'Okay, son,' said Stiles, stepping back. 'Sorry to have bothered you. You can go now.'

'Hey,' objected Daz, 'you can't just let him go. He must have hidden it somewhere. What about what he did to my friend? He must have...'

He dried up as Stiles gave him a look that would have crinkled iron. 'He's clean,' said Stiles. 'There's no crime here. Of course, I could always arrest *you* for wasting police time,' he added dryly.

Daz gulped.

'Go on,' barked Stiles. 'Hoppit, before I change my mind.'

Daz threw Denny a look of pure venom before hopping it.'

'Could be trouble there,' said Stiles. 'I know his type.'

Denny nodded. 'It's okay,' he said, 'It's not as if he knows where I live or anything.' They turned to go, and Denny turned back for a moment. 'Thanks Jack,' he said, then walked swiftly away, leaving Stiles looking puzzled and a little worried.

* * *

'I didn't know you chewed gum,' said Tamar, referring to the contents of his pockets. She was determined not to mention Denny's ill-advised parting comment, if he did not know how stupid that was, she was not going to be the one to tell him.

Denny grinned. 'I don't,' he said, tucking the packet of gum back into its sheath.

* * *

'Look on the bright side,' Denny said to her back in the file room. 'I know you didn't like it, but at least they didn't play any "Take That".'

'I rather liked "Take That",' she said, causing Denny to feel superior to her for the first time since they had met. He contented himself with a look of contemptuous disbelief, making Tamar feel as if he had looked through her record collection and found an A-ha LP.

'Anyway,' she said quickly to cover her discomfort. 'What I'm worried about is you changing your past like that. You shouldn't have done it, you know.'

'Well?' he asked. 'We're okay aren't we? Nothing happened did it?'

'We don't know yet what the consequences will be,' she said seriously.

* * *

'Who the hell are all this lot then?' stormed Stiles – who was clearly working himself up to a heart attack.

'Displacement,' said Hecaté wearily.

Six new people all clearly from different periods of history were ranged about the room in varying states of distress and/or fury.

'Jesus!' screeched Stiles. 'What the ...' He stopped when he caught her eye. She was clearly close to tears. 'Okay,' he said in a much milder tone. 'Send 'em to sleep and we'll try to work it out.'

'I made a terrible mistake,' she told him. 'And it looks as if it is not going to be as easy to put it right as we thought.'

'We can do it,' Stiles said reassuringly.

He thought for a moment. 'Okay, it seems to me that what happened was this: Denny and Tamar would enter a file and cause the displacement, therefore, sending some random person from that file to where there was a gap for them, i.e. – *here*. When they left the file – the person was naturally taken back to where they came from. But – when that person did *not* get taken back to where they belonged – someone else from here was put there instead to fill the gap that Tamar and Denny left behind and to make room here. Right so far?' he asked.

Hecaté nodded.

'Okay, so when you sent the people back to their own files, there were already people there filling the space and ... and...' he floundered.

'It caused another displacement,' said Hecaté. 'A *random* displacement, just as before,' she clarified just to make certain he understood.

'So it's all just a colossal mess,' summarised Stiles. 'Just because a person *started off* here, doesn't mean they will be "displaced" *back* here. Oh Christ!' another horrible thought struck him. 'We don't even know if the people we sent back ended up in the right files.'

'Please!' begged Hecaté.

'But they probably did,' amended Stiles, still thinking out loud. 'No, what's happened is, that instead of sending back the people who replaced the ones we kept here – the people from here – the universe "compensated" randomly as before and sent this lot here instead.'

'So, we have a maximum of six people from here, who are out of time somewhere,' he said. 'Maybe even five or only four if one or two of them were big chaps, or possibly the odd horse or something ... Well, that's not so bad really, is it?' he smiled encouragingly at her. 'We can sort that out. 'Course we can.'

'It's not just that,' she told him.

'Oh?' Stiles frowned.

'There will now be historical anomalies in many different files,' she told him. 'We have no way of telling one from another, no way to find the monster and no chance, any more, of tracking Tamar and Denny. They are on their own now.'

~Chapter Nine ~

'HOW MUCH LONGER are we going to keep this up?'

The thin man looked at his subordinate in surprise. He might well be a little taken aback. Such a question from a mere lackey was an unprecedented occurrence in his experience. He blamed the one called Clive, he had begun it, and now an insidious culture of free thinking was spreading slowly through the entire organisation.

He considered a sharp reprimand and then decided against it. It might, after all, in some circumstances, be considered a fair question.

He frowned, therefore, to show his disapproval, but answered reasonably enough, 'I take it, you are asking why, with all our resources, we do not simply *give* them their answers?'

'Or at least, send them in the right direction instead of letting them wander about history in this untidy manner,' affirmed the lackey. 'They are making a terrible mess of things,' he added.

'Nothing that they can't clean up,' said the thin man tersely. 'It's good experience for them, all of life is a learning curve.'

'But ...'

'There is no "but",' broke in the thin man. 'You asked a question, and I am going to give you an answer and then let there be no more of this matter, understand?'

'Yes sir,' said the lackey meekly.

'Very good. Now then, firstly we cannot simply *give* them the answers. That would be to violate their free will. We are not even supposed to be helping as much as we are.' He looked shrewdly at his subordinate. 'But of course, we both know that that is a lot of nonsense really. It is the official line, and we must be seen to be adhering to it. The reality is, that we *are* helping them so why, you are wondering are you not, do we not simply help them a little faster and get this thing over with? I will tell you.

'We give them clues, knowledge etc. For example, they always know when they are in the *wrong* place. If we can do so much, why not simply tell them where is the *right* place? We can't!

'There are two reasons. One: they are being steered on a course that has its own inevitable end, and it is simply not time yet for the answers to become apparent. You will note that I said "steered" and not "driven". Ultimately they have to do this on their own, but given the right amount of help at the right moments, they will reach the correct solution at the correct time. What you perceive as a lot of messing about and time wasting is, in fact, a carefully controlled and timed sequence of events that must take place in order for the desired result to occur[*] and the consequences will reach much farther into the future than just the outcome of this one pursuit.

'Destiny,' said the lackey, catching on.

'Exactly, that is what they call it. We have a whole department on it, as you know. "The planning department" as it is more properly called. They have sent us a detailed analysis of the projected outcome of the situation, and we are working to that. But you never heard me say that, understand?'

The lackey nodded.

---

[*] And if you believe that you'll believe anything

'However,' continued the thin man, 'you have heard of the saying "The best laid plans of mice and men ..."?'

'Yes,' was the eagerly given answer, 'It postulates the admittance of random and unforeseen events which can disrupt the working of the destiny – I mean the planning department's er ... plans.' He screwed up his face in confusion. 'But how...' he began.

'Even the planning department cannot control the will of humans, unfortunately,' The thin man told him, 'especially these particular humans I have to say, who are incorrigible and unpredictable to the *nth* degree. And indeed it is a fact that the whole concept of so called "destiny" hinges on the implementation of free will and *vice versa* actually. The many worlds theory depends on it – the concept of choice you see. But we won't go into that now. And so, occasionally, it does happen that a "spanner" to make use of a humanism, is hurled into the works and "destiny" takes a sharp turn in the wrong direction. Which brings us to our second reason.' He steepled his hands and looked judiciously at this audacious questioner of authority. 'Human behaviour cannot be that closely controlled. Give them too much information and who knows what they will choose to do with it.'

'But haven't we already given them the answer,' interrupted the lackey. 'Well, indirectly anyway,' he amended.

'Some information has been "delivered" yes,' said the thin man cautiously. 'As you say, indirectly – not to them. But it is of no use to them at present, and it is not in their hands as yet anyway, it's not time yet as I believe I already told you,' he added with a hint of impatience.

'The stage has been set, and the players positioned,' he ruminated, 'and all else is in the hands of the gods – so to speak. Destiny and the planning department are not as fixed nor as absolute as the pawns – I mean the humans involved seem to believe.

'Humans can be steered however, and often with better results, as we have seen, than when they are told what they must do, in which case sheer human perversity usually makes them do the exact opposite.' he rolled his eyes. 'We have made such mistakes before and even when that is not the case, things can still go wrong. We do not know for example, what this Askphrit character might suddenly decide to do, he has fooled us before. The truth is that in dealing with humans, anything at all can, and often does, happen. Best we do not interfere too much in case something of the kind happens again. In this way, we leave our options open to change our plans if necessary, even up until the last minute.'

'And we can disclaim all knowledge if it all goes horribly wrong,' added the lackey shrewdly.

The stern and humourless face of the thin man creased suddenly into a wink.

'Now you're getting it,' he said.

* * *

On the other side of the next door, they found themselves in Liverpool, circa April 1912 according to Tamar.

'How do you know?' asked Denny 'Hey, what's wrong?'

For answer, she pointed a shaking finger at the dock, and he followed her gaze and saw ... The Titanic.

Denny nodded. 'You know that ship then?' he surmised.

Tamar stared at him in bewilderment. 'It's the Titanic,' she said eventually.

Denny shook his head. 'Whatever it is,' he said. 'I'm sorry I'm not picking it up from you this time. What about it?'

'Well,' she said, apparently thinking hard. 'It's the TITANIC.'

'I'm going to shake you in a minute,' said Denny. He was picking up on her distress, but no facts were coming through at all. 'What *about* the bleeding Titanic,'

'It sank,' she told him baldy.

'Oh!' he said. 'That's a shame,' he said lamely. He really was not that interested.

'A shame?' said Tamar incredulously. 'The most famous wreck in history. 1500 people drowned, and you say... all you can say is ... you never heard of it did you?' she realised suddenly.

'No,' he admitted, 'and that's a problem isn't it?' he added, suddenly catching on.'

They both turned to gaze at the ship.

'1500 people drowned?' asked Denny.

'Yes,'

'Shit!'

Tamar told him the story of the Titanic; he was flabbergasted.

'That's terrible,' he said 'what a momentous cock-up.'

'Are you sure it's real though?' he added.

Tamar nodded uncertainly. 'I see what you mean,' she said. 'One of us has got it wrong, that's for sure.'

'How could that happen?'

'History must have changed,' she said. 'And for some reason only one of us remembers the original version,' she shrugged.

'So what *is* the original version?' asked Denny putting his finger squarely on the nub of the problem.'

'That's the fifty thousand dollar question,' said Tamar glumly. 'Will she sink or won't she?'

'And is she supposed to sink or not anyway?' Denny added to the confusion.

'Dunno,' said Tamar unhelpfully.

'Why do we remember it differently?' said Denny. 'If changing history changes our memory of it, as you say, then why…?'

'… Does one of us remember it the way it was *before* it was changed?' Tamar finished for him.

'It's got to be you,' he said. 'I mean who's the Djinn around here anyway? You never saw the world like humans do and anyway, you were alive when it happened, I wasn't.'

Tamar reluctantly agreed to this. She did not like it at all, because it meant that the ship was meant to sink in order to fix the timeline and that they would have to be the ones to make sure it happened, because it clearly was not going to happen on its own.

'It doesn't matter why,' she said. 'We may have been the ones that caused it in the first place ...'

'Or Askphrit.' put in Denny.

'Either way, it's got to be all this jumping around in history that's done it,' she said.

There was a silence.

'So what do we do?' asked Denny eventually.

'Nothing?' said Tamar hopefully.

'Um,' said Denny and scratched his nose meaningfully.

'Well look,' said Tamar. 'We don't even know for sure that I'm the one remembering it right. Maybe *you* are. So we don't even know for sure what's going to happen here, I mean not really. Just because I was here at the time doesn't mean my memory now is right. In fact, now that I think about it, it's far more likely that it's you that's got it right not me.'

'Explain,' said Denny tersely

'The change must have happened while we were in mainframe, which means that it's more likely that the memory you took with you into mainframe was the right one. Because I was living at the time it happened, *my* memory will have altered along with the timeline – if it didn't, then I would be remembering something that never happened.'

'So she's going to sink, and we have to stop it from happening?' said Denny eventually. 'Because it's more than likely our fault anyway.'

'Even if it wasn't ...' began Tamar

'Yes, yes, I know,' said Denny testily. 'Funny how you weren't so keen to fix the timeline when we thought *you* might be the one remembering it right.'

Tamar looked down.

'Because if the timeline changed from a massive disaster to a happy ending then you would rather just leave it that way?' he pressed on mercilessly.

'Fifteen hundred dead, Denny,' she said plaintively. 'Fifteen hundred!'

'It doesn't make a difference,' he said sternly. 'Surely not mending a rift in time when you know about it is just as much a crime as deliberately causing one. Especially if there's a good chance that we caused it in the first place'

Tamar just looked stubbornly at him.

'You can't always play the hero,' he said gently. 'Sometimes you have to do the right thing.'

'Gosh that was deep,' he added to himself. 'Practically Zen, in fact.'

'Nah,' said Tamar allowing herself a smile. 'Zen's that thing where you talk a lot of bollocks in order to confuse yourself into believing just about anything isn't it? What you said actually made a lot of sense.' She sighed. 'I wish it didn't.'

'Here's some more sense for you,' he said. 'It's pretty clear that the timeline has changed, right? So whatever is going to happen is the wrong thing. Therefore, it doesn't matter who's right or wrong. Whatever happens on that ship, we have to be there to put it right again. Fancy taking a cruise?'

'And if the ship *doesn't* hit the iceberg?' said Tamar.

'Then your memory was the right one. The ship sank, and there's nothing we can do about it. We'll just have to face it and ...'

'And what?' said Tamar.

'Well, sink the ship obviously.'

'How?'

'Um ...'

It'd be easier to make sure she *doesn't* sink,' said Tamar gloomily. 'I mean just from a practical point of view even.'

'I know,' said Denny. 'Spot the iceberg and shift it out of the way – easy.'

'Exactly, but if there is no iceberg ...'

'Damn!'

'There are always going to be a lot of people to say something weird happened,' pointed out Tamar. 'Doesn't mean anyone will believe them – we know that.'

'So we just ...'

'Make a huge great iceberg out of nowhere.' affirmed Tamar gloomily.

'Bugger!'

* * *

'Bugger!' said Stiles

'As you say,' agreed Hecaté.'

'Right!' said Stiles pacing again. 'Right! So ... we can fix this. I just have to ... Okay, let me think for a bit.'

He continued pacing up and down the room muttering to himself. It was not in his nature to give up and accept things and besides, for one thing, they had promised Tamar and Denny that they would keep an eye on them, and how could they do that now, in the "time soup" that had been created? And for another, if they did not fix this, the historical ramifications could be horrendous. He could just imagine Tamar's fury and Denny's sarcasm. Oh no! Anything but that!

Besides, Stiles liked a good conundrum to solve; it was the policeman in him.

Hecaté maintained a respectful silence while she waited.

Eventually he stopped pacing. 'Right,' he said again. 'It's obvious really. We have to get in there and put this lot back where they belong and get the people who are in the wrong files back where *they* belong'

Hecaté raised an eyebrow 'Just like that?' she asked.

'No, not "just like that",' he said. 'I never said it would be easy, but there's no other way. We have to go into the files. I mean we can, can't we, now that we have the password? We can get in from here.'

 Hecaté nodded 'The hands on, practical approach?' she said, 'mmm.'

'The *human* approach,' said Stiles. 'Sometimes it works you know.'

'So I have learned,' she said. 'I admit it would not have occurred to me to take such an arduous route.'

'Sometimes you need to do more than just snap your fingers,' said Stiles. 'That's life,'

'Very well,' she said humbly. 'How do we begin?'

'By tracking the historical anomalies of course,' said Stiles with a grin.

* * *

Denny bounded up to the prow and balanced on the rails, fastened to the rail was a notice bearing the mystery "No persons beyond this point". 'That's all they know,' said Denny. He outstretched his arms and yelled. 'I'm the king of the wor-r-r-ld!'*

'Pillock,' said Tamar contemptuously, 'do you *want* to draw attention to us?'

'Ha!' retorted Denny. 'If shifting a bloody great iceberg out of the middle of the ocean doesn't draw attention to us, I don't know what will.'

'Keep your voice down,' she hissed. 'If it comes to that, we'll be long gone by the time anyone notices that.'

Denny subsided; he knew this was a strain on her. 'How long have we got?' he asked quietly.

'Tomorrow,' she said in a strained voice.

'And not a sign of any ice at all,' said Denny

'I know,' she said gloomily.

All that day they could feel the tension mounting. They barely spoke at all, and Tamar was beginning to get that look on her face that Denny interpreted as "I don't give a stuff what the universe says, I'm doing it my way."

This was worrying. He knew damn well when she was up to something. He decided to tackle her before it was too late.

* * *

He got straight to the point. 'You know if that iceberg doesn't appear by 11.30 that we have to... that you have to manifest it don't you?'

'Why?' said Tamar bluntly.

'Tamar!' he said warningly.

'Oh sod off!' she told him. 'I'm not killing fifteen hundred people just because...'

'I know how you feel,' he told her. 'But we can't save all the people all the time. What are you going to do? Spend the rest of your life hurtling through time, stopping disasters, and preventing wars and assassinations? What's next? Atlantis?

---

* He was obviously picking this up from Tamar although he did not know it.

Pompeii? JFK? The day the Beatles split up? All those things have already happened. It's too late.'

'Don't be silly,' she snapped, 'of course I'm not, and I know that, but this is different. It hasn't happened yet – not as such.'

Then the penny dropped for Denny. She knew – had known all along, that the ship was meant to sink and that she intended to do bugger all about it. She had lied to him. He lost his temper.

'You're rationalising and you know it,' he snapped – he intended to say a lot more, but Tamar turned on him in sudden fury.

'Yes, I know it, so what? Anyway, you can't stop me, so sod off and leave me alone!'

Denny was startled at her vehemence; she sounded like she hated him. He walked away in silence.

* * *

He wandered to the other end of the ship and leaned over the back, contemplating whether or not to throw himself overboard. He was feeling depressed, and it was more than just the fight that was behind it. Perhaps he was getting sick of this kind of thing. Wouldn't it be nice to have a couple of weeks just watching the telly and eating crisps and not having to worry about all this stuff? He was getting weary of it.

'Fifteen hundred people, Denny. Fifteen hundred,'

Denny jumped.

'I can't just let them die, Denny, I can't.' Tamar was behind him suddenly, sobbing. (She had become, since humanity had hit, a very soggy person.) 'How can you be so callous?'

'Oh you know me,' he said, 'I'm a completely heartless bastard.'

She looked at the floor. 'I *do* know you,' she said. 'That's why I don't understand.'

Denny was silent for a long time, 'Okay,' he said, eventually, 'do what you want! To hell with it.' He rubbed his forehead wearily. 'Remember what happened the last time I said that?'

* * *

The world felt strange around him; he recognised the feeling from somewhere. The air felt thick with destiny, perhaps because he knew what was going to happen. No, that wasn't it – he could *feel* it – history was changing because of Tamar's determination to change it, or rather not to change it back to what it ought to be. The reverberations were making themselves felt already. His memory of the events was the same, but it was as if he was looking through a window at the world as it would be after she had done it – as if he was in both worlds at once. This, he realised was the power of the Athame. He weighed it in his hand; 'I just wish I knew what would happen if she goes through with it, what the consequences will be …'

* * *

It was eleven thirty p.m. And still nothing. Denny's stomach lurched. This was all wrong. He found Tamar staring stubbornly out to sea. 'Come with me,' he ordered, roughly. 'There's something you have to see.'

'What? What the hell is wrong with you? What do you think you're doing?'

'Showing you the consequences.'

He faced her grimly. 'The world is splitting,' he told her. 'Like it did when Askphrit went back to face himself and changed his own history. It's splitting into two worlds and look.' He drew out the Athame, and cut a symbol in the air, which shimmered and then faded. 'There's the world you're about to create, where all these people survive.'

'What ...?'

'Look!'

She looked. It was like a screen seen through a window, while wearing 3D glasses. And she saw ... 'The future?' she looked at him questioningly.

'From our perspective it's the past. But see ...'

'Hitler, Jack-booting through Europe unfettered. We didn't stop him, why?'

Denny handed her the Athame. Then she understood. 'I see, because a man on this ship, who should have died, didn't.

And his son became a Nazi spy. One man made all that difference.'

'No! One *woman* – you. There are other things too. I'm sorry.'

'I don't need to see any more.' She handed the Athame back to him. 'Close it.' She ran away from him.

'Tamar!'

She turned back briefly, 'don't worry, I'll do it,' she said, and left him standing there, feeling guilty and depressed as the warning bell rang out.

* * *

The ship lurched sickeningly as it hit the berg, why the hell Tamar had insisted on remaining until it was over, was a mystery to Denny. 'It's morbid,' he had said. But she had been adamant, and so he had not pushed it. Apart from that, she was not speaking to him – and that he *could* understand.

It was strange, but it seemed that it was true that the majority of the passengers really did not seem worried at all yet.

Denny leaned against the rail and watched their excitement and fun (they were actually playing hockey or football or something with the chunks of ice – Denny was not a sporty person, so he could not identify the game). He was overcome with a terrible depression. All too soon, there would be panic and screaming and death. Why had she wanted to stay, when they could not interfere, not even in the smallest way? Where was she anyway? He looked about him, but there was no sign of her. *Bloody hell!* He ran.

She was down in steerage freeing the trapped passengers. Denny grabbed her by the waist in a fury and slung her aside. 'What the hell are you doing?' he screamed in fury. 'You lied to me!' He came closer in that moment than he ever had to hitting her. A different kind of man would have.

'I didn't – I wasn't – *listen* to me.'

'How could you? After what I ... when I showed you ...'

'I'm not! This is different, these people are *supposed* to get out, but we changed it somehow, *trust* me.'

Denny sagged. 'We shouldn't even be here, if we weren't ...'

She nodded. 'But we are, and we have to put right what I made wrong. There's a reason why those files aren't supposed to be accessed by the likes of us.'

He looked unsure.

'Use the Athame,' she said. 'You'll see, I'm telling the truth.'

Denny drew it out and weighed it in his hand. Then he brought it down on the lock, and it split. 'Let's get out of here,' he said.

The word best used to describe the experience that followed, from the point of view of Tamar and Denny, was "cold". As they bobbed in the freezing water, Denny eventually asked. '*Now* can we go?'

'Close file.'

~ Chapter Ten ~

'THERE,' SAID HECATÉ, 'that is definitely not right.'

'No kidding,' said Stiles dryly. 'So we've found one?'

Stiles's idea was to search for the historical anomalies that might represent a person out of time, just as they had been searching for Tamar and Denny. What made it easier in this case was that they already knew which files to search. Unfortunately, though, Tamar and Denny were still moving on and as they did, more and more people from different files kept appearing and then suddenly disappearing back to where they came from. This was all fine as far as it went, but it was distracting in the extreme and made the search for previously visited files more than necessarily confusing.

'All right,' said Stiles. 'Send me through, I'll go and fetch him.'

'My God!' he knocked himself on the head suddenly. 'How stupid we all are.'

'What?' said Hecaté, alarmed. 'What is wrong?'

'Don't you see?' he said irritatingly, since she clearly could not. 'We can get into any file we like, straight from here – any file at all, now that we have the password.'

Hecaté's eyes widened. 'But how foolish we are,' she said.

'That's what I said.'

'We must get this done and done quickly,' she said. 'So that we can find our friends and bring them back here to end this.'

'Amen to that,' said Stiles. 'Send me in.'

The moment Stiles disappeared into the file one of their "guests" vanished – hopefully back to where he had come from.

Stiles reappeared looking harassed. 'I did what you said,' he told her. 'I grabbed him and said "close file", but I must have lost him or something ...'

Hecaté smiled. 'All is well,' she told him. 'Both are now back where they belong.'

Stiles rubbed his head ruefully. 'I hope you're right,' he said.

* * *

'Knock, Knock.'

'What?'

'Knock, Knock,' repeated Denny. 'Just humour me.'

Tamar sighed. 'Okay, who's there?'

'Sahara.'

'Sahara wh... do we *really* have time for this?'

'Sahara who.'

'Sahara who?'

'Sahara the hell did we end up here – no that didn't really work did it? Sorry.'

'I don't think we're in the Sahara,' said Tamar pragmatically. 'I'm pretty sure we're in Egypt.'

'Ah, close but no cigar. What makes you think we're in Egypt?'

'Well, those Egyptians over there were my first clue.'

'How do you know they're Egyptians? They could be... er ... they could be ... I got nothing.'

'They're building a pyramid.'

'How can you tell it's going to be a pyramid? So far, it could be anything.'

'I can just tell.'

'Well, whatever. No one's seen us, for a change, so we might as well get out of here.'

Tamar grabbed his arm. 'No,' she said, 'there's something here, something … I think we might have found him.'

Denny was excited. 'Really?' then he frowned. 'What makes you think so? And what the hell would he be doing *here* of all places? I'm bloody certain I haven't got any ancestors in ancient Egypt.'

'Which question would you like me to answer first?' Firstly, I can sense him, or something very like him, which is worth investigating, don't you think? And no, I don't know why I can. Secondly, how the hell should I know why he would come here? But you know as well as I do, that nothing is ever simple with him. Maybe he's got some other plan up his sleeve.' She took a deep breath. 'Or, maybe, you *do* have ancestors here, how the hell would you really know? You didn't know that you had ancestors in Troy, did you?'

Denny gave in. 'Okay, so what do you want to do?'

Tamar hesitated. Well …'

'I guess the first thing to do is to blend in,' suggested Denny. 'What *is* the well-dressed ancient Egyptian wearing about town these – those days?'

'Something like this,' she said, snapping her fingers. Denny gasped. He was accustomed to Tamar's beauty, but this was something else. She was stunning in gold and white, which left little to the imagination. Her customarily pale skin was golden and seemed to shimmer in the sunlight. The black wig, square cut over her brows, emphasised her eyes, which were heavily rimmed with charcoal or something, making them look huge. The whole effect was hypnotic. He was sure that he did not look nearly so impressive. For one thing, he appeared to be wearing a nappy. He was just glad he could not see himself.

'So, what now?' he asked, biting back the impulse to drag her behind the nearest sand dune and ravish her.

'Well, not that,' she told him, picking up on his thought. She smiled. 'Maybe later.'

'Let's just look around,' she said, sounding a lot more certain than she felt.

As they drew nearer to the crowd of men working on the nascent pyramid, Denny was staggered at how like modern construction workers they seemed. They lounged about drinking, laughing and chattering. He heard loud music coming from somewhere and, as they approached, he would not have been at all surprised to hear one of them wolf whistle at Tamar, at whom they were staring with unconcealed interest.

There were no slave driving gang bosses with whips, nor did they see the ropes and pullies that have been hypothesised by archaeologists. How was the work being done? Actually, these men seemed to be in no hurry to be getting on with the work at all (rather like council workers.) Denny was even sure that he saw one man reading a paper. 'Tea break?' he wondered aloud.

In the distance, they saw a cloud of dust approaching at some speed. It reminded Denny irresistibly of a truck rattling along one of those dusty roads in American road movies.

A man who was, in any guise, quite unmistakably some sort of foreman, starting shouting through some sort of megaphone and waving his arms about, all that was missing was his hard hat. His voice had the distinctive distortion that one expects through one of those thing, and he could have been saying anything, but the gestures were remarkably explicit. "Get off your lazy arses," was one, and "get out of the way," was another. The men all rose slowly and carelessly and looked expectantly towards a point beyond where Denny and Tamar were standing. Like people who join a crowd all looking up at the top of a building, Denny and Tamar followed their gaze.

As they watched, over the horizon, they saw what appeared to Denny, to be a large JCB, hove into view. His mouth dropped open. Tamar did not look at all surprised, and only Denny could know what that was costing her.

Denny had no such scruples. 'What the hell is *that* doing here?' he hissed. Then he slapped his forehead. 'It's *him*, isn't it?'

I don't know,' she admitted. 'I can't see why, though. I mean, what's the point?'

'What does it matter? He's obviously here. This proves it.'

Tamar shook her head. 'I'm not so sure,' she said.

Denny shook his head impatiently. 'You said you sensed him here, and now this! What more evidence do you need? What else could it be?'

She shook her head again. 'I don't know, but I just think that we shouldn't be too hasty. There could be a dozen explanations for this'

A dozen?' Denny rubbed his chin wearily. 'Okay, name one.'

Tamar opened her mouth and then shut it again, and then, 'I've got a better idea,' she said.

* * *

In the end, they got quite a lot of information out of the workmen, who, after the fashion of workmen everywhere (and everywhen), liked nothing better than to loaf about expounding their views and generally informing the ignorant, rather than get on with some work.

The men told them, in slightly condescending tones, as if they were simpletons, that the equipment (by this time, there was a vast array of fork lift trucks and earth diggers – the trucks that had arrived contained scaffolding) came from the "sky men". These were gifts from these great beings to honour their Pharaoh. Yes, they had seen them with their own eyes, everyone had. They were also teachers. Their fathers remembered them also. No, they were not the gods, they were told, when Denny asked. They were just men who came from the sky – giant men perhaps ten or twelve feet high; some were bigger. They came from the sky.

Even with all they had seen, Tamar and Denny were inclined to take this last piece of information with a pinch of salt. As Denny pointed out, all this talk of giant sky men did not prove a damn thing. Askphrit could still be behind it. Particularly as, when pressed the men admitted that the gifts came from the sky men, but ultimately through the grace of the gods, from whom Pharaoh was descended and with whom he talked on a regular basis.

Tamar said that this was an early example of a religious method, which still existed into the present day, among natives in Africa and Papaya New Guinea and Paui etc, known among the practitioners as "Cargo Cult", whereby the natives of the land would pray to their god to deliver to them the trappings of western civilisation, such as wristwatches and telephones and even trucks and aeroplanes, believing that all such things came from heaven and belonged to everyone. The fact that it seldom worked, she said, did not put them off, they had obviously just not worded the prayer correctly. The white men, who had plenty of "Cargo" obviously knew something they did not. Pidgin, the language used by many of these people gave an interesting insight into their beliefs at times, she said. A helicopter, for example, they called a "mixmaster belong Jesus Christ".

Denny yawned. He was more interested in where the giant men came from. Were they Aliens (as seemed most likely) or were they a product of Askphrit's overheated imagination? If so, they needed to find out, in Denny's opinion, since this would represent a huge problem. And a possible opportunity.

Tamar thought it unlikely that the giant men had anything to do with Askphrit, but she was even more sceptical about the possibility of their being Aliens. She was quite scathing on the subject, and Denny was crestfallen, until he realised that she was upset with him about the yawning.

'So, what are they then?' he demanded.

'If you really want to know,' she said, with an elaborate yawn. 'Why don't you ask them?'

Even though he knew that she was not being serious, Denny thought that this was a good idea.

'I *do* really want to know,' he said. 'And, after all, what harm can it do really? They seem to be benevolent. And we can always get out of here at any time, if we need to anyway.'

'If they are Aliens or some – "thing" that bastard thought up to cause trouble,' said Tamar. 'What makes you think they'll admit it?'

Denny grinned. 'Oh ye of little faith.' he said.

* * *

It was against Tamar's better judgement that they went to find the Giant Sky Men.

Further questioning had revealed that the sky men lived among them and even took wives sometimes from among the populace. Their tall houses were pointed out to Denny and Tamar, who saw them standing stark and austere against the skyline. They were elite. A sort of nobility, but the men assured them that they would be made welcome if they went seeking knowledge. The sky men were a benevolent race.

Tamar was interested in the fact that these men apparently wished to mingle their DNA with that of the people. 'The Vikings have a myth of Giant men also,' she said. 'And they believe that they are the descendants of these men. Suppose it's true.'

This time Denny did not yawn. 'We need to find out who they are,' he said

'I think I might know,' she told him.

* * *

They were welcomed into the house by a man who was tall, but by no means a giant, and asked to wait in a small chamber. 'My lord Tempe would be with them shortly.' The man disappeared.

Tamar and Denny looked at each other and without saying a word they both rose and left the room to follow the man. To be received when their hosts had had time to make ready for them, was to lose their advantage, they both felt.

The man passed by several doors and stopped at a hole in the wall, which Tamar realised after a few moments thought was an intercom of some kind. 'Indoor plumbing too, I bet,' she muttered inconsequentially.

'I wouldn't be surprised,' Denny agreed.

'There's archaeological evidence to suggest that certain ancient peoples did have it,' she told him. 'They had to on account of them living in high rise apartment buildings.'

Denny yawned. 'Is that important?' he asked. 'We already know that historians have consistently underestimated the people who lived before them. God, you've got *me* at it now.'

'It might be important,' said Tamar. 'Then again, it might not. We just have to …'

She broke off, listening. 'What's that?' she hissed

Behind one of the heavy doors they could just make out a heavy thumping beat. Denny cocked his head to listen. 'Motown,' he said eventually.

Tamar nodded.

She went to push the door open, Denny held her back. 'Wait,' he said. 'We might be you know…' he went through a series of facial tics and knowing looks, 'interrupting something.' He winked. 'You know. I mean it's *Motown*,'

Tamar looked blank, but Denny knew she understood him, she did not often play dumb, but when she did … Denny shrugged, he knew when he was beaten. He stood aside, and Tamar raised her arms and the doors flew open. Denny thought that this was unnecessarily dramatic. But Tamar knew what she was doing.

The words of the song floated over the stunned silence. "Look out baby 'cause here I come. And I'm givin' you a love that's true, so get ready, 'cause here I come …"

The Giant men – and they really were (there were giant women too, they now saw) and many people of ordinary size stared at the intruders. Denny broke the ice. 'The Temptations,' he opined '"Get Ready" William "Smokey" Robinson, 1966'

'– AD,' he added inconsequentially. Denny knew this kind of thing. Who would have thought it would ever come in handy?

The tension broke, and a giant man with wavy brown hair and blue eyes who looked vaguely Irish laughed suddenly. With a wave of his hand, he dismissed all but the other giants.

'Well, Well, Well,' he said, in English. 'You appear to have caught us.'

* * *

They were from the future, they said. What would be, on our calendar, the late 35th Century. They were humans, philanthropists who had discovered the secret to time travel and had come back in order to secure their own future. They did this in various stages of ancient history and all over the world. Yes, they had been among the Norse men and many others. Some cultures remembered them, and some did not, it did not matter. When Denny objected that it was dangerous to tamper with history they laughed at him.

'But we had already done it.' They said. 'Who do you think brought fire to the cave man, Prometheus?'

Evolution, they said was a circular phenomenon. 'Without us, civilisation would not exist as we know it, and if it did not, we would not exist as we are. We are the creators of our own future. We know this. If we had not come we would have broken the cycle. We are our own ancestors, our own ancients and the teachers of our past generations. This is how it has always been, did you not know?'

They knew nothing of magic; this was technology, they said. And they had heard of the various gods but had seen nothing of them. They were not gods to the people they taught – neither had they ever pretended to be.

Their people no longer lived on Earth, this accounted for their greater height, they said. They had removed to a planet with a lighter gravity – they would not say its name – many thousands of years before they came back to Earth. They would not say why they had abandoned the Earth.

'How did you discover all this?' asked Denny.

It was not remembered now, but the truth of it had been proved again and again. The circular nature of evolution mirrored that of time itself and was a part of it. It was possible to look back over the history of the world and see that everything that had happened had also happened before and everything that was going to happen would happen again.

'We read of the ancients and knew that it was of ourselves that we read. Round and round we go and each time, our pupils learn a little faster and a little better. And each time, we ourselves are a little further ahead because of it. This is not an interference in history. It is the nature of things. We hope that eventually we will eliminate many evils from the world such as poverty and war and malaise and also reality TV.'

'How did you discover the secret to time travel?' asked Denny. 'I mean without that, you couldn't have done all this.'

'Well, in one sense you might say that we already had the secret, we only had to look into the past, it had all been done before. But, in a sense, you are right, in each cycle the discovery had to be made and who knows now how many times this has happened. But I will tell you. The secret was discovered in some old writings that were unearthed in the middle of the 29th Century. Long before we knew what use we would be putting it to. The secret was kept to prevent abuse of this power until our destiny was revealed to us.'

'And what was the secret?'

The giant spokesman looked at him curiously. 'And do you not know it yourselves? You are not of this time – that is clear'

'Well,' Denny began. Tamar dug him in the ribs. 'No,' he said, turning to her. 'It's a fair enough question.' He addressed the Giant. 'It was a sort of accident,' he said, 'us ending up here. We don't know how we did it. But really I just wanted to know, what the writing was, you know, who wrote it in the first place.'

'It was written by one who had discovered the secret, many centuries before. And the writing contained many vehement exhortations never to abuse the knowledge that she had found.'

'*She*?' they both said together.

'Yes, she. And although you may find it strange, she had addressed the writing to the very man who eventually discovered it. Called him by his very name. But after all, it is only to be expected, if you think about it.'

'What was his name?' asked Tamar to avoid asking the other burning question that was in her mind. And absolutely *not* because she thought she might ever need to know it.

Denny asked it. 'What was her name?'

The Giant took the questions in their due order. 'He was called Roderigo Alvarez II. And her name was Tamar Black – but the maiden has fainted.'

'Close file.'

* * *

Tamar did not want to talk about it. 'We don't have time to ponder the nature of the universe right now,' she said testily. 'We have more important things to do.

'And why did you have to close the file before we found out how they pinpoint their destination? That could have been useful.'

'We could always go back and ask them.'

Tamar shuddered. 'No, they'll know now that we lied to them about how we got there, besides ...' she shrugged expressively. Denny nodded, he too had found them creepy – unnatural was a better word. Perhaps he was more xenophobic than he had thought. It was just that they had been so – so ...

'Patronising,' supplied Tamar, breaking in on his thought, 'superior – condescending?'

Denny shook his head. 'No. More, sort of, too perfect, too polite and too goody goody – inhuman, no vices or weaknesses. I just ...'

'Whatever, we're not going back, besides we'll find him, I know we will, and if what they said was right, I'll find the way to locate the files myself. I'm the one who discovers it, they said so.'

This was an encouraging thought, so Denny just nodded 'Okay,' he said. 'You're the genius. Pick a number, any number, go on, I dare you.'

'I never said I was a genius, anyway, it's your turn, we agreed to take turns, I'm not taking all the blame. Egypt was my fault. The next disaster can be down to you.'

'It wasn't exactly a disaster, but okay. Um, this one.' He pushed open a trapdoor. 'Have you noticed,' he said as he entered the file. 'Whoever chooses the file has the most to do with what happens when we get there? I mean I chose the Viking file and the one in the nightclub, didn't I?'

'Coincidence,' scoffed Tamar. 'Besides that's a generalisation. What about King Richard?'

'We decided on that one together.'

'Oh shut up.'

* * *

Denny was actually about to be proved wrong in his theory for when they landed in the file Tamar immediately recognized it as Ancient Greece. A far more Ancient Greece however than the one she had known. The coastline where her home town would stand seemed a prehistoric landscape, yet clearly it could not be, for these were *historical* files, weren't they?

'Well, there's nothing much to be seen here,' said Denny after a few minutes. 'What do you think? He can't be here! There are no people.'

It was Denny's day to be proved wrong. Just at that moment a figure appeared. That of a young woman carrying a box as carefully as another woman might carry her baby.

She was a tall woman and almost as beautiful as Tamar, but her face seemed to have no expression. One got the impression that she was unscathed by experience or emotion, untouched by life and yet she did not look vacant or silly, just inhumanly serene. Denny was fascinated, Tamar nervous. There was magic at work here, or she was a monkey! Big magic. She tugged at Denny. 'Let's go,' she hissed. The woman – you really could not call her a girl, (although she looked no older than about sixteen) she was so tall, looked up.

'He gave me this box,' she said in a sing song voice. 'He told me I must not open it up.' For the first time, an expression flitted across her face. 'I am his to be commanded,' she said. 'So why do I wish to disobey?'

Tamar started violently. 'Don't interfere,' she hissed at Denny. 'Say nothing, we shouldn't be here.'

Denny sighed; it was the same old song. 'We never should,' he said. 'Just once I'd like to end up somewhere that we *are* supposed to be.'

'Shhh.'

The woman was clearly talking to herself. The feeling that they got, was that she only ever talked to herself – that she had no one else to talk to. But in that case, thought Denny, who was the "He" who had given her the box?

'I must not open it,' she muttered. 'But then, if I must not, why was it given to me to keep? Surely if it is my own box, I can do with it what I wish. I wonder what it contains? One little peep cannot hurt. No, I promised, oh but how silly, it is only an old box.'

'She knows what's in it,' said Denny. 'I can tell.'

'Yes,' agreed Tamar, 'She's just talking herself into it, justifying herself.' She tugged at Denny's arm again. 'We should go now.'

'Why? Do you know what she's got in there?'

'I'm not sure, but I think, I think that that's Pandora.'

For a moment Denny looked blank, and then he went white. 'Oh God!'

'Oh Zeus!' responded Tamar.

The woman appeared to have come to a decision. 'I *will* open it.' And she lifted the catch.

'RUN!' yelled Tamar, already halfway down the beach. Denny followed, not fast enough. It was horrible.

To be caught in a maelstrom of all the ills of mankind is indescribable. But I will try.

On the one hand, there were the physical effects. It was like being caught in a huge whirlpool in the middle of the worst storm ever. He was cold and dizzy and sick, more sick than any human being ever was or will be. His head pounded with the noise, and he was pulled in every direction, it felt as if his body were being torn apart. And this was nothing compared to the emotional effects. To feel all the pain of what the whole of mankind would ultimately suffer with just one heart to take it, was unbearable. To feel the evil that men would feel and inflict, the misery and the jealousy and the cruelty, the grief, hunger, death and betrayal.

Denny thought, and hoped, that he was going to die. It lasted only a few seconds, each one an eternity, and then he lay on the sand. He was very still.

Tamar ran toward him on wobbly legs. She had been away from the centre of the storm, but she had caught the backlash of it, so to speak, before it had dissipated.

As she reached him, he sat up. 'Crimeny,' he said and threw up violently. Then he grinned. 'I don't half wish *you* had chosen the file,' he said.

'Are you okay?' she asked in disbelief, she had felt it, a tiny portion of it anyway. She could not even imagine what it had been like for him. He would be changed forever. She was surprised he was not catatonic.

'I'm fine,' he said. 'Just a bit you know, seasick.'

'*Seasick*?'

'Yes, but otherwise, just the same.'

'Just the *same*? But you *can't* be, not after that, after feeling all that. I'm sure it would have driven me insane.'

'I always knew it, you know,' he explained. 'I'm human, so it's always been inside me, all that stuff. It's in every one of us, I suppose. No surprises there.' He grinned again. 'It's just a bit much to take all at once like that, you see, but I'm okay now. Just feel like I've got the world's worst hangover,' he laughed. 'I tell you, mead's got nothing on that box. Shall we get out of here? I could use a stiff drink. No chance of that I suppose?'

Tamar shook her head, not in negation, but in disbelief.

Denny misinterpreted this gesture. 'Thought not,' he said 'You're probably right. I daresay it's the last thing I need.'

'Huh?'

He got to his feet. 'Come on. Askphrit's not here, let's get on. And *you're* choosing the next file,'

~ Chapter Eleven ~

IT MAY HAVE BEEN noticed by the more observant reader, that after terrific experiences such as the one Denny had just been through, he and Tamar often refused to talk to each other about it afterwards. I'm sure psychiatrists would have a lot to say about this attitude. They would bandy words like "repression" and "isolation" about like nobody's business, but I would like to see any person, even a psychiatrist, handle such an experience any better. One must not assume that Denny and Tamar withdrew after these experiences because they were not close to each other; I personally have a different explanation for their reticence. You can disagree if you like, or perhaps you do not care. After all, it is not as if you are being paid to care, like the aforementioned head quacks. However that may be, I think it likely that there was, for them at least, nothing much to talk about really. All that could possibly be said was already understood by the other, due to their common experience and their telepathic link. And as to the rest, the uniqueness of the experience, could not be explained in any wise, so there was no point trying. In any case, Denny said no more about Pandora's Box, and Tamar did not ask.

Tamar chose the next file, as instructed, and, as usual, at random.

They appeared to be in London and yet, despite the fact that it was early evening, the streets were eerily deserted. A loud siren was going off.

Tamar recognised it. 'Air raid,' she said tersely.

As if to confirm her words, a man came running around the corner and repeated what she had said, and added. 'Run for the shelter.' He disappeared around the corner, and then the bombs started dropping.

'Bit early,' Tamar mused. 'It's still quite light.' There was no question of them running for shelter, and they stood curiously watching the piecemeal destruction of the city, having a view from amongst the dropping bombs that must, I think, be unique. Being both on the ground, and yet not running away.

'It's the blitz,' said Denny excitedly. 'WWII, do you realise what this might mean? It depends on the date of course, but we're damn close.'

WWII, you will remember, was the time Askphrit had chosen to despatch Denny's granddad.

Tamar frowned. 'The date, yes. That's the question, isn't it?'

'If it's before 1941, we're ...'

'Tut, man,' scolded Tamar. 'Look around you. Look at the cars – didn't you notice the clothes that man was wearing? If this is the '40s, I'll eat my knickers.'

Denny looked around him, casually at first, then in shock. He showed Tamar a very white face. 'B-but, this, this is – *now*!'

Tamar nodded, calmly enough. 'Near enough, yes.'

'But this is *impossible*.' This from a man who knew, without a shadow of a doubt that *nothing* is impossible. Except possibly not finishing the last of the choc chip cookies once the packet's been opened. Or getting a politician to give you a straight yes or no.

Tamar grimaced. 'I don't know about impossible,' she said. 'But there is definitely something funny about this.'

'Funny!' Denny was outraged.

'Strange then,' she amended.

'You don't say,' said Denny sarcastically. 'Strange you say, well that clears that up then, I'm so glad you're here to explain these things to me. *Strange*! Of course it's bloody strange, strange enough I should say.' He paused. 'Strange,' he said again. 'Strange, strange – no, the word's lost all meaning.'

Tamar was tempted to slap him, to bring him to his senses, as they do in plays. But since she was feeling much the same way, she forbore.

'Let's try to think this through logically,' she said.

'*Logically*?' Denny threatened to start all over again. Tamar slapped him.

'Sorry,' said Denny, rubbing his face. 'I'm okay now.'

Tamar pursed her lips. 'Hmm – okay, we need to find a newspaper, find out the date. It's either the future somehow, that we've got into, in which case I want to know about it, or ...'

'How can it be the future?' Denny protested. 'These are historical files, aren't they?'

'Depends,' said Tamar cryptically. 'Or, as I was saying, it's the past, as is more likely, and Askphrit's done something. In which case, I *really* want to know about it.'

'What do you mean, "depends"?' Denny homed in on this remark.

'On which point you started from. Time is circular. Our descendants said so. You know – the one's we met in the *past*.'

'Yes, but ...'

'Watch out!'

At this point, a building collapsed on Denny effectively putting an end to this line of speculation for the time being. There's nothing quite like having half a house fall on your head to clear the brain, after all.

By the time he had climbed out of the wreckage, he had had time to think about it somewhat, and he thought he understood. After all, he reasoned, every file they entered represented the present to the people who were living in it. This presumably included the present that they knew as the present, which was not the end of time, hopefully. If time is circular, then the files were accumulative. They flowed into each other. Past, present and future were just entry points in the system.

If this were true, then it made their task all the harder. He could not help hoping, that his speculations were wrong. He looked at Tamar. She just nodded. 'Got it now?' she asked. 'Let's find out when we are.'

No, Denny shook his head. 'I'd rather not know,' he said, 'let's just get out of here.

They stopped for, a moment, to watch, as Big Ben was struck, and crumbled slowly to the ground.

'After all,' he explained, 'what can we do about it, anyway? If it's the past and Askphrit has changed it somehow, the best thing we can do is catch him and hopefully prevent his doing it again. And if it is the future, well, we can't change it, and frankly, if it is, I'd rather not know. I've learned my lesson about seeing into the future. It's nothing but trouble.'

This was indisputable; Tamar nodded. 'Okay, if that's what you want, let's go.' She caught his hand and they took another look around at the devastation of war, and both said a silent prayer that it would never have to happen. And then – 'Close file.'

~ Chapter Twelve ~

'I THINK WE'RE GOING about this all wrong,' said Denny.

'Oh yes? Illuminate me.'

'Well, Miss Sarky Pants. Askphrit's using the files like us, isn't he, to move through time? So hasn't he got to open and close files the same way we do? Which means, doesn't it, that he has to come back here to enter another file? Why don't we just wait for him here?'

'Hmm, it's a good idea in theory, with just one problem. We don't know that he *is* moving through time, he might just stay in one place – or rather time.'

'But we're never going to find him like this, just jumping into files at random, he could be anywhere! Isn't there some better way?'

Tamar thought about it. 'No.'

'You know, I thought at least the numbers of the files would go in some sort of order that we'd be able to work out, but they seem to be just random.'

'Yes, I've noticed that. The numbers must relate to something else, not the chronological order. It's beyond our means to find out what it is though.'

'What about those personal files?'

'How's that going to help?'

'Maybe if we find the one for my Granddad ...'

'And how are we going to do that? Besides, how do we even know that he's still there? Maybe he's moved on to some *other* ancestor of yours – Christ he could be in Troy by now.'

'Will you stop going on about Troy. Besides, how the Hell would *he* know about that anyway?'

'He knew about Grandpa!' Tamar pointed out.

'Well – that's a lot more recent.'

'Ha! That depends on where you're looking from.'

Denny didn't have a good answer for this. 'Well okay then, these files, isn't there some kind of key? We never know *where* we're going to end up, until we get there. It's ridiculous. Why isn't there a door marked 'Help'?'

'How should I know?'

'Well I'm fed up with the whole thing.'

'We'll find him. I know we will.'

'Huh, s'what *you* say.'

* * *

Stiles was becoming quite adept at file jumping; he was even beginning to enjoy it. It was a shame, he thought, that he could not have gone with Tamar and Denny – seeing the past, albeit briefly, was kind of fun. On the other hand, he had to admit, it was probably just as well that he had not really.

If he had not come back, then they might never have worked out how to access the files properly, and Tamar and Denny would probably have ended up hunting through time randomly for the rest of eternity.

He had now sent all the displaced persons from history back to where they belonged. Whatever the various ramifications of their little adventure might be, was out of his hands now, and he would just have to hope that it was not too serious. Now it was time to find Tamar and Denny and bring them back.

* * *

'Okay, we'll try the personal files,' said Tamar. 'But first, I think we should try mainframe.'

'I thought we were *in* mainframe,' said Denny, perplexed.

'I mean the central files. Like you said, maybe there's a key to these files and ... shh, someone's coming!'

Denny opened a file at random, and they scrambled in.

They were falling through the sky, as if from an aeroplane except that there wasn't one and also people who jump out of planes usually take the precaution of bringing a parachute. 'Who the hell designed these files?' bellowed Denny over the sound of the screaming wind.

Tamar did not answer; she was busy panicking. When she tried to use her powers to teleport safely to the ground, she found that she could not. She no longer had them. Denny did not know this of course. He himself vanished in a small whirlwind and landed safely on the ground. He watched Tamar falling and wondered in a detached way why she was not on the ground already like him. By the time he realised that she could not do it, it was almost too late he was about to shoot into the air to catch her when ... Was it a bird? Was it a plane? No, it was Mega Man! No way!

Denny actually rubbed his eyes as the caped crusader (no – that was Batman) swooped through the sky out of nowhere and caught Tamar just before she hit the ground, to a round of wild applause. He then swooped away taking Tamar with him. Denny thought that he might well faint too; this was impossible! Where the hell was he?

* * *

'I think they are in trouble,' said Hecaté, tapping anxiously at the keyboard.

'What makes you say that?' asked Stiles.

'Just that they should have shown up somewhere else by now, at least I think so. I find it unlikely that the monster is to be found in this region of history, so they should have moved on.'

'But you don't know?'

'No.'

'Where are they now?'

'That is what I am telling you, I don't know.'

'I meant where were they last?'

'I think, in the early 20th century.'

'Can you pull them out?'

'I am trying, leave me be.' She flapped at him irritably. 'Wait! A temporal anomaly, they may have moved on. But – it could be the monster.'

'No, he wouldn't let himself be caught out like that. He's hiding; Tamar and Denny *want* us to be able to track them, don't they? It must be them – like waving at the security cameras. Where are they?'

'That's odd,' said Hecaté.

'What is?'

'It cannot be them.'

'Why not?'

'This is impossible!'

'What is?' Stiles lost patience and looked at the screen. He could just about make sense of what he was seeing. He gasped. 'B-but – that's impossible!'

'That is what I said.'

'What the hell could it be?'

* * *

Tamar opened her eyes in a hospital bed and said. 'Where am I?

'Megalopolis General,' said a voice, she snapped her head round and saw the meekest hunk in the world. The man, despite being large and muscular, with fairly handsome features, managed to give off an air of complete and utter awkwardness and unattractiveness. It was almost as if he was doing it on purpose.

Tamar sat up, unsteadily, to get a better look at him. He did not look like a doctor.

'My name is Kent Clark,' said this enigma, and Tamar understood as she remembered the swooping and the cape. She smiled knowingly. Kent looked at her. He had that look on his face, the look that was all too familiar to Tamar. So much for "Lori Lain"

She grinned, then hurriedly wiped it off her face, now was not the time. 'How did I get here?' she asked, her memory was fuzzy for some reason. 'Did I already say, "Where am I"?'

'You were falling, and Mega Man caught you,' he replied. 'Can't you remember where you fell from? Mega Man told us that there was no aircraft around that you could have fallen from.'

Tamar tried to stop herself from laughing at this pathetic subterfuge, even if she had not already known, he was giving himself away with every word and gesture.

Tamar leapt gracefully out of the bed and snatched his press pass from his pocket so suddenly that he had hardly realised what she had done before she was reading it out to him.

'Kent Clark – Press pass,' she read in a mocking sing song tone. 'Press?' she frowned 'I see. So you aren't here to see if I'm hurt or anything. You're here because my little escapade has got people worried. No plane or helicopter or even a balloon to fall from. Well...' she fixed him with a steely eye, 'just why the hell should I tell you anything?'

'Well...' he stammered. 'I was just hoping that you might ... that is to say if you wouldn't mind ... I thought ... if you would consent to enlighten ... I'm sorry to have bothered you miss... er? I'll be going now.'

But Tamar had just realised the gravity of her situation and had decided not to let him leave just yet.

'You know,' she said as he turned to the door. 'It's just a personal opinion, but I think you could do with a better disguise.'

'What?' said Kent Clark amiably but with a hint of concern in his voice.

'Of course,' continued Tamar ignoring this. 'It does seem to be working for you. So maybe I'm wrong.'

'I think maybe you are still in shock, Miss,' said Kent. 'You appear to be rambling. I'll send a doctor in on my way out.' He opened the door.

'Thank you,' said Tamar. 'For saving my life today. Pretty cool.'

Kent turned back, all concern. 'You are confused miss,' he said. 'I didn't save you – Mega Man did.'

Tamar winked wickedly at him. 'That's what I said,' she agreed.

He stared at her as if she were mad. It really was a pretty good act thought Tamar. Time to ring down the curtain. With another quick gesture, she snatched his glasses off his face. 'Give it up mega– boy,' she told him. 'You aren't fooling anyone.'

He slammed the door hastily.

He looked around nervously and waved his hand at her. 'Keep your voice down,' he urged.

Tamar waved a hand dismissively. 'If these fools haven't worked it out by now, why then, they probably wouldn't believe it if I wrote it in the sky in letters of fire. How many coincidences can people believe in? I'll tell you, shall I? As many as it takes to keep their world from imploding. Trust me, I know.'

Kent looked unconvinced. 'So, how do you know?'

Tamar smiled. 'Funny story,' she said. 'It has to do with how I fell from nowhere out of the sky. Off the record?'

* * *

Denny was wandering around the – as far as he was aware – entirely fictional city of Megalopolis. He knew where he was because of the myriad signs telling him so, and admonishing him to keep it tidy. It *was* tidy, astonishingly so, and so were the people. He felt as if the signs were directed specifically at him, as if he were making the place untidy just by being there. He felt like this in a lot of places, even – since he met Tamar – in his own home.

All this taken into account, he could not do what humans usually do in these situations, which was to tell himself that he had just imagined it. The fact had to be faced, he had seen Mega Man, really seen him. He tried to work out what it all meant. Could it be that Mega Man really had existed once? Did we just pretend afterwards that it never happened?

There were strong arguments for this thesis, not least that, according to Tamar, that's what humans always did in the event of a piece of history that they did not want to have happened. Add to that, the fact that this was the sort of thing humans tried to deny even when it was happening right in front of them, and it seemed more than plausible as an explanation. Tamar would know.

Question was: where *was* Tamar? Denny – not the sharpest tool in the box at the best of times – and these were not the best of times by any stretch of the imagination, took a good twenty minutes to reach the conclusion that he should begin his search at the nearest hospital. The result of this brain lag was that he arrived at Megalopolis General too late. She was already gone.

'What the hell happened to the simple plan we had?' he thought dolefully, 'just pop in and out of each file, no messing about. Why does this keep happening?'

* * *

Tamar's memory was hazy. She knew what had happened in a vague way – that is, that she knew she was in a place that she should not be in, with a fictional superhero. But she had no idea how she had got there, or that she was supposed to have super powers of her own. She had forgotten all about what she was meant to be doing; she had forgotten Askphrit, and she had completely forgotten Denny. This may have been because, technically, none of these things existed in this version of reality.

Since she had no ID or money, her new friend had had no option but to take her home with him – well he *was* the good-guy. Besides, he had strong reasons for wanting a private talk with her *and* to keep her where he could see her.

He rounded on her almost the moment they walked through the door. 'Okay,' he said. 'How do you know who I am?'

'Because I'm psychic?' she said, impishly. 'Okay, okay, I'm sorry, I'll try to explain.' She thought for a moment and said, 'parallel universes.' (Tamar's memory may have been compromised, but her intelligence was as sharp as ever and she had already worked out what must have happened – in theory. Although, how it had happened remained a mystery.)

This was a cryptic enough remark, typical of Tamar's manner of communicating. Denny would have got the point immediately, being used to her staccato sentences, augmented, as they usually were, by psychic transmissions. Not that she remembered any of this, but she looked at her interrogator expectantly, as if this remark should clear the whole matter up.

'What?' he said, disappointingly.

She sighed. 'I'm from a parallel universe – you know? The multiverse theory?'

He looked blank.

'Anyway,' she resumed. 'In my universe, where I come from, you – Mega Man – are ... well – um, how do I put this tactfully? I can't! You're fictional I'm afraid. A story. There are movies,' she added helpfully.

'What are you talking about?'

'You're like Batman.'

'Batman?'

'You know? Not real – like Zap Fordham – he's my favourite – not that I don't like you too ... you're not going to hit me are you?'

Kent Clark aka Mega Man drew in a deep breath to calm himself down. After all, clearly the poor girl was trying to be helpful and did not mean to be the most irritating person he had ever come across in his entire existence. She was no doubt rambling in this manner because of a blow to the head. He had to be patient.

'Let's try this again,' he said, forcing himself to smile in what he hoped was a soothing way. In his current frame of mind, the result was more of a constipated grimace. Tamar could not help laughing, the frown returned.

'You know?' she said dreamily. 'You don't look at all how I would have expected, isn't that funny?'

He did not look as if he thought it at all funny.

'You're right,' she said. 'Let's try this again. Oh it's such a bore having to explain things. Okay, so, I'm from a parallel universe I don't know how I got here so don't ask. You do know about parallel universes don't you?'

* * *

Plan A was simply to close the file and hope. Hope that Tamar exited the file at the same time as him from wherever she was. There was good reason to suppose she would. The problem with this idea was that there was still someone in the file room waiting for them. The other problem with this idea was that he had no idea where she was and whether or not she might just vanish right before someone's eyes.

Plan B was to leap off a tall building or a bridge shrieking wildly in the vain hope that a flying man in a cape would come to his rescue, thus enabling Denny to ask a few pertinent questions such as. 'Where did you take my girlfriend?'

How else could a stranger in town hope to make contact with a Superhero?

Well, said a sarcastic voice in his head. *If you know his secret identity, you could always try looking him up in the phone book, stupid!*

* * *

'Take unicorns,' Tamar was saying.

'Unicorns?' Kent was stupefied at this sudden change of tack.

'Right, they're not real are they?'

'No, so what?'

'Except that somewhere, in another universe, they *are* real, everything exists somewhere ... I'm not explaining this very well am I?'

'Actually,' he rubbed his chin thoughtfully, 'I think I'm beginning to get the idea. In your world, I'm like a unicorn – somebody made me up, and now I exist for real?'

'Or maybe it's the other way around, I don't pretend to understand it all – God that hurts.'

'You're injured?' he asked solicitously.

'Only my pride. I meant that it hurts to admit I don't know something.'

'Oh.'

'What was I saying? Oh yeah, maybe when a thing doesn't exist in one universe in reality it exists as a story or a myth instead, perhaps the universes sort of leak into each other.

Maybe everything exists everywhere after all just not in the same way. I mean the popular theory is that multiple universes are created by choices people make. For every choice you make you *could* have made another and that choice and its consequences exist too. Maybe you're only a story in my universe because that's the way you want it there.'

'And the unicorns? They like to preserve their anonymity too?'

Tamar shrugged. 'I said I didn't really know. You don't have to rub it in, besides it still works in a way. Unicorns *do* exist here, just not in reality. But you've heard of them. You could draw me a picture of one.'

'I could draw you a picture of an elephant, doesn't mean they really exist.'

'Of course they exist … oh!'

They looked at each other and laughed.

* * *

Having found the address, Denny could not decide what to do next. This indecisiveness was not new to him, but it was usually mitigated by having Tamar around to whom the phrase "bull in a china shop" would not be an inappropriate description. She had plenty of decision. Not for the first time, he realised that they made the perfect team. He wondered what she was blundering into without him to hold her back. Time to find out.

* * *

'Len Lowther?'

'Never heard of him.'

'Lori Lain? Lanni Long.?'

'Why do all these people have the same initials?'

'I don't know, I didn't make them up. Jerry Kite?'

'Nope.'

'Timmy Jolson?'

'Give it up.'

'But you do work for the "Daily Globe", don't you?'

No, I work for the Megalopolis Star.'

'Oh.' Tamar was disappointed. 'But you grew up in Minorville, right? Tell me, you grew up in Minorville.'

'Yes, I did.'

'On a farm?'

Whatever the answer to this question it was extremely effectively interrupted by a small whirlwind in the living room. Both Tamar and Kent were flabbergasted by the advent of an indoor tornado, neither of them having any memory of ever seeing any such thing before. Before the dust had settled, and Tamar had not even had time to quip 'I guess we're not in Kansas anymore.' Which she had been thinking of doing? Which just goes to show, you can take the Djinn out of the girl ... or something like that only more pertinent? Kent had whipped off his specs and become the eponymous hero in tights just as Denny emerged from his dustcloud.

'Kraptonian!' accused Mega Man.

'Bollocks!' said Denny with more truth than elegance.

'Then you are some kind of super villain, what do you want of me?'

Denny ignored him. 'Tamar, what are you doing here? We have to get out of here – now!'

Tamar looked at him curiously and slightly fearfully. 'Do I know you?'

Denny groaned. 'Oh great,' he said. 'Amnesia! Like we don't have enough problems.' He paused to leisurely push Mega Man to one side as he tried to make a grab at Denny, and then continued. 'I'm Denny – remember? – You don't remember, of course you don't, oh hell!'

'Sir,' said Mega Man, pompously. 'I'm afraid I'm going to have to ask you to leave this young lady alone, or face me.' He balled his fists and struck a fighting stance, with his chest stuck out and a fierce expression on his face. Tamar and Denny looked at each other, and both laughed. Mega Man dropped his arms sheepishly.

'It's all right,' she said. 'I must know him – he knows my name; maybe he can help us sort out what happened to me.'

'You trust him?'

Tamar looked at Denny. 'Yes,' she said, simply.

'Even though he's clearly not human?'

'You can talk,' said Denny, affronted.

'So this Ash – pit...'

'Askphrit.'

'Whatever! He's a god.'

'Mad god.'

'Who used to be a jinx?'

'Djinn, as in genie.'

'Huh?'

'Look, just come back with me, I'm sure it'll come back to you.'

'Back where?'

'To the archives – mainframe – whatever.'

'What?'

'I already explained all this.'

Kent stirred. 'If I may just interject here ...'

Both Tamar and Denny turned to him. '*No!*' they said in unison.

'But it seems fairly obvious to me that ...'

'No!' This was Tamar.

'All I want to say is ...'

'Just shut up.'

'Tamar ...' began Denny.

'Both of you,' she said fiercely. She put her head in her hands. 'I mean you!' she pointed at Denny. 'I don't know who you are or what the hell you're talking about or what you expect me to do. And you!' she looked at Kent. 'Aren't even a real person, so I don't see why I should listen to either of you.'

At this point, Denny lost patience. It had all just been too much for him. Having relied on finding Tamar and having her explain things to him, it was just too hard. She did not even know who she was for God's sake! But she would remember, he was certain – well almost certain – if he could just get her out of here. Something about this file had made her lose her powers, that much he had been able to ascertain, and also any memory of ever having had any powers. It was possible that Askphrit had something to do with it. After all, he was going around changing history and Tamar had explained that this would alter people's memories. But if he could get her back into mainframe, which was stuck, in the same second of eternity, maybe she would go back to normal.

It would not occur to him until later that if she had forgotten her past, because it never really happened, then why it was that *he* still remembered it?

Anyway, that was the current plan, and she wasn't having any of it. So, in a moment of desperation, he did what was probably the most stupid thing he could have done, he lost his temper and said. 'Sod this, let's go. Close files.'

The world vanished; he opened his eyes and said. 'Oh Hell!'

Tamar rubbed her eyes in disbelief. 'Where did he go?'
Kent shrugged.

PART TWO – TO HELL AND BACK

~ Chapter Thirteen ~

'WHAT THE HELL could it be?'

Hecaté shrugged – as perplexed as Stiles. 'It does not make sense. It would have to mean that there is another one of them out there, someone else using the files to travel, but that is impossible.'

'We covered that. The fact is, there is an anachronism showing up in the present, and it can't be Tamar and Denny or Askphrit, since they all came from here.'

'I know, I know. So, who is it? And are they a threat? Maybe it is nothing to worry about.'

'Where are Tamar and Denny? Can you find them?'

'No, but that just means that they are blending in, because they do not need any help.'

'Well – that's good – right?'

'Indeed, but ...'

'We should try to find out what's causing the anachronism in the present, in case it's a problem,' said Stiles. 'It couldn't be caused by the time freeze could it?' he added, hopefully.

'No,' she said, looking at him as if he were stupid.

'Well, I don't know, do I? This is all new to me, but what I *am* good at is detecting. What exactly are we looking for?'

'There are several reports here of a man in strange clothing, who appeared suddenly in York, in a shopping centre. There are pictures – look. Since we've only just picked this up, we have to assume that this has happened since they left, in a manner of speaking. If you understand me.'

'I think so, you think it might be because of something they, or Askphrit did.'

'Yes, possibly, now that the files are open, who knows what may happen?'

'Still, there's no rush is there? I mean, he's frozen in time now, just like everyone else.'

'Yes, I suppose he is, but still, we should try to find out why he is here, what brought him here. Maybe he needs our help.'

'I agree, I guess I'm going to York.'

'I will send you.'

* * *

'It's all gone wrong,' moaned a weasely figure from the back of the room.

'Patience Molbus, patience,' soothed the tall thin man. 'It is out of our hands now in any case, but we must have faith in our champion. These unforeseen circumstances were to be expected in some ways, we are after all, dealing with an extremely cunning adversary.'

'But ...'

'But, we would not have sent her, had we not had confidence in her powers. She is extraordinary.' He broke of and stared dreamily ahead, like a man trying to pierce the veil of mists ahead. 'I think,' he said, 'I really think she might be the one.'

There was a solemn and portentous silence as this sunk in.

After a long while a voice was heard from the back of the room. 'The one what?'

The thin man sighed. 'Chimps!' he said. 'I am working with chimps.'

'Yes, but the one what?'

'You be careful Tibyd,' said the thin man. 'I may have to promote you – anything to get rid of you,' he muttered.* It seemed fair to him. It was after all how he had ended up with most of this bunch in his division in the first place.

Tibyd beamed. 'Thank you Sir.'

* * *

'Do you think he'll come back?'

'I don't know. He looked pretty mad.'

'Why, do you think?'

Kent looked ruefully at her. 'Can't imagine,' he said eventually

'So, what do we do now?'

'I guess I'll make up the spare bed. You hungry?'

Tamar opened and closed her mouth a few times and finally said. 'Now you come to mention it, I'm starving.'

Kent grinned. 'Maybe later I'll take you flying.'

'Cool!'

'If you like, that is.'

'Well yeah.'

'And I'm sure that if he wants to, he can find you again, so don't worry about it.'

Tamar wrinkled her brow. 'Who are you talking about?'

Kent glanced at her strangely. 'Oh, no one.' He said eventually.

'You're not afraid?'

'No, this is great.'

'Cold?'

'I really hadn't noticed.'

'You're really taking to this flying thing. Even I was nervous the first time I did it.'

'I wish you hadn't said that.'

'Trust me. So where do you want to go?'

'Um.'

---

* This of course being the time honoured method of getting rid of incompetent employees without risking an unfair dismissal trial and all the attendant publicity. This explains a lot about upper management

'Want to head back?'

'God no!'

There was a scream in the night. Mega Man swung round sharply, causing Tamar to wonder if her spleen was really a necessary organ, because she was not sure that it had not rocketed out of her body. 'Hey!'

'Sorry, I'm not used to passengers.' He paused listening. 'Fire at the foundry, I have to go, I'll just drop you off at home …'

'Won't that waste precious time? Better just leave me here – there on that building. I'll be fine, just don't forget to come back for me.'

'I can't just leave you here, you'll freeze to death.'

'Don't argue, just go, I mustn't be the reason you don't get there in time.'

He nodded shortly and swooped off into the night.

Tamar shivered; it was bloody freezing.

* * *

It was dark, and everything was still, there was no sound – really no sound at all, not even the sound of his own breathing. 'Oh Hell!' he said again. Again no sound came out, but he thought he heard the echo of his words, very faint and from a great distance. Now he was really scared, a fear that was building up slowly to primal terror. Very slowly, after all, there was no point wasting his adrenaline all at once – he might need it later on, for when things got really bad. Because technically nothing bad was really happening to him at this point, nothing was happening at all, in fact, but later on there might be monsters. 'Am I dead?' he wondered, 'strange, I expected more pitchforks.'

It was like being in a black hole – that is, if he had known what a black hole was like, this was what he might have expected – except there was no sense of gravity and no whirling stars, such as you saw on Star Trek. No, it was more like being nowhere at all. He remembered Tamar describing a half-remembered experience of the same type.

'I *am* dead!' he thought. 'Oh shit! I haven't got time for this. Let me out, I'll be dead later.'

He pondered for a while, got bored and decided to do something about the situation. After all, if this was the afterlife you could keep it. He dug around in his pocket and pulled out the Athame. He had faith in this toy, if anything could get him out of this ... It had never let him down before. He weighed it in his hand and grinned without amusement in the darkness.

Then he heard a voice. 'Hey you! Are you all right in there?'

* * *

'Bloody freezing! Bloody, bloody – stop thinking about it, he'll be back soon.' Tamar flapped her arms around herself to keep warm, and looked down at the world so far below her. There was something familiar about this view that she could not quite put her finger on. Something ... Suddenly without warning the large skyscraper opposite lit up like the world's hugest Christmas tree. After a few seconds, the flashing lights resolved themselves into words. It read "CLOSE FILE"

'Close file?' she murmured. 'What the hell does that...' she was back in mainframe before she finished the sentence. '...Mean? Oh yeah.'

'That was bloody convenient,' she thought. She was now more certain than ever that they were being helped. She suspected Clive – he was always in the middle of these things, but whoever it was, well, she agreed with Denny, a little *more* help would come in handy right now. And to hell with interfering with free will.

* * *

'I will send you,' said Hecaté.

'How?' asked Stiles. 'I mean doesn't teleportation rely on time, I remember Cindy telling me...'

'Hmmph!' it was an impressive snort even for Hecaté. 'Witches!' she added in a derogatory tone. 'They may have to rely on such chicanery moving between dimensions, but I,' she drew herself up impressively. 'I *am* a goddess.'*

'Okay, okay.' Stiles held up his hands placatingly. 'I know I know.' But still, he looked at her interrogatively.

She smiled. 'You do not believe in me? That could be a problem you know.' (Deities rely on belief for their powers and indeed their very existence)

He looked sheepish. 'I just wanted to know how you would do it. It's the policeman in me.'

'Moving things – or people – through space is not a problem for me. I do not rely on the astral plane it did not even exist when I was – born. I simply will it and it is done. Do you trust me?'

'Of course.'

'Good.'

She closed her eyes, and Stiles instinctively did the same. A chill went down his spine a creepy crawly presentiment; he snapped open his eyes and grabbed his gun of the table. Hecaté raised her eyebrows but said nothing. There was a flash (gods tend to be showy) and he was gone.

When he opened his eyes again, it was on an eerie, sepia toned, frozen world. The second of time he was in had gone mouldy, it seemed. He shivered.

'Don't touch anything,' she had warned him, even disturbing the dust would change things, but that could not be helped. 'Just don't pull down anyone's pants or put them in funny positions with their finger up their nose or suchlike.'

Stiles had been indignant. 'How old do you think I am?' She had looked shrewdly at him. 'I think that, compared to me, you are a child and anyway, I know you, so heed me.'

Stiles conceded; there's no point arguing with a woman, even a goddess, perhaps especially a goddess. He did not even bother to point out the grey at his temples and the crow's feet

---

* For the full explanation of this statement see 'Tamar Black - Reality Bites.' in brief it goes like this. To teleport instantly from one location to another one must move into the astral plane where there is no time and simply travel in the normal way (the normal way for a witch of course is to fly) to your intended destination. You can of course see where you are going from the astral plane, but it is all done instinctively anyway. It's amazing how convenient magic can be

around his eyes. There were times when she appeared to consider him a sort of ante-pubescent Just William (or Bart Simpson, for those of you under thirty, and if there are any under thirties reading this book – What's the matter with you, why aren't you out getting drunk?)

He moved carefully between the immobile people, being careful not to disturb so much as a fallen leaf. It was slow going and all around him was the feeling of dread expectation that one usually associates with nightmares. His hand tightened on his gun and he moved forward at a frustratingly slow pace. 'It would help if I knew what I was looking for,' he thought. 'Maybe I'll know it when I see it.' But he doubted it; his coppering instincts were against the likelihood of such chimerical operations. Things just did not happen like that.

He had forgotten what he was dealing with; much like Denny still did on occasion. They both still tended to view the world in a hard headed, practical, common sense way despite all the evidence to the contrary that they had seen. And they were both capable of being surprised by coincidences, even though these turned up these days with the same regularity as they did in bad action movies.

As soon as he saw it, he knew he had found it, a – he almost choked on the word – clue. He almost spat on the ground, but he remembered Hecaté's injunction just in time. Clues! What am I, Sherlock Holmes? Stiles believed in clues in the same way he believed in coincidences, on the other hand … it was undeniable.

Just ahead of him was a crowd of people all staring in the same direction, that they were standing still was a given in the situation but there was a suggestion in their attitude that this had been pretty much the case before time had stopped. And the expression on all the faces was unmistakable to Stiles. It was the expression you saw on the faces of people when confronted by a particularly gruesome traffic accident or shootout, but also, grimly enough in Stiles opinion, when witnessing a celebrity having an embarrassing incident in public. A mixture of shock, fascination and curiosity. These were the faces of people who had witnessed, sorry, *were witnessing* something both horrible and compelling at the same time. The only problem was – they were apparently looking at nothing more interesting than the display in the window of Bennetton, and whatever you might think personally about this, people are used to such horrors. Stiles was disinclined to think that even the poster in the window bearing the legend "We're all the same inside" with the appropriate graphics to complement it, could account for the large crowd it appeared to have attracted. You see worse every day – or was that just him? He did not think so.

This then, was the place where their mystery man had appeared, possibly with a flash and a bang, or – no, the incident had been reported. This was no doubt the last place he had been, though, before time had stopped. What had he been doing? And more importantly, where the hell had he gone? Was it possible he had disintegrated or vanished before people's eyes? Accounting for the shocked expressions. There were no answers here, why couldn't clues turn up when you needed them? On the other hand, Stiles had a bad feeling about this. All his instincts told him to worry excessively, and that even mild panic would not be out of place. People did not just vanish – at least not in normal circumstances, not without magic – even when they were out of their own time, at least he did not think so, he really needed Hecaté's input here, she would know. He concentrated and called on her with his mind – he just hoped it would work.

~ Chapter Fourteen ~

A GNARLED HAND reached through the blackness and grabbed at Denny's hair. He yelped. 'Hey, watch it.'

'Jus' tryin' ter 'elp,' said a disembodied voice gruffly. 'Sod yer then, yer ungrateful bastard. Stay there if yer'd ruther, see if I care.'

'Um, I'm sorry,' ventured Denny. Actually, I'm not even sure where I am, and I'm a bit ... please help me.'

'Doesn't even know where 'e is,' muttered the voice. 'Where do they get these idiots? You been drinkin'?' he added a little louder.

'I wish.' muttered Denny. 'No, I haven't been, er drinkin', I'm just lost. I think ...'

'Lost?' said the voice in wonderment. 'Lost?' it repeated. ''E says 'e's lost, by Beelzebub that's a new one. You sure you ain't been at the gold top?'

'Gold top?' thought Denny. But he did not have any more time to wonder about that as he was pulled out into the light by his horns. '*Horns*? Here, wait a minute.' Then he saw where he was. *Double, double shit! With a horse apple on top.*

'Ogod,' he said. 'No, I mean – I didn't mean ... no, noo-oh shiiit.'

* * *

'Thank God that's over,' breathed Tamar. She heard footsteps.

'One thing after another,' she thought, as the guard folded up neatly with a small sigh and she dusted off her hands. 'That's what we should have done in the first place,' she thought ruefully, but Denny had an unfortunate tendency to panic. And now... well where was he? Surely, he would not have carried on going through the files without her. Would he? Perhaps if he had panicked again ... no. So ... where...? Damn!

Two choices now lay before her, did she wait here and hope that he turned up. Or did she... what? What *was* the other choice ?

Okay, thinking logically, if he wasn't *here* then he must be ... aaagh!

Okay, start again. What was the last thing he had said? "Close file" obviously, so ...? Wait, he *hadn't* said that had he? What he'd actually said was "close *files*". What did that mean? Maybe he was out of mainframe altogether. That would be okay, as far as it went, if he was back in the world. But she could not count on that. There were other places outside of mainframe, as Tamar knew only too well. Besides, think about it. The world as we know it is actually, technically a part of mainframe, well, one of the files anyway. So if Denny was *outside* of mainframe, then he could be anywhere, or nowhere, he could be ... oh no, it did not bear thinking about. Tamar wrenched open the main file door and started to run.

* * *

'He does not belong *here* anyway,' said Satan, frowning from his sagging armchair. They were gathered around him on a square of carpet, like children at story time. (Hell took this idea directly from teachers – every evening the sinners were tortured with readings from Enid Blyton or Harry Potter.) His minions trembled as well they might, such a frown had been known to cause earthquakes and/or floods, and they knew what was coming. (Famous Five do something incredibly boring – in a boat).

Another cock up! And frankly, they were sick of taking the blame.

'Doesn't he?' asked Snarkle before the others could silence him. 'How can you tell?' (There's always one). Several minions – all of them, in fact, hit the ground running, but Old Nick (which no one ever called him to his face – those sinners who had called him that in life were singled out for extra special punishments – Beatrix Potter) merely frowned a little deeper – he was more puzzled than anything.

'Well, for one thing,' He said, shaking his head in deep perplexity, 'he's still alive'

* * *

After five minutes hard running, Tamar suddenly stopped. This was not because she had arrived. She did not really know where she was going, after all, nor what she was looking for. Neither had she realised this and decided to think sensibly and stop panicking. Nor had she merely run out of breath. In fact, she was distracted, by raised voices behind a nearby door. She skidded to a halt and listened, fascinated.

'I am the real Robin i' the Hood,' said one voice

'Scurvy knave,' objected another. 'Would you give me lie to my very face? I gentlemen, am Sir Robert of Huntingdon ...'

'Ah, you see?' interrupted the other voice. 'He *admits* it! He is not even called Robin. I, on the other hand, am. I am Robin of Locksley ...'

'A *peasant*,' said the other voice, scornfully.

'Well?' said the first voice.

'Peasants cannot be heroes,' said the second voice. 'Well known fact.'

'Why not?'

'This is surely all academic,' said a third voice. 'I am the true Robin i' the hood, and I will suffer no pretenders.'

'Is that a threat?' said the first voice. Move him forward a few centuries and he might have been saying "come and have a go, if you think you're hard enough."

'A challenge,' confirmed the third voice, languidly.

'Right, you ponce!'

There was the sound of a scuffle. Tamar grinned; this was a famous historical cock up, and she had always wondered how it would be resolved. Now maybe she would find out, she gently pushed open the door.

Inside she saw a small conference room. There were three burly men fighting like cats in a sack on a Persian rug. There was a lot of scratching and biting and hair pulling. They ought to have been ashamed of themselves really. Behind a large oak desk, were three accountants, or possibly they were clerks, all dressed in identical grey suits and wearing identical expressions of alarm. They were remonstrating ineffectually with the "heroes" along the lines of. 'Oh I say...' and 'Oh really – gentlemen – please.' And flapping their arms feebly.

Tamar acted on instinct. That is: she leapt into the fray.

She emerged, not a hair out of place, holding on to the ears of two of the protagonists, her foot on the third one's head.

'Ow, ow, ow, ow.' they whimpered.

'Had enough?' she snarled.

'Mmm, mmm.'

Okay.' She released them and they stood upright, gingerly fingering their ears.

'You call yourselves fighters?' she said contemptuously. 'I've seen more vicious three year olds. Much more vicious actually,' she added thoughtfully. 'Those little bastards really go in for the kill.'

The Robins had the grace to look ashamed. They looked at the floor and twisted their feet around each other. Tamar had to fight back the urge to laugh.

One of the little grey men came forward and cleared his throat. 'Ahem,' he began. 'I'm sorry, I don't quite know who...?

'Tamar,' she snapped. 'Historic amendments.' There was a tense silence, during which she wondered if she had said the wrong thing. Then she saw it; the little men were looking at her in awe. She had clearly made them nervous. Good.

'Who's responsible for this mess?' she snapped.

'Well – ma'am,' stuttered one. 'It looks as if *you* are.'

'I meant whose *fault* is it?'

The three stooges looked at each other and shrugged. 'We don't know,' said the chattiest of the three. 'We just get handed the problem, and well …'

'And you're doing a sterling job, I can see. But if I might make a suggestion?'

They leaned forward eagerly. Tamar gazed thoughtfully at the three Robins. 'A challenge,' she muttered under her breath. 'Not a bad idea. Winner takes all, 'specially if we can arrange it so that they *all* win.'

'You lot,' she barked. 'How do you feel about an archery contest?'

The Robins looked at each other. 'Do we have a choice?' asked the one who had issued the challenge and whose head was bleeding.

'No.'

* * *

Tamar whistled as she strode down the corridor. That had gone rather well. The three claimants would be inserted back into history at slightly different intervals, all believing that they had won the right to be remembered as 'Robin i' the hood'. For the beings who spun the cosmos, arranging three separate archery contests, all identical, should be a piece of cake. Of course, there would always be pedantic historians who would dispute the true origins of the legend, but so what? It would give them something to argue about and keep them out of mischief. And at least the Robins were happy.

But best of all, she had managed to swipe one of the clerks access cards. She strode along singing 'Merry men, merry men, merry men, men, men, men,' to the tune of "The Lone Ranger".

* * *

'He *looks* like one of us boss,' said Snarkle. (Some people never learn)

The Lord of hell only smiled. (Later he would listen to the tale of Johnny Town Mouse *and* the Flopsy Bunnies.) 'Yes, it's intriguing really – a classic case of morphic resonance. He's obviously not an *ordinary* mortal. Perhaps he's on the demon fast-track.'

Denny panicked; it couldn't be ... could it? And do I really look like them? He glanced at the devils and imps around him in horror. Then he mentally shrugged. Oh well, he had never been what you would call handsome.'

'Mind you,' mused his Anti-Holiness. 'I don't seem to have a record of him, perhaps he's a...' he spat the word. '*Hero.*' (Heroes deserved Jackie Collins)

The imps shuddered impressively.

'Well, if he's not dead,' said Snarkle, really pushing his luck now. 'Don't we have to send him back?'

Satan pinched the bridge of his nose wearily. 'Judas,' he addressed a weaselly man on his left, 'what's the directive on that one?'

'Nothing in the rules says you have to be dead to be here boss.'

'Hey!' objected Denny. 'I'm not supposed to be here, I didn't sign up for this. I'm not a bad guy.' Uneasily he wondered if this were, true. After all, nobody's perfect, and only last year he had turned his landlord into a statue. He wondered if leaving the loo seat up was a cardinal sin; Tamar certainly seemed to think so. However, it appeared that this was not the point. The crucial phrase here, as it turned out was "didn't sign up for this."

'Didn't you?' Satan furrowed his brow. 'Judas – check that, will you?'

After an apparently endless search through a huge tome, while Satan fidgeted and complained about the ruddy software, and why did the "other lot" get regular upgrades? Judas informed the company. 'He's right, no contract.'

'Damn.' Lucifer thumped his hands on the sides of his armchair. 'So what the Hell's he doing here, spying?' He looked so thunderous that Denny cowered. 'Speak mortal.'

N - no, I'm just lost – honest.'

The devils laughed. 'Lost – lost, that's what he said before.'

'Load of rubbish, you can't get lost here. – Well, you can if you're a lost soul of course but ...'

'Let's put him in the lava pits, soon get the truth out of him.'

'We can't.' said Lucifer. 'He's out of our jurisdiction.'

Denny breathed out. 'Look,' he said, 'I was in mainframe ...'

Satan actually went white – a difficult feat when your natural hue is a sort of reddish plum colour. He gulped. 'Oh Gawd,' he spluttered. The imps stared. 'What?' he said. 'It's just a *saying*.

'Anyway,' he rallied, 'get him out of here. I'm getting one of my migraines. This was a good attempt at nonchalance, but Denny was not fooled. 'I want ...' he began. Then he felt a hundred horny little hands grip him and drag him away.

* * *

Mainframe – central files. Now what? Tamar sighed; she had no idea what she was looking for. Well, Denny of course, but ... this was unlike the other files in that it was not a file really, it was a – there was no getting around it – it was a cloud. Her own personal cloud apparently, although she had seen someone come in just before she had. There was no sign of him. 'Oh God,' she groaned.

'Yes, can I help you?' came the reply.

Tamar nearly fell off her cloud, until she remembered that it was only data, and so was she. 'Oh shit,' she breathed.

'Sorry,' came the reply. 'Command not recognised.' And now she noted the slightly sing-song quality to the voice. 'The most common password in the universe,' she thought, wryly. Although, here there was clearly more to it.

'I need some help,' she asked tentatively. She was finally beginning to feel out of her depth.

'Ask me anything.'

'Um, I need to find someone.'

'Who?' Wow this was really sophisticated software; it was like having a normal conversation – almost.

'Denis Sanger, he's …'

'Fifty nine - hundred files found – specify by date and place of birth.'

Tamar counted on her fingers muttering under her breath,' so if he's 25 no 26 now, that's 1978, and he was born in London somewhere'

'Thinking – twenty seven files found, specify exact date and place of birth.'

'Thinking,' responded Tamar mischievously. But "God" apparently had no sense of humour, and infinite patience.

Tamar shugged. 'Okay, 12th Dec 1978 …'

She got no further. 'Denis Alexander Sanger, born 12/12/78 11:58 P.M at King's Cross Hospital, Ward 22 – Mother Alice Meriam Sanger, Father Julian David Sanger, not found. That is to say, his current location is not known – that is odd.'

'Very odd,' agreed Tamar. She was thinking, at the same time, that she had just found out, in ten seconds, more about Denny than he had told her in two years. 'Does that mean he's dead?'

'Thinking.' And this time Tamar could have sworn she heard a slight whirring sound. 'No record of death – Denis Sanger has fallen out of the matrix – he could be in one of the archives – checking ... Ah here it is. Not an archive exactly. Denis Sanger is in Hell.'

'Oh, well, that's okay then.' This news was surprising, but not too worrying. If anybody could get out of Hell, it was Denny; at least he had the Athame. He was probably slicing demons into mince at this very moment, probably having a whale of a time.

A nasty thought occurred. 'And you're *sure* he's not dead?'

'Positive.'

'Thank God.'

'You're welcome. Can I help you with anything else?'

'Actually …'

* * *

The boatman was stunned. 'Take him *back*? You've got to be kidding. Nobody goes back. Unless you count Hercules – young Trevor as his Dad called him – of course, back and forth like a bloody fiddlers elbow that one, but …' He stopped.

The imp was nodding. 'Charon, just take him, okay?'

Charon shook his head. '*Him*, really? Well Heroes aren't what they used to be, an' that's the truth. They used to be taller. Well, get aboard young feller, got any money?'

'Um.'

'Huh, you are a typical hero after all,' he said. 'They never pay their way. Oh well, let's go, I haven't got an eternity you know.' He chuckled hoarsely.

'By the way,' he added, 'you might want to lose the horns if you're going topside, might make you stand out a bit, if you see what I mean.'

* * *

The cloud vanished; then two things happened. First, Tamar expected to find herself hurtling through the air, and second, this did not happen, she was once again standing on nothing. 'God?' she tried, experimentally. Silence. Not even the whirring sound of "thinking".

She tried 'Oh shit.' But no reprimand was forthcoming.

'Help,' this was a formulaic response, she did not really expect any help, naturally. I mean, since when did a computer help anyone, even under normal circumstances?

She sat down on empty air and began to worry. There were two possible explanations for this turn of events, and neither of them was encouraging, and both meant that she was in serious trouble. It could be A, a computer meltdown, which meant that, sooner or later, someone would fix it, and she would get out just in time to answer a lot of awkward questions about what she was doing in here in the first place. Still, there was probably plenty of time to think up something. She expected it would take between a millennium and an eternity before the engineers were called, a bit like being trapped in a lift in a multi-storey car-park.

Explanation B, was, of course, that she had been caught, and was being held for questioning. This was slightly less worrying, at least someone would be along shortly, and she had been in worse jams. Still it was kind of eerie in here; she wondered uneasily if she would begin to run out of air, but that was silly, she was mere data in a file. She did not need air. This argument, however, was not persuasive, and she began to feel panicky.

'Mind over matter, mind over matter,' she told herself, 'it's actually quite nice in here, the peace and quiet, the sunshine ...' Then, in the grand tradition of broken lifts everywhere, the lights went out.

* * *

'Gone?' Hecaté was understandably perplexed.

'Yes gone,' said Stiles. There were only so many ways of saying it.

'And, and please do not take this the wrong way, I have every faith in your abilities, but you are certain that ...'

'No, I'm not bloody certain,' he snapped, 'maybe they were watching a mime who submitted to spontaneous combustion, but I doubt it.'

Hecaté nodded gravely. 'As do I,' she said. Although intelligent in many ways – preternaturally so, in fact, Hecaté was unable to grasp sarcasm, possibly because under normal circumstances sarcasm is not used on gods. Grovelling, in fact, is the accepted manner of addressing a deity if you want to keep all your extremities intact and where they are supposed to be.

Stiles let it go. He should not have let his temper get the better of him, if he was not so tired and worried ... but it was not her fault. And even if his normal way of dealing with worry and stress, learned from his days on the force, was to spread it around, it was different with her, she was ... special. And she never lost her temper even when he was being irritable or just downright obnoxious; she never complained – well hardly ever – she just put up with him, and apparently loved him. It worried him sometimes – what did he ever do to deserve it? He glanced at her there was a slight frown on her face, she looked worried too. A pang of remorse went through him.

She caught him looking at her and gave a wan smile. 'Do not worry,' she told him, 'we will solve this.' *she* was trying to comfort *him*. It was unbearable.

'We will.' It was a statement, made with an absolute confidence and certainty that he did not really feel. But it convinced her; her brow cleared. This time the smile was genuine.

'I really must try harder,' he thought, 'not to be such a grouchy bastard.'

'We should go back to the – how would you put it? – "The scene of the crime",' she said.

He grinned.

'Maybe I can pick something up,' she continued. 'Although …' she glanced at the screen, uncertainly. 'Maybe I should not leave my post.'

'It won't take us long,' said Stiles. 'I really think we should go. I have a feeling this is important, we need to find this guy.'

'Or at least look for him,' said Hecaté with a gentle smile.

* * *

Tamar was getting worried. She did not know how long she had been sat in the dark but at least, in a way, it was less unnerving than the light. This way you could not see that you were sitting on absolutely nothing.

A nasty thought occurred to her. 'I've been in this situation before; I'm being deleted! Maybe I'm just going to be left here forever.'

Suddenly the light came on, and she found that she was sitting on the cloud again. 'Here we go,' she muttered. A shaft of sunlight hit her square in the eye. 'We have ways of making you talk,' she thought. There was utter silence. 'Psyching me out?' she wondered.

Then she heard the voice. 'File update complete – what's so funny about that?' For Tamar was laughing hysterically in her relief.

Eventually she recovered herself. 'God?' she asked.

'Yes?' there was a definite hint of petulance in the voice this time.

'Where is Denis Sanger? I mean, current location of ...'

'He is on the River Styx'

'Coming or going?'

'Going. Anything else?'

'Oh good – I mean yes. Can you help me to find a person called Askphrit? Well not so much a person ...'

Before she had finished the sentence, she found herself in a dark street with the rain lashing down on her. Just ahead of her was a shuffling figure, head down, shoulders drawn in against the rain and cold. The figure seemed vaguely familiar. 'It *can't* be!'

She followed him anyway.

As she looked around she tried to estimate the year and location. There were street lights and neon signs, so obviously the 20th century or later. There were cars on the road, but they were going by too fast for her to be able to see them, and anyway identifying cars was not her strong suit. Denny would have come in handy right now. She pushed the thought aside and continued to follow the tramp-like figure that, unlikely as it seemed, *had* to be Askphrit. They rounded a corner, and she realised where she was. So, what the hell was he doing in Denver? What was the old villain up to?

He turned into an alley and sat down, pulled a few sacks over him and pulled out a bottle from which he took a long draught. Then light dawned.

* * *

'Okay, let's get some answers, let's go find this guy.' Stiles looked grim.

'Or at least look for him,'

'There's really no need,' the voice came from behind them.

'Looking for me?' the man said, as they turned to face him. 'How nice, but as you can see, I've found my own way here. Do you think you could help me out?'

Stiles and Hecaté looked at each other in shock. Stiles was the first to recover.

'What the hell are *you* doing here?'

* * *

Denny emerged into sunlight, in what appeared to be New York. One of the seven entrances to hell, Charon informed him. He was not surprised.

'This is the one closest to home for you,' said Charon, (Denny did not believe it for a second) 'We aim to please. Come back soon.'

Denny did not bother to answer. He sat down on a handy step and breathed in deeply. 'Well, change my shorts,' he said.

After a while, he stood up; the world was frozen around him, no chance of teleporting home, unless … maybe there was someone who could help. He started to walk.

~ Chapter Fifteen ~

DENNY HAD TO break in, of course. They would obviously be in no condition to answer the door, being frozen in time, like the rest of the world. It was only when he thought of this that he realised that he had no idea how to unfreeze them.

Cindy was in front of a mirror evidently applying lipstick (so- no surprises there) and Eugene was watching TV. Well at least they were both home (and not doing anything revolting). Thank God they had relocated to New York, it had taken him two hours (except it had not – it had just *felt* like it had) to get here on foot, imagine if they had still been in London. On the other hand, what frigging use were they as statues? As he pondered this he fingered the Athame, strange to tell, he had forgotten all about it. Of course! 'I wish I knew how to unfreeze them.' And he did.

It was so simple really, all he had to do was move them, and this was not as easy as it sounds. Moving someone who is frozen in time is comparable to pulling someone out of a black hole, except gravity is a puling infant compared to time when it comes to holding something down. If he had not had demonic strength – literally – courtesy of the Athame, he would never have managed it.

'Bloody hell,' he gasped, collapsing on the floor with Cindy gazing down at him perplexedly. He had started with her on the assumption that as, the lighter of the two, she would be the easier to move. He had not bargained on being so exhausted afterwards that, even with her help, he did not think he would have the strength to move Eugene. Then again, he had time to recover while he explained the situation to her, he had nothing but time when you came to think about it.

* * *

Cindy, being a witch, grasped the situation easily, but said she could not think of a way to help him really. 'We could fly of course,' she said. 'But without the use of the astral plane it would be pretty hard going. On the other hand, we can take our time I suppose.'

'We?'

'Yes,' she said firmly. '*We*. Now help me move this big lump, we can't leave him behind.'

Flying, thought Denny sourly, I could have come up with that on my own if I'd had half a brain, I needn't have bothered these two. Denny did not particularly like Cindy, and wondered how he was going to put up with at least three days – or the equivalent at least – of her company.

* * *

'Second star to the right and straight on till morning.' Denny had now heard this particular "joke" at least six hundred times since they had set off two days ago. 'It wasn't even funny the first time, how *does* he put up with her?'

He floated on his back above the clouds, leaving Eugene – in the form of an eagle – to navigate. This way he did not actually have to spend much time with Cindy – Eugene he could just about tolerate, under normal circumstances. But at the moment, any company was unwelcome; he wanted to be alone to fret.

Cindy appeared beside him; he forced himself to smile.

'Don't grimace at me like that,' she told him. 'I know you don't like me, you don't have to pretend.'

Denny scowled. 'It's not that,' he lied. 'It's just that I've got a lot on my mind at the moment, it makes me moody; don't take any notice of me.'

Cindy nodded. 'Fair enough,' she said. 'Except I *am* a witch you know – perhaps I'm not a very good one, but I did pick up on your desire to rip out my tongue.'

'Oh – well, look it doesn't mean …'

'Listen, I *could* care less,' she interrupted him. 'But only if I were dead.'

Denny grinned. 'That was quite funny,' he told her.

'Yes well, I do have my moments you know, but you have to keep it simple around Eugene – he's a lovely bloke, but he has the sense of humour of Homer Simpson'

Denny actually laughed. Then he looked thoughtful. 'I think I may have under-estimated you.' he pinched his fingers together, 'just a little bit – maybe.'

'Like I said, I don't care. Well –,' she mimicked his previous action, 'maybe a little bit.' They both laughed.

'The thing is,' she continued. 'We have a problem here. I just want to help out if I can. So we have to at least try to get along, do you agree?'

'What do you think you can do?' he asked. 'I mean, really?'

'I don't know yet, but you never know. Anyway, *you* came to *me*, didn't you? You must have thought I'd be *some* use.'

Denny nodded. 'Okay, I'll try,' he said. 'I'm just so worried about her.'

'Me too.'

'Well, I'll try not to take it out on you. Good enough?'

'She'll be okay you know. If anyone can take care of herself …'

'I know, I know.'

Eugene appeared on the horizon. 'Need a course correction,' he said, turning right. 'This way, wheee! Second star to …'

'Shut up Eugene,' said Cindy.

Denny threw her a grateful look. She was all right really.

He looked down through the clouds; they were nearly there. Wasn't that York just below them? Just a few more hours and he would be home sweet home. And that, he thought, would be when his problems would really start.

For some time, he had been watching birds skimming past without noticing them. After all, what was so unusual about birds in the sky? Think about it.

* * *

That damn computer had done it on purpose she was sure. Not that it wasn't her own fault too. She now realised her mistake. All mainframe had done was what she had asked it to. It had taken her literally, when she had asked to find a "person" called Askphrit. So, it had sent her to him – so far so obvious. The real bugger was that this Askphrit was the wrong one, the human version of him who had existed briefly in that period after she had taken his powers and before he had got them back.

A "*person* called Askphrit". It was what she had said. She could not deny it. Only she was sure mainframe knew perfectly well that this was not the only version of him out there and that there was at least a chance that this was not the one she wanted. On the other hand, this was the present – one version of it anyway – it was the logical place to send her. Except she had not asked to be sent anywhere, at least she had not meant to. So why hadn't she left yet?

She knew the answer to this question as well as you do. Here was the perfect opportunity to get rid of Askphrit once and for all. He was mortal – vulnerable. She could kill him now and never have to worry about him again. It was a God-given opportunity. She smiled grimly, "God-given" indeed. Again, the feeling of a power working behind the scenes came over her. Had she been sent here on purpose to do this very thing? Did somebody *want* her to do it?

Just do it, a voice in her head urged her. *You know you want to; he's evil, a monster. Think of all the things he's done. He's trying to kill Denny.*

'Denny!' she thought, '*he* wouldn't want me to do this. Askphrit's mortal now – defenceless. It would be murder.'

So what? How many has he killed? How many more? Think of all those you could save. Denny never needs to know.

She felt like a puppet. The only question was, who was pulling the strings?

Did it matter? She had been put in this situation for a reason; she could end it here and now, that was the point. She now felt more certain than ever that this was a task she had been given. It was her – she almost choked on the word – destiny.

Bugger that!

* * *

'See what I mean?' said the thin man, 'We show her a clear destiny and what does she go and do? Humans – Pah!'

The lackey nodded sympathetically.

'Spanner! Clang!' he added savagely. 'Oh well, get me the planning department.'

* * *

'What the hell are *you* doing here?' gasped Stiles.

'Ah so you *do* know me then?' said their visitor. 'It's been so long. At least it seems that way; time is relative, so I'm told. Well that makes things easier. There won't be any of that tedious explaining and so on. As to what I'm doing here, can't you guess?'

Hecaté now found her voice. 'Th – the monster!' she croaked.

Askphrit looked hurt. 'Now – is that nice? I'm offended. I'm not a monster. However, I'm afraid I might have to put you to some inconvenience, if you won't co-operate. And I see that you won't, oh well – *don't even try it sister.*'

Hecaté had come forward with her hands raised, and begun to chant a binding spell.

'I have, currently, more followers than you, therefore, I have the greater power, and you know it.'

Hecaté bowed her head. She did know it.

'Now then,' said Askphrit, beaming, benevolently. 'You asked what I'm doing here. When I'm supposed to be floating around history causing no end of trouble.' He laughed. 'You good guys, so predictable. I assume that the bane of my life and that "sidekick" of hers have gone haring off into the archives to track me down? I can see by your faces that they have. Good. So all I have to do is this ...' He ambled over to the computer and leisurely closed the file.

'No!' cried Hecaté and Stiles together.

'Well that's them taken care of,' he said. 'Trapped!' He turned to them, grinning. 'You lot,' he spat contemptuously. 'What a lot of blundering misfits! Did you really think that if I had wanted that boy gone, that I wouldn't have got it right the first time? I'm insulted! I really am. On the other hand, I was depending on it.'

He sat down in an armchair. 'Well, isn't one of you going to say it?' he asked.

'Say what?' asked Stiles.

'Why, say "You'll never get away with it" of course.'

'Oh I think that goes *without* saying,' said Stiles.

'Ah ha, ha, very good, yes.'

'Get away with what?' asked Hecaté. 'I mean, you have not revealed your dastardly plan yet.'

'Haven't I?' said Askphrit, surprised. 'How very remiss of me. I suppose that's why you haven't tried any futile attempts at escape, or is it that you both have enough sense left to realise that you can't? Still can't be too careful eh?' He manifested a cage around Stiles. 'I know I can't cage *you* darling,' he said to Hecaté. 'But I think I'm right in assuming that you won't run off and leave your lover to my tender mercies.' He looked at her. She nodded mutely.

'Well now, let me see. Where were we? Oh yes, obviously I didn't want to kill the kid. Otherwise, I would have done it. No, what I wanted was to create a near enough miss that they would feel the reverberations, and come after me. I wanted them safely in the past, so I could trap them there, where they can't cause me any more trouble, and now they are.

'I could have erased his existence, and that certainly would have worked too, except that would have changed my past too. I didn't want that naturally. That would have put me back in that deleted file, still hiding, still waiting for her to find me. This way is better. She may have stripped me of my Djinn powers, but at least I am still a god. World domination is within my reach again. And best of all, that woman, is trapped forever in the archives of history; I finally have my revenge. She'll realise, sooner or later, how she has been fooled, but there won't be a damn thing she can do about it.'

'The world is frozen in time,' said Hecaté. 'And only Tamar can undo it. How does that fit into your plans for world domination?'

'It's factored in,' responded Askphrit. 'In fact, I anticipated it. I needed the time it would give me to reach you, and to set things up, since I am not affected just as you were not.'

You see I know that it's not true that only *she* can undo it. In fact, the spell is already weakening here and there since she has become trapped. The universe compensates as you would say. However, this all takes "time" – if you will excuse the pun, and I am, unfortunately, short on patience. But you also have this power over time, you can speed things up considerably for me. I do not have this power, but I have Ran-Kur's memories, and I know all about you, enough to know that you *will* do it.'

'I will not,' she said, defiantly.

'Oh I think you will,' smirked Askphrit, directing a blast of energy at Stiles, who screamed in pain. 'I truly think you will.'

* * *

'Okay,' said Denny putting down his guitar reluctantly. (The ability to manifest is at best a mixed blessing) 'I won't play anymore, if you promise not to tell anymore awful jokes, deal?'

'What's wrong with my jokes?' said Cindy

'What's wrong with his playing?' asked Eugene.

Cindy gave him a dirty look. 'Whose side are you on?' she barked, whereupon Eugene turned himself into a mouse and ran up onto her shoulder, nuzzling apologetically until Cindy started to laugh.

Denny sighed, feeling lonely.

They were only a few miles from home – Denny's home, that is, but Cindy had begged for a rest, she had been apologetic about it, but she just did not have the strength to go on, she said. She might be a witch, but she was only human. Sensing his impatience, she had suggested that Denny go on without them, she knew her way from here, after all. But Denny had gallantly refused. The truth was he had an uneasy feeling, caused by – who knew what? And he was unwilling to leave her alone with only Eugene, who was a very worthy fellow in his own way, but not much use in a crisis – he tended to panic and cower. 'I was like him not so long ago,' Denny thought. 'People *can* change – but still …'

He thought he had better stay with them – just in case. Just in case of what, he could not say, but Tamar relied on her intuition, and it rarely steered her wrong.

'I didn't even know I *had* intuition,' he thought. 'Probably, it's just the heebie jeebies.'

Still he kept alert through the next few hours (not to labour the point, but with there being no actual time etc. etc …) while Eugene and Cindy slept. He was glad he did.

After a few hours (we're going to have to think in real-time, just to keep the narrative flow) Denny noticed a squirrel; it was hopping along a fence. He did not think much of it at first, and then it hit him. Suddenly he remembered those birds. His heart stopped – what the hell could it mean? Was Tamar back? Or was she …? He dredged up a half-remembered conversation between Cindy and Stiles, hadn't she said that if a spell was properly sealed only the one who cast it could reverse it, unless they died, then it automatically reversed itself, as the universe compensated? *Oshit!* He woke Cindy.

'She probably didn't seal the spell,' Cindy soothed, but Denny could see that she was worried.

'So, what?' he argued. 'Even if she didn't, who would be reversing it, and why?'

Cindy shrugged. 'Didn't you say she was in a parallel universe – without her powers?'

'Go on, make it worse.'

'No, I mean maybe that's why the spell broke.'

'It was still working when I got back.'

'Maybe you got back *before* she entered the parallel universe.'

'What?'

'Time is relative, particularly in hell I would have thought. Besides, the spell hasn't completely broken – look.' She pointed to a motionless cat. 'Maybe it's just wearing off.'

'I have to get back – now!'

'Agreed, I just don't think it's time to despair, not yet. There could be a million reasons for this.' The cat wandered off.

'That does it.' said Denny. 'If time's operating again, maybe I can teleport again.'

He vanished then reappeared again, scowling. 'Well that was a waste of time. The effect's pretty local,' he said, 'I ended up in the shopping mall'

* * *

Tamar backed into the shadows as another figure wandered into the alley. No whoever he was, he strode purposefully toward the slumped figure, behind him was another smaller figure. Tamar tensed; were they going to rob him? To think she was actually contemplating rescuing Askphrit of all people. *People* ... of course, that was the point, he was now only a person.

The taller man bent down and seemed to examine Askphrit; he turned to his companion. 'Another one,' he said, 'poor soul.' He shook Askphrit gently who woke with a start.

'Huh, hey mmph I didn't do nothin', le' me 'lone,'

'Hello friend,' said the man, 'don't be alarmed, we're here to help, as is our duty and the duty of all good servants of the Lord.'

'Huh?'

The other person spoke. 'Let me talk to him Brother Bartholomew,' she said.

Tamar grinned in the darkness, Bible thumpers. No doubt, they ran some kind of shelter. Hot soup and a bed for the night, as long as you took the pledge and promised to behave yourself. "Say your prayers and you shall have a cookie." She knew Askphrit well enough to know what he would think of *that* idea. On the other hand, if you're cold and hungry …

The woman was talking to Askphrit in a low voice and then the two of them hoisted him to his feet and guided him down the alley. Filled with an almost insatiable curiosity, Tamar followed.

~ Chapter Sixteen

'DID ANYONE see you?' asked Cindy anxiously.

'Well ...' then he stopped suddenly; Cindy was frozen stiff in front of him. He spun round. Eugene was in a similar condition. Just to confirm Denny looked up at a flock of geese, all frozen stiff in the sky above him. What the hell was going on?

He considered leaving them there. He wondered why he had not been frozen too. He wondered if he was going mad. He decided he did not care if he was. Okay, Eugene first this time. He summoned all his strength and spun and kicked Eugene's legs from under him. Denny landed on the ground gasping, Eugene had barely moved, but he *had* moved; that was the main thing.

'Looks like we're back on track anyway.' said Cindy cheerfully.

'We don't know that,' snarled Denny. 'We don't know *anything*. I want to know what the hell is going on, and I want to know now!' He flung the Athame at a tree, the blade sank through the trunk up the hilt and then it met the irresistible force of time and stopped, quivering resentfully.

'You'll never get that out now,' said Cindy calmly.

* * *

Askphrit stopped gloating for a moment and frowned. He turned to the computer and typed for a few moments then turned back to Hecaté and Stiles with a malevolent grin. 'Almost forgot about that,' he said. 'I can't have those buggers in mainframe watching my every move, not now. Now is the time for a little privacy – don't you agree?'

Neither Stiles nor Hecaté had the least idea what he was talking about, so they had no opinion on the subject, and gazed blankly at him.

However, Stiles did notice that the sun appeared to have gone out.

* * *

'It looks as if murdering the old swine was not the actual destiny we had in mind for her after all,' said the thin man. 'Typical planning department cloak and dagger stuff.' He snorted impressively.

The lackey had been watching Tamar for some time now and had his own opinions on her tractability. He doubted very much whether she was being "steered" as much as the planning department, or his boss, thought she was. He suspected that when the final dénouement came, it would be as unexpected to them as it would to anyone else involved; although they would never admit it of course.

Suddenly the thin man swore and thumped the air. 'Oh bugger, bugger damn, damn, damn,' he said. 'Would you look at that! What did I say about spanners?'

'What?' asked the lackey perplexed.

'Look!' screeched the thin man in fury and frustration, 'Look at that – nothing! Not a glimmer, not a squeak'.

The lackey gazed curiously at the screen – the thin man was right. He had never seen such a thing before – ever!

'What does it mean?' he asked nervously

'It means,' said the thin man edgily, 'that some bastard's turned the security cameras off.'

'Keep an eye on things, said the thin man – somewhat redundantly in the circumstances. 'I've got another meeting to go to. I hate bureaucracy.'

'You're in the wrong job then aren't you?' muttered the lackey under his breath.

* * *

Tamar had to stuff her fists into her mouth to stop herself from laughing at the sight of Askphrit singing 'O' holy day', apparently with ardent enthusiasm. Wait till she told Denny about this.

He was then baptised, with no great show of reluctance – he had his eyes on the prize, a hot meal and a warm bed. No doubt, it all seemed worth it.

The preacher boomed about sin and salvation and asked the congregation to welcome brother "Fred" (Fred?) Into the arms of Jesus, and "Fred" seemed more than happy to be received. He wiped his eyes, theatrically and made a tremendous show of penitence, promised to abide by the laws of the Church and called himself a wretched sinner.

'You never said a truer word,' muttered Tamar under her breath.

And generally conducted himself as the biggest humbug who ever lived, as is the accepted procedure on such occasions. Tamar could hardly tear herself away.

Eventually, and with considerable reluctance, she decided that she really had to go. There was another, far less innocuous, Askphrit out there somewhere, who had to be found. She took one last look at this fraud mopping up soup off his beard and sighed.

'Close file.'

~ Chapter Seventeen ~

TAMAR FOUND HERSELF back in the historical file room – not a total surprise. She pondered for a minute whether to leave mainframe and go back for Denny, who ought to be back at home by her reckoning, by now, or to go back to central files and try again.

Go get Denny, she decided. She might need his help, and there was less chance of a cock up in communication if he were there. He and computers talked the same language – so to speak.

So she made her way back to the deleted file and said the magic words.

Nothing happened. She tried again. Nothing then she used some distinctly un-magical words. She was trapped.

* * *

'Pull,' grunted Denny, tugging futilely on the Athame. Behind him, hanging on to his waist was Cindy, and behind her was Eugene, all heaving and grunting like that strange family who were so determined to pull up one rather obstinate turnip.

They all fell to the ground in a heap. Denny was cursing.

'Well, it's your own fault,' Cindy told him.

Denny glared at her. 'You can go off a person you know,' he said.

Cindy smiled pertly, 'I think I'll live,' she said. 'It's not as if you ever liked me all that much in the first place.'

'Maybe if we had a few more of us ...' put in Eugene.

'Oh yes, and a donkey,' said Cindy.

Denny laughed and suddenly slung an amiable arm over Cindy's shoulder. She blushed in confusion, causing Eugene's ears to redden.

Denny removed the arm. 'One more try?' he asked, hopefully. 'I really don't want to leave it behind.'

They groaned, but hopped to it, or rather, shuffled to it.

'One, two, three, heave.' The tree came down. But the good news was that the Athame, having been moved, now slid out easily. Several birds shot out of the canopy squawking indignantly.

'Okay, now let's get out of here before anything else happens,' said Denny.

'Amen to that.'

Denny weighed the Athame in his hand; something was bothering him. He stopped, and then he slapped his forehead. 'Wait a minute,' he said. God I'm such an idiot, why didn't I think of it before? We don't have to schlep all the way home. We never did. *Any* computer will get me back into mainframe. I've got the codes. Well, one of them anyway.'

'And you couldn't have thought of this sooner?' Cindy was exasperated.

'I know, I know, I just said, I was an idiot, didn't I? I'll say I'm sorry if you like, but don't you see ...?

* * *

For the first time in, perhaps, ever Tamar felt like crying – not with anger or frustration, but with fear. Even in her worst moments, she had never felt this helpless, perhaps because, more recently, she had always had Denny around. It occurred to her that she was beginning to rely on him too much.

'Whatever happened to the good old days, when I didn't need anyone? I've been in worse jams than this, before I even met Denny. There's always something you can do. Besides, Denny's not here. It's up to me this time ... What would

Denny do …? I miss Denny … What was so good about not needing anyone anyway? It was lonely. Okay pull yourself together … Think!'

There are always choices, even if it's the choice between getting killed now, or not getting killed until later. What are my options?

She decided that she could A, stay here and rot – maybe not.

Or B, leave the file, go back to the historical files and continue the search for Askphrit (the bastard) alone – better.

Or C, go back to central files and ask for help.

Then there was secret option, D – give herself up and take her punishment like man – save that for later.

She decided on option C, which was, after all what she had been planning to do after she had found Denny anyway. This still left the problem of her being stuck in mainframe, (Q. Why was she stuck in mainframe?) But she could worry about that later. She still had a job to do, and at least now she had a plan, of sorts.

* * *

'There's not much use in a computer that you can't turn on,' observed Cindy dryly. 'No power you see. Everything's stopped.

Denny grunted. 'Okay, so I didn't think it through.'

Cindy snapped her fingers. 'What we need is a laptop.'

Denny whirled round. 'That's brilliant! Hell, even a mobile phone would probably do. You are a genius.'

Cindy tried, unsuccessfully, to look modest. 'And you thought I wouldn't be any use,' she taunted him.

'Okay, I'll say I'm sorry if you like. I've definitely been a bit …'

'Forget it.'

The file appeared to have been closed again for some reason, but it didn't take Denny long to get in this time, and, within a few minutes, he had the screen up that read ...

< WELCOME TO MAINFRAME >

<Ready

Once the jubilation was over there was the decision to be made. Who was going? Cindy wanted to go, and Eugene, quite obviously, did not, although he tried hard to hide this. But Denny wanted Cindy to stay behind to monitor the situation, much as Hecaté had done, and would have been quite happy to go alone. Despite his recent lesson in judging people, he still could not envisage Eugene being much use to him where he was going. He had enough to worry about, without having to baby-sit that big coward.

'I need you to stay here,' he told Cindy. 'From here you can pull me out if necessary.' He sighed. 'Eugene, you can come with me if you want to,' he said, reluctantly. 'Eugene? ... Where's he gone?

'AWOL, I'd say,' concluded Denny, after a short search. 'Just what we need, another missing person, as if we don't have enough problems.'

'Well,' said Cindy, bravely, blinking back tears, 'you'd better get going.'

'Going?'

Cindy nodded to the screen. 'To find Tamar. After all, she needs your help. *She* didn't run away, and I know you want to get on with it, and I'm still here to keep an eye on things at this end.'

'Oh don't be stupid,' snapped Denny, 'we don't *know* he ran away. He might be in trouble, and even if he's not he might get himself into some. We have to find him; we can't just leave him behind.'

'I think I may have misjudged you,' said Cindy. 'I'll say I'm sorry if you like.' She smiled though her tears; Denny put an arm round her. 'Don't worry,' he said, 'he's probably fine, and he can't have gone far.'

* * *

They were sat under a handy tree; Denny wrapped his jacket around Cindy's shoulders, and she put her head on his shoulder with a sigh. They sat in silence for a moment.

'Thanks for trying,' said Cindy timidly, sensing that he was not in the best mood.

Denny grunted. She glanced up at his profile. He was frowning. She remembered how afraid of him, she used to be. It seemed ridiculous now. It was strange, he still did not look like much, but she could sense the power within him, and not just from the Athame. Ever since she had known him, he had seemed permanently tensed, like a coiled spring, and he never seemed afraid, even when he *must* be.

'Tamar is lucky,' she said. 'I wish Eugene was more like you.'

Denny was startled; this was unexpected and rather awkward. 'Um,'

'I mean, it's funny really,' she continued, oblivious to his discomfort, 'he looks like everything a woman could want, but inside, he's like a little boy. Whereas you ...'

'Cindy ...'

'You *look* like, well, like the victim of some wasting disease – by comparison anyway, but you're, well, you're a man.' She gave a little sigh.

Denny shifted uncomfortably, just because he was learning to tolerate, nay even to like Cindy, did not mean he was ready for *this*.

Funny, this had been happening more and more lately. It was weird; after all, he looked just the same as he always had. Cindy was right about that. Too pale and skinny, and badly dressed – the drug addict look Tamar called it. The only changes were on the inside – he no longer cared, for instance, what people thought of him (he had never cared what he looked like – it would be like caring that he wasn't a lion – pretty pointless.) He had more confidence now. But people could not see that. Or could they? It was true that he no longer shuffled through life slightly apologetically.

'I always judged people on the way they look,' Cindy was saying. 'Guess I'm learning a few lessons too.' she smiled at him.

'Look... Cindy – this is all very flattering, but...'

'Oh don't look so worried,' she laughed. 'I know you don't think much of me. And even if you did, I wouldn't *dare* go up against Tamar. I just meant, well I wish Eugene were more like you. Or that I could find someone that is.'

'I used to be like Eugene,' Denny told her. 'Afraid of my own shadow I was.'

'You?'

Denny grinned, 's'true,' he said. 'Scouts honour. Funnily enough I was thinking about that earlier, people can change; maybe you should give him a chance.'

'If we ever find him.'

'Ah good point. And ... just for the record, you're not so bad. Compared to my sister-in-law, you're heaven.'

'Well thank you ... I think.'

'You're welcome.'

'You don't think ... no.'

'What?'

'It's silly really. But you don't think Eugene might have ...'

'What? Come on, you know him better than I do, if you've got an idea, let's hear it.'

'It's what *you* said, actually – about people changing. You don't think he could have gone into the file, do you?'

'Why would he, on his own? Why not wait for me? I was going in anyway. He wouldn't know where he was going.'

'Well he's not very bright at times you know. He probably just didn't think it through. He's very jealous of you, you know.'

'Oh.'

'Oh no, not because of *me*. Just because, you know, what I said before. He probably wanted to prove he wasn't afraid.'

'But, he *was* afraid.'

'That's why he wanted to prove he wasn't. You're a man – surely you understand that.'

'Not really, but I'll take your word for it. Why don't we check in the files?'

'Both of us?'

'Yeah why not? Don't you want to give him a smack upside his head, when we find him?'

'No!' she said, indignantly. 'Well, yes, maybe just a little bit.'

Denny staggered suddenly and went pale.

'What's wrong? What is it?'

'I don't know, something's happened, didn't you feel it?'

'Feel what?'

'Like the world … I don't know, I felt it.'

'A disturbance in the force "Obi Wan"?'

'Actually, *yes*.'

'Oh.'

'And look,' he pointed up.

'Uh oh.'

Denny panicked and slammed the laptop shut and picked it up – effectively closing the file again. 'We have to get back to the house now!'

~ Chapter Eighteen ~

THE FIREWALL WAS back in place, but that was no problem for a girl armed with a piece of chalk. Suddenly she was aware that she was not alone. She spun fast and kicked. If in doubt kick first and ask questions later.

'Ooof,' came a voice in the darkness. 'What did you do that for?'

'Eugene?' There are not sufficient adjectives to describe the disbelief in her voice, so you will just have to imagine it.

'Hi Tamar.'

*

'Do you mean to tell me the file's open again?' Tamar was delighted. 'That's great, let's get out of here. Close file ... close file. Damn, not again!'

*

Tamar was outraged. 'I can't believe it! You came in here because you thought Denny – *my* Denny, was after Cindy, how stupid are you?'

'No, she likes him though. She thinks he's more of a man than I am. She forgot, I think, that I could read her thoughts.'

'Oh, yes, I forgot about that too.'

'Everybody does.'

'Well I can't read yours, so explain it to me. How was this supposed to help?'

'She thought I was afraid. So, I thought I'd show her that I'm not.'

'And leave her alone with Denny, who I think she's actually a bit scared of, good job.'

'She's not scared of him anymore, oh no, thinks he's the bees knees, now. You should have seen them, heads together all the time, always whispering, making plans, leaving me out. Poor Eugene's too stupid to help,' he said, bitterly. 'I can't get a read on *his* thoughts for some reason, but don't you think it's a bit funny that he's closed the file after me? He was supposed to be so all-fired keen to get in here to find *you*. So where is he?'

'Something must have happened,' she said. But she sounded uncertain.

'Like what?' said Eugene sceptically. 'The world is frozen in time, what could possibly have happened? Nothing *is* happening.'

Tamar nodded. He had spoken her thoughts aloud.

'I wish he'd stayed in Hell,' said Eugene.

Tamar looked horrified.

'Okay, no I don't, but I wish he'd left us out of it anyway.'

'How did he get out of Hell anyway?' asked Tamar. 'Did he tell you?'

'They had to let him go, apparently. Something about legislation or jurisdiction or something.'

'Because he wasn't dead yet?'

'No, something else, something about his not having a contract. Denny said he didn't understand it, and frankly, I don't either.'

'*Jurisdiction*?' muttered Tamar. What did that remind her of?

* * *

Cindy stumbled and gasped and clutched at the stitch in her side. 'Why are we running? What's going on?'

'Something very, very bad. I don't know what, but you saw it too.'

'The sun?'

'Yes, the sun doesn't turn black for no reason. Especially when there's no time for it to happen in. Something's gone horribly wrong.'

'All right – STOP!'

Denny wheeled round, frowning. 'What?'

'Tamar,' said Cindy. 'And Eugene of course,' she added, almost as an afterthought. 'Though I say nothing about him. He's *my* problem.'

'And mine,' said Denny gloomily. 'You're right of course, it's just …'

'Whatever the problem is here,' Cindy said, 'I think we'd be able to handle it better with Tamar's help. Don't you?'

Denny sighed. 'I suppose you're right.' he shrugged. 'I hate that.'

'So, are we going in to get them?'

'I am,' Denny said in that tone that you don't argue with.'

'*What?*' Cindy was outraged. 'You can't just leave me behind, you might need me. Okay you probably *won't* need me, but, I mean you can't just leave me here! I mean it's not safe.'

Denny ignored her. He opened up the laptop and typed busily.

Cindy paced behind him. 'Are you just going to ignore me? Do you even know what you're doing there? And what are you going to do once you get inside? What am *I* going to do?' What are you doing anyway? *Denny*!'

Denny had reached the file and had stopped, puzzled. 'Hum,' he muttered. 'I forgot. I don't have to go in the long way now. I have the password I can go directly to the historical files, what *was* that damn password? Ah, yes, there we go… My God!'

'What?'

'My God, this is brilliant.'

'*Denny*!'

Denny finally looked up. 'Look.' He pointed at the screen.

'I don't …'

'Look at the menu,' Denny yelped excitedly.

'Uh huh.'

'Oh you don't understand, actually, I forgot, you wouldn't understand would you. This means I can search for any file I want. We couldn't do that before.'

'Oh. So how does that help you to find Tamar?' We don't know which file she's in.'

'I don't need to find her. We'll have plenty of time to find her after I sort out Askphrit.' Denny looked at Cindy's blank expression. 'Don't you see? This means I can find him and end this.'

'How?'

'Well, he made the mistake of messing up his timing when he went after my Grandfather. He gave himself away, so I know exactly where he's been. Which means I know exactly where to find him. If I go into the file and prevent him from killing my Grandfather, then I'm guessing that none of this will ever have happened.'

'Actually, I meant how are you going to stop him when you find him, don't you need Tamar for that?'

'Actually, no. It was always going to be me that killed him, if I could. That's what this is for.' He held up the Athame. The blade looked strangely dull.

Cindy looked sceptical. 'It's an impressive weapon, no doubt,' she said. 'But it won't kill a god.'

Denny smiled. 'Not the blade,' he told her. 'What's *on* the blade – Harts blood'

Cindy blanched. 'Does Tamar know you have that?'

'No.'

'She's going to kill you.'

Denny shrugged. 'Under the circumstances, I think it's just as well that I *do* have it, don't you think?'

Cindy looked dubious.

'Look, I took some of the blood, in case something like this happened. I think I knew that it might be down to me in the end. Now I have him in the hollow of my hand.'

'If you say so.'

'I *do* say so. My Grandfather died on October nineteenth, 1941 in his back garden during an air raid. I don't know the exact time, and I don't know exactly how Askphrit pulled it off. But I know he'll be there somewhere, and, thanks to this very helpful menu, I know exactly how to get straight there. And since I have the file number, I literally have all the time in the world to get him.'

'If at first you don't succeed etc. etc?'

'Precisely.' Denny tapped in a long number, double checked it and then looked at Cindy, his finger poised over the "Enter" key. 'Aren't you going to wish me luck?' he asked.

'You're really just going to leave me here?'

'You'll be safer here,' he muttered. 'Trust me.' He hit the key.

'Good luck,' whispered Cindy to the empty air.

~ Chapter Nineteen ~

'OVERTIME'S A BITCH,' thought Clive. And Tamar and Denny's interesting trek through the files of history was causing more overtime than that clerk had ever known. He had picked up on their journeying almost immediately, because he had watched and influenced all their movements closely for many years. He was confident that he was the only clerk to have picked up on what they were doing now. Management would, obviously, be oblivious, and he certainly was not going to tell them.

The worst thing about this overtime was that it was self-imposed and, therefore, unpaid. But he felt that it might be worth it.

At the moment, he was watching Denny.

An old man was creeping up behind him. He was carrying an axe. Clive had a bad feeling about this. He did a quick search and came up with a name for the old man. He groaned; this had the potential to be really, really bad.

The old man struck Denny on the back of the head with the butt of the axe head and gave a cowardly whimper when Denny conspicuously failed to go down like a sack of potatoes, but instead, turned to face the old man with a look of terrible ferocity.

'What the hell …' he roared, then he saw the old mans blanched face. He lowered his voice 'What did you do that for?' he said in fairly reasonable tones

The old man gathered his courage. 'Well, what are you up to?' he demanded, 'You're trespassing on my property in the middle of the night. I've a right to defend my home and family.' He glanced suspiciously at Denny taking in his outlandish attire. 'And my country, for that matter,' he added.

Denny smothered a smile. It was obvious now; the man thought he was a German spy.

'Dad?' both men turned, a skinny young man had appeared from inside the house

Without warning, he fired a shot straight at Denny. With an instinctive dexterity which his best friends would hardly have credited him with a few years ago, Denny spun and threw the Athame into the man's heart.

The old man gave a cry. 'John!'

From his place in the shadow of a large oak tree, Askphrit gave a satisfied smile and turned to leave.

And suddenly Denny had a horrible feeling of destiny, but not for long, as the young man drew his last breath and Denny ceased to exist.

He did not really notice though. Since he did not exist, he could not have caused his existence to be erased. And so it was not. Until he did it again, except he could not have, so he did not. This could go on all day, or for the rest of eternity.

* * *

Peirce was lounging against a pillar grinning toothily and enjoying the show. Askphrit predictably, had released him, and Hecaté had, somewhat reluctantly, unfrozen him. It was either that or watch Stiles die. But she was painfully slow at unfreezing the rest of the world and Askphrit was getting impatient and throwing the occasional energy bolt at Stiles to speed up the process.

I cannot go any faster, please leave him alone,' she pleaded.

'You shouldn't be doing it at all,' admonished Stiles. 'He's just going to kill me anyway as soon as you're finished. And then God knows what he'll do!'

'Besides,' he continued, with a confidence that was completely unjustified in the circumstances. 'Tamar and Denny *will* get out of mainframe eventually, whatever this lunatic thinks, and then – well, we'll just see, won't we?' he finished lamely.

Askphrit chuckled. 'They won't get out,' he said. 'I have taken some rather elaborate precautions to make sure of it. The last time I saw him, he was very effectively cooking his own goose – or rather his own grandfather, I should say.' He gave an evil laugh.

Stiles shook his head. He did not believe it. Tamar and Denny could get out of anything that this maniac could cook up. He admonished Hecaté again.

Hecaté ignored him and continued muttering spells, pausing only to flinch as this remark earned Stiles another blast.

Peirce grinned again. He did not like Stiles. He did not like anyone much – well he *was* a vampire.

'I don't know what you think you're grinning about,' said Stiles. 'As soon as I get out of this, you'll be the first to die.'

'Ha! Big talk for a man in a cage,' said Peirce. 'But even supposing you do escape. One, I'm already dead, and two, in case you forgot – you can't stake me unless you can find my heart, and I don't even know where it is.'

Peirce had had his heart removed (well it was not as if he was using it) and stored, so he said, in a vault somewhere.

Stiles had indeed forgotten about this, and he shifted uncomfortably. 'Well, anyway,' he blustered, 'you'd be amazed what you can live through.'

'Not really,' yawned Peirce. 'I lived through death didn't I? After that, nothing much really surprises one.'

Askphrit interrupted mildly. 'Please, please, enough of this. You will disturb the lovely lady in her meditations. And Peirce, our friend is right, should he escape you will indeed be the first to die, *I* shall make sure of it, now shut up.'

'Go on my dear,' he said to Hecaté. 'Oh and stop re-freezing time whenever you think I am not paying attention. I am not a fool you know.'

'What is that word that Tamar is so fond of using to describe you?' muttered Hecaté, who had indeed been doing this at intervals. 'Oh yes – Bastard!'

* * *

'We have to find another way out of mainframe.' Tamar was saying. 'We obviously can't count on the file being opened again from the outside, and for that matter, we don't even know why it was closed in the first place.'

'Or the second place,' said Eugene mournfully.

'Exactly,' agreed Tamar. 'If something's happened to Denny, I want to know about it. Besides …'

Eugene's silence was eloquent.

Tamar turned on him fiercely. 'He wouldn't have abandoned us here if he could help it,' she said firmly in a cold voice. 'You may disabuse yourself of that idea right away. Right, so we need a plan to get out. Any ideas?'

'What about finding the file for the present, say the day before you froze time. Then we'd just have to wait a bit to catch up with ourselves – oh.'

'Exactly, it would cause a paradox. There'd be two of us in the same time. Two of each of us I mean,' she explained.

'I know,' said Eugene affronted. 'Still, he mused, there'd only be two of us until the other two of us entered mainframe again, then we'd be back to one. Wouldn't we?'

'No, there'd be one of us in here and one of us out there. Anyway it's not practical. Do you have any idea how long it would take us to find the right file? They aren't named. It's all a bit hit and miss you see.'

'Oh, I didn't know.'

'On the other hand, I can't see any other way out unless there's a way out from central files.'

'What's that?'

'Just what it sounds like. In fact, I think that's the best idea, but we'll have to be careful not to get caught. I think they might be looking for me there.'

'Sounds risky, how do we get in anyway? It must be guarded.'

Tamar held up the pass key. 'With this.'

'You stole it?'

'Of course.'

'Then I think you're right, they *will* be looking for you, are you sure this is a good idea.'

'Can you think of anything better?'

'Well, what about the way Denny got out?'

~ Chapter Twenty ~

THERE CANNOT BE many people who try to get *into* hell. *Out* of hell, certainly. Plenty of those, there is after all, only so much Enid Blyton a grown man can take. But trying to get *in* is pretty rare, though not unheard of. There is a section of society that think that Hell is all wild parties and racy leather underwear. They know nothing of the horrors that really await them. After all, it is supposed to be a punishment.

Tamar had never been to Hell, but she had a pretty shrewd idea of what it was going to be like; it made her nervous in a way that she was entirely unfamiliar with.

If the punishment was fitted to the crime, then what the hell was *she* in for? An eternity of having her every wish fulfilled? Ugh, horrible. Still, if Denny had managed to get out … Anyway, there was no other way.

Eugene had surprised her; it really was a pretty good idea, one that she herself would never have thought of, being inclined to over-think things. Eugene, on the other hand, apparently took the simple route through life. And sometimes the most obvious solution was the best.

That did not make her any happier about it though.

Eugene himself did not seem all that worried about it. He had, after all, got the most powerful being in the world beside him. Besides, as he said, 'I never signed no contract with the Devil either. And I certainly ain't dead.'

Tamar knew that this was oversimplifying matters a bit too much. Hell is full of sinners, not poor fools who signed away their souls for a mess of pottage – whatever that was. Still, if it kept him happy.

The problem now was how to get into Hell. Denny had ended up there by accident, and although Tamar knew how it had happened, she was not sure whether it would work again. Denny had been thrown clear of the filing system and had landed in Hell. She and Eugene might end up anywhere. It seemed a bit hit and miss to her.

The alternative was to find the actual file for Hell, if there was such a thing. Technically, hell was not part of the world.

Where to start looking? – Admitting that central files was out of the question.

Hell is another world, but not an alternate reality, which would just be another version of this world. There are also many different hells, from what she had heard. Denny had been to the Christian Hell. Although all hells surely would lead back to the world, just as all hells are accessible *from* the world. And suddenly she knew how he had done it.

She grabbed Eugene by the hand and giving him no time to argue, said 'Close files.'

When she found herself in the nothing between the worlds, she almost panicked. She could almost hear the echo of Denny's last words when he had been in this place 'Oh Hell!' she repeated.

Nothing happened; her voice made no sound. 'Oh Hell,' she said again. 'Hell?' then she heard a voice from above her head. 'Not another one; where the Jesus are they all coming from?'

'Two this time,' moaned the devil. His Dark Lordship's going to have an aneurysm.'

'Not dead?' asked another one.

'Not dead. Not on the list. Not supposed to bloody well be here. What are we going to do with them?'

'Let's kill them.'

'It won't make any difference,' moaned the first devil. 'I tell you, they're not on the list. Alive or dead, we can't keep them.'

'I like killing things,' sulked the other devil.

'How would you know? You've never done it. They're always dead already when they get to us – well usually.' He looked irritably at Tamar. 'No, the only thing to do is to get them out of here as fast as possible and hope that He doesn't find out.'

Tamar heaved a silent sigh of relief.

'Come on youse two,' snarled the devil turning on his heel. 'This way to the river Styx, keep quiet, keep your heads down and no arguing. I don't suppose you brought any money with you?'

* * *

'Agggh!' Stiles was still suffering stoically. Living proof that lightning *can* strike more than once in the same place, particularly if it is guided by a very vindictive and pissed off god, who thinks he is being screwed around. Stiles was smoking gently from the ears like the wily coyote after he has just swallowed a stick of dynamite. It is pretty fair guess that he felt like it too.

'If you do not desist,' said 'Hecaté. 'I will do no more.'

'Fine,' said Askphrit. 'I'll just kill him then shall I?'

'Ooh, let me,' said Peirce.

'Do so,' bluffed Hecaté. 'Then, where will your leverage be?'

Hecaté had forgotten that Askphrit was totally insane. He called her bluff.

* * *

Charon was, predictably, not at all pleased to see them, but after some huffing and puffing, he agreed to let them cross. 'They'll have to wait, though,' he said. 'I've got some incoming to deal with first. They'll have to keep out of sight, while I bring them across, it could cause unrest that sort of thing, if they see me ferrying people *out*.' With that he turned the boat around and Tamar and Eugene were left on the shores of the river Styx shivering in the perpetual fog. The devils who had escorted them left without a word.

'Could have been worse,' said Eugene, flapping his arms around him to keep warm, although there was no keeping warm in that place. The cold seemed to be a part of your very soul. 'It was quite easy in the end,' he continued, cheerfully. 'Won't be long now, before we're out of here. They seemed quite keen to be rid of us, didn't they?'

'Mmm,' Tamar was thinking about something else. 'What do you suppose they meant "they're not on the list?".'

Eugene shrugged. 'That we're not dead yet I suppose.'

'No, that wasn't it,' she said. 'And after all, why should it matter, this is a place where they keep your immortal soul. Just because most people don't arrive here until they die, doesn't mean that it is a necessary pre requisite – apparently. The body isn't the part of you that stays here anyway. No, it's something else. Something about – what did you say before? Jurisdiction.'

'Yes, so what? I mean as long as they let us go, what does it matter?'

'It matters, I'm sure of it. I'm just not sure why.'

'Well, perhaps it's because we aren't Christians,' said Eugene. 'This is the Christian Hell, isn't it?'

Tamar looked thunderstruck. 'My God!' she said. 'Could it really be that simple?'

They were distracted by the arrival of Charon's boat looming through the fog. It was a chilling sight now. Filled with hundreds of pallid ghost like figures, seeming to each take up no more space than a breath of air, yet each one a distinct personality, or rather a distinct sin. Eugene grabbed Tamar and pulled her behind a rock. 'He said we have to keep out of sight.'

They hid, but they watched – could not help but watch, as the crowd disembarked and began a long forlorn procession along the dreary banks of the river up toward the caverns of Hell. Tamar could not tear her gaze from them; they all looked so bewildered and frightened. On each face, was an expression of confused surprise. "This has to be a mistake." "This is not for me surely?" They tried to cling to one another for comfort, but found that they could not; they had no more substance than smoke. That would change when they reached Hell proper, and it would not be a change for the better. Lost souls indeed. It was horrible. Tamar felt paralysed with an inconsolable pity. What had they done? If they had committed sins as great as her own, she would be surprised. And yet, here they were, and she was to go free. 'There but for the grace of God,' she muttered. Except that was wrong, wasn't it, the wrong way round, it was by the grace of God that these poor souls were condemned. Again, she felt that thought, curling its way around the edges of her mind. This was important in some way. But she could not quite catch hold of the idea that was forming in her brain. Then all rational thought ceased, as her attention was arrested by a familiar face in the procession.

'Jack?'

~ Chapter Twenty One ~

DENNY HAD, BY Clive's reckoning, erased his own existence and re-existed, seventy five thousand whole times and seemed set to go on until time itself ceased. You had to admire his tenacity.

An hour later (from Clive's viewpoint) he was not admiring him nearly so much. An hour later still and he was not admiring him at all and was wondering how on earth to stop all this.

He wondered where Denny had gone wrong. Surely he had gone back to the day when his grandfather had died anyway, at the hands of Askphrit, too late to affect the future. He supposed that it did not really matter, but out of curiosity, he checked the dates. Denny turned out to have checked into the file a mere day earlier than his grandfather's original demise. More than enough time to make a significant difference, a conception is usually achieved in only one night after all. The real question now was, had Askphrit planned it that way? It was a masterly stroke if so. A masterpiece of timing and finesse. Or was it a just a monstrous coincidence?

And if Askphrit *had* planned it, how the hell had he known?

Of *course* he had planned it, Clive thought. The evil cunning sod. And why he had done it was pretty obvious too. But how had he pulled it off?

It turned out to be staggeringly simple when Clive looked into it. He had changed the file numbers round. After he had killed the man once – he simply switched it so that when Denny finally found what he thought was the correct file (and it made no difference to Askphrit how long this actually took, it would all happen instantaneously from his perspective anyway) he was actually in the file for the previous day. And on that day Denny's grandfather had faced and shot what he thought was an enemy spy – Askphrit himself of course.

He had clearly been banking on Tamar or Denny or both actually finding the codes at some point – but apart from that, he had left nothing to chance.

Clive was inclined to blame "them upstairs" for this. He was sure they had handed the codes over somehow (no doubt in some unorthodox and totally untraceable manner. And, had Clive but known it, Askphrit had been pretty sure of this too. As he had said to Stiles and Hecaté – good guys are all so predictable.

Still, none of that mattered now. It was done, and Denny (and by association, Tamar) were stuck in a time loop. It was fortunate, Clive supposed, that Denny had not really touched many lives in any significant fashion. The resulting mess, had he been a political icon, for example, or a contestant on "Big Brother", would have been inconceivable. Still it was bad enough as it was, and what was to be done about it?

He considered simply pulling the plug on mainframe and switching the universe off. Maybe when he plugged it back in, it would go back to startup mode, and he could put this – and a whole host of other things, now he thought about it – right.

Bad idea! Someone would have done it by now if it were possible. Maybe someone had, he thought. After all, how would anyone really know?

He decided that it was too risky, besides he was not sure where the plug was.

He checked the alternate realities, but Denny it seemed was a remarkably consistent character. There was no universe out there that Clive could find where he had not taken exactly the same path – the aggravating creature. The only exception was the universe that had split off when Askphrit had dramatically changed his own destiny – and that was clearly impossible. It was not even the same Denny.

If only he could insert some extra time into the file. Just a few seconds would do it. Just long enough to break the cycle, in those few seconds Denny would both exist and not exist at the same time and Clive was quite certain that he was astute enough to see what was happening and stay his own hand. The problem was that time is not a commodity that one can just shift around at will. Although humans treated it that way, file clerks knew better. Humans talked of saving time or wasting time, of losing time and even – gross conceit – "making" time. Of course, humans did not actually "make" time they merely pinched it from other tasks.

Hmm, maybe they were on to something there.

* * *

The procession stopped abruptly as Tamar ran out heedlessly from her hiding place to where Jack Stiles had now stopped his slow shuffle towards eternity. He was, quite possibly, the first person ever to have done so. But not the last.

Charon was speechless with indignation this was unprecedented. The march toward eternity (as it was officially called) halted for no man – or woman.

Stiles stared blankly at Tamar, his eyes dull and uncomprehending. She stared back shocked and disbelieving. Not Jack! – Not *here*. The pain of it was unbearable; she felt like she could not breathe. She began to sob uncontrollably. The parade of the dead stared.

Suddenly Jack smiled – another first – lost souls do not smile. 'Tamar?' he said haltingly as if the word, as if speech itself was an unfamiliar concept. 'What are you doing here?'

Tamar gave a watery smile. 'I was going to ask *you* that.'

'I'm dead,' he said simply.

'But- but, this is Hell!' as soon as the words were out of her mouth she realised that she could have put it more diplomatically.

Stiles seemed unconcerned, however. 'Is it? Well, I can't say I'm all that surprised. My mother always said I wasn't a good Catholic boy.' He leaned forward conspiratorially. 'I used to steal cookies,' he said, with a sickly grin. 'And once – I killed a man.'

'I'm sure you didn't mean it,' said Tamar her heart wrung with pity.

'Doesn't matter does it?' said Stiles. 'Thou shalt not kill, and thou shalt not steal. I suppose it's all one down here. I broke the rules.'

'The rules?' murmured Tamar, more to herself than anything else. There was that thought again, really clamouring for attention now. If only she had time to think.

By this time, the whole crowd of souls were crowded round them listening with their mouths open.

Charon had so many things he wanted to say, that the processes of his thoughts had brought his mouth to a standstill. He was choking on his own breath.

''Course, it was really my mother who promised that I'd keep the rules, not me,' said Stiles, darkly. 'Nobody asked *me*. But I suppose once you've been baptised into the Faith, that's it.'

A door in Tamar's head flew open and the thought marched in crying. 'SEE ME!'.

She turned to the spluttering figure of Charon. 'I want to see the boss,' she told him. ' RIGHT NOW!'

* * *

From the point of view of Denny, it happened something like this –

Time slowed down, stopped and reversed, just about a minute he thought. Then it stopped again. He saw, in reverse as it were, what he had just done. No, he *experienced* it in reverse; that was more like it. Whatever it was, it was clear that he could stop himself this time. For some reason, he had been given a second chance. He had no idea what the consequences of his actions would be, beyond guilt. But Denny was no murderer and guilt was enough to stay his hand when time began moving forward again. It occurred to him that time, in the normal way of going on, stops for no man and that there must be some really weighty reason why it had for him. But even if he had not thought of this, he still would have changed his actions.

* * *

Denny and the young man stared at each other for a few seconds weighing up their options, although with very different thoughts. The shot had gone wide, and Denny had not been hit.

A moment later a policeman appeared, hurrying round the corner and took Denny by the elbow. 'Come along sir,' he said. 'I've been looking for you.' Denny offered no resistance. He recognized the voice. It was Clive.

'What's going on?' asked Denny, quite naturally.

Clive shook his head. 'Search me,' he said.

'Clive!'

'Now then Denny, you know better than that,' Clive admonished him. 'I can only guide, I can't interfere. Besides, I don't really know an awful lot.'

'You're lying,' said Denny baldly. 'But never mind, if you're here to guide me, what do you suggest that I do now?'

'Hmm,' mused Clive. 'Good question. I suggest that you get out of this file. You won't find your quarry here. He's flown, and he won't be back. In fact, it's as if he was never here, if you follow me.'

'Because of what you did to the time?'

'In a way, yes.'

'Can't you tell me anything? Where can I find him?'

'Ah, that is more than I can tell – no really, I don't know.'

'So, what happened, why did you stop time for me?'

'Think about where you are,' said Clive. 'Can't you guess?'

Denny suddenly saw the whole thing. 'O-oh m-my G-God,' he stammered.

'Quite.'

'I guess I really owe you one.'

Clive inclined his head. 'Least I could do,' he said.

'But now I suppose I'm back to square one.'

'Perhaps.'

'Unless ...' Denny's face creased with the effort of thought 'Askphrit will be here tomorrow won't he? To try to kill my Grandfather himself, won't he?'

'I doubt it.'

'So do I?' sighed Denny. 'That was never the point, was it? The point was to get me here to do it for him. And now that has failed ...' he left the sentence hanging.

'Who knows where he might be now.' Clive finished for him.

Denny sunk his head in his hands. Clive shook his head. 'Now is not the time to give up,' he said.

'Denny looked up. 'No, you're right, I suppose I should get back to Cindy, she might be in trouble now that things haven't gone back to how they were before all this started. And then, I suppose, it's back to plan A.'

He looked curiously at Clive. 'Just one thing,' he said. 'How did you do it?'

'I borrowed some of your spare time. Don't worry, I took it from when you were sleeping, you'll never miss it. Now, close the file.'

'Close file.'

* * *

Cindy simply could not get her head around it, but she did pick up on what she thought were the main points.

'So, Askphrit tricked you?'

'Yes.'

'And now he could be anywhere?'

'That's right.'

'But as far as he's concerned, you are stuck in a time loop in mainframe, and Tamar too?'

Denny thought about this. His face darkened into a frown. He thumped his palm with his fist. 'That little bastard,' exclaimed. 'He lied to me,'

Cindy was puzzled. 'Well, I don't know if I'd call him *little*, exactly,' she said tentatively.

'Not *him*,' said Denny, confirming what Cindy had thought. 'Clive,' Denny thumped his palm again.

'What are you talking about?' said Cindy patiently. She knew she would get there in the end.

'Clive, that clerk, you know?'

'Yes, I know who you mean.'

'He knew, don't you see? He must have!'

Cindy sighed. 'Knew what?'

Denny looked at Cindy penitently. 'Oh sorry,' he said. 'I'm so used to Tam being able to follow my train of thought I've forgotten how to explain myself. Let me see ...' he stopped to organize his thoughts. 'Okay, Clive knew what you just said, about Askphrit thinking that I'm still stuck in mainframe. Like you said, as far as *he's* concerned, his plan worked, which means that there's no reason for him to go back and change it. So when I said that he wasn't going to be in the file to go after my Grandfather and start this whole thing off, Clive *knew*, I was wrong, but he *said* I was right, do you follow me?'

'I - I think so.'

'Or at least, he let me *think* I was right, which amounts to the same thing. I could have waited in that file for another day and finished this for good after all, if he hadn't convinced me that there was no point. The treacherous little swine.'

Denny stabbed the Athame viciously into a tree stump as if he wished it was Clive's head.

Cindy shook her head. 'How can you be so sure that Askphrit doesn't know that his plan didn't work? It seems to me ...'

'Because it *did* work.'

'Huh?'

'Because we *did* go into the files after him, because Tam *did* stop time.' He gestured to the frozen birds above them. 'And because we're still here, and Tam and Eugene are stuck in mainframe, just like before I went back into the files. Nothing's changed. Don't you understand? The only thing Askphrit *doesn't* know is that I escaped. And that means ...'

Denny frowned biting his lip. He turned to Cindy, his eyes shining. 'I know where he is.'

~ Chapter Twenty Two ~

'WHAT ARE you *doing*?' hissed Eugene.

Tamar looked withering scorn at him. 'I'm going to save my friend,' she said. 'You go home if you like, I won't stop you.'

'I think you've got delusions of grandeur,' said Eugene. 'I know you're powerful, but what do you really think you can do against *Him*?'

'I know what I'm doing – I think. Anyway, I have to try. You don't have to come. I don't need you,'

'Of course I'll stay, I just want to know what you're up to.'

Tamar smiled. 'You'll see.'

* * *

Charon, rather reluctantly, led them up through the many caverns and levels of hell, saying 'it's your funeral – or rather your eternity of torment.' He was rather bemused by this turn of events, and part of him wanted to see how it turned out. Besides, it does you good to get out and about occasionally. In any case, Tamar had threatened him with dismemberment, and he was not entirely sure that she could not manage it. Satan himself had no direct power over Charon, any more than he had power over Death himself, but Tamar was scary.[*]

---

[*] Tamar was powerful, but her greatest gift was her unlimited self-confidence. People

He left the new arrivals (all but Stiles) on the shore. He would pick them up later; after all, they were not going anywhere.

It was a long journey and Eugene tried to make conversation. He turned to Charon. 'So, what's your name?' Even Eugene realised that this was a lame beginning, but one had to start somewhere, and Charon was not an approachable figure.

'Charon,' he grunted.

'Sharon?' said Eugene. 'That's an unusual name for a – a person of your persuasion.'

Charon looked at him curiously. 'Is it?' he said in a lugubrious tone.

'Er, well …'

'As far as I know, I am the only one of my kind.'

'Oh, I see.'

Tamar smothered a smile.

Eugene was about to give up, but Charon was actually quite flattered by this unaccustomed attention. Nobody, in all his long years, had ever asked him about himself before. 'I am the ferryman of the dead,' he informed Eugene sombrely. I ferry all the dead from the world to their various destinations, so it has always been.'

'Oh.'

'Yes, indeed. I belong to the underworld, and the underworld belongs to me. It is my special task until all worlds draw to a close.'

'Fascinating.'

'Ah, we are here.'

Satan looked up from his armchair. 'What?' he snapped pettishly.

Tamar stepped forward. 'I've come to make a deal,' she said.

Satan cowered.

* * *

with far greater powers than hers, often viewed her with alarm and uncertainty, simply because she always acted as if she could do *anything*

'You monster,' Hecaté sobbed over the pile of ash that was her former lover. 'Do what you will with me,' she cried dramatically. 'I shall help you no longer.'

Askphrit frowned. 'Hmm,' he said. 'I suspect you mean it too. I do seem to have been a bit hasty here, don't I? Tch, Tch, what to do? Peirce?'

Peirce ran forward, 'Yes master?'

'Sweep that up will you?'

'NO!'

It was not the obsequious Peirce, who uttered this declaration, naturally. It was Hecaté, who flew at Askphrit furiously 'Jack was right,' she screamed at him. 'They will escape, and he will be avenged. They will stop you, they will …' she broke off sobbing. Pierce stopped to watch interestedly.

Askphrit was surprisingly gentle as he said. 'No, no, my dear. Did you think I was merely boasting when I said I had taken precautions against that? They are trapped forever in a time loop that I created. He has killed his own ancestor, and from that, there is no escape. And she is bound up in his fate, as long as he is trapped, so is she.' He allowed himself a chuckle. 'And he cannot *possibly* escape.'

'Guess again.' It was Denny, who had kicked the door in with an impressive crash, and who now stood, dramatically framed in the shadow of the doorway, the Athame clenched in his fist, and a look on his face that would have turned gorgons to stone. For once he had made the entrance of a lifetime, and the impression that he had intended. Askphrit was speechless.

Denny kicked Peirce out of his way and strode up to Askphrit. 'Well, Well, Well,' he said, 'you seem a little surprised to see me.'

Askphrit replied with a sickly grin while his eyes darted hither and thither like a trapped animal seeking an escape route. He was also looking for Tamar, who he assumed would not be far behind.

Denny glanced around at the scene in the room. The still smoking pile of ashes, the tear stained face of Hecaté, now frozen in shock. It did not take a genius to figure out what had happened. This was fortunate, since even with the Athame, Denny was no genius.

'You appear to have murdered a good friend of mine,' he observed coldly. Neither angry nor sad – just stating a fact. 'I think you'll find that was a mistake. One of many you have made recently I might add.' He turned to Hecaté. 'I'm sorry I didn't get here in time to prevent this.'

She looked at him in wonder. 'At least you are here now to avenge him,' she said.

Denny nodded. 'Any last words,' he said to Askphrit, 'before you exchange time for eternity?' He raised the Athame. Askphrit did not even try to escape; he seemed transfixed by Denny's gaze, like a deer in the headlights.

'What no quips?' jeered Denny. 'No funny remarks? Not even a wholly inadequate attempt at justification? Well!'

'Don't gloat dear – it's not in good taste.'

Denny spun round. 'Explanations later,' said Tamar. 'For now, just wait.'

'Wait? Wait for what?' He raised the Athame again.

'No don't kill him. There's really no need – isn't that right?' she addressed a cloaked figure which had emerged from the shadows in the corner. It nodded silently.

'He deserves a fate *worse* than death,' Tamar continued, 'and that's exactly what I've arranged for him.'

The figure threw back his hood and stalked over to Askphrit who suddenly found his voice.

'You fools,' he said. 'Do you think you can scare me with this ridiculous hobgoblin? What's the game eh? The figure took no notice of him. He turned to Denny, 'Hello again,' he said.

Then he snapped his fingers and held out a claw. 'Judas, the list,' he snapped. From a hole in the air, a skinny hand appeared for a second holding what appeared to be a scroll made of smoke. 'Special effects,' said Satan, 'good eh?'

He ran a long fingernail down the scroll. 'Ah, yes, this all seems to be in order. Askphrit AKA Fred Jones, baptised a

Christian on January ninth 1991. Broke his first commandment on January tenth and indeed all of them by the end of that week. Seven deadly sins all committed, and, then indeed, some really quite spectacular sinning thereafter. Says here – consorting with demons and vampires. Worshipping false gods i.e. himself. Dear me, worse and worse. Trying to take over the world. My word, I've never seen a record so fine. Christians are usually so half-hearted with the sinning. It's as if they can't be bothered. We should have some fun with this one. I'll take him.' He stretched out a claw toward Askphrit.

'Don't look,' warned Tamar.

The room grew cold, and an icy blast blew past them. When they opened their eyes, Satan and Askphrit were gone. All that remained was a gust of cold wind that blew out the door sweeping away the pile of ash that had once been Jack Stiles P.I.

~ Chapter Twenty Three ~

DENNY, HECATÉ and Tamar stood for some minutes in flabbergasted silence.

Tamar was the first to speak. 'Hey,' she cried, apparently to the empty air. 'A deal's a deal.'

For a moment, the room chilled again, and from the empty air, it seemed they could hear the sound of cold laughter. Then it was gone. Tamar sagged.

* * *

It had happened like this –

'I want to make a deal,' said Tamar.

Satan cowered. He recognized her as a demonic entity, yet alien, not of his kin and, as such, she was a powerful threat.

'Oh yes?' he managed. It was usually he who offered to make demonic deals; to have someone come to him in this way was a novel and unnerving experience.

'Yes,' she said. 'Two souls for one.'

Satan leaned forward interestedly. 'Go on.'

Tamar grinned. 'Well, to begin with, if you accept I want him back.' She pointed to Stiles.

Satan inclined his head noncommittally.

'No, I need an answer,' she insisted.

'So, lay it on the line for me.'

'Okay, I have a soul for you, that I think hasn't even crossed your radar, even though he belongs rightfully to you. He's an evil sod the likes of which you have never seen before in this place, I guarantee it.'

Satan looked dubious.

'Seriously,' Tamar insisted. 'He's the business.' She looked at Eugene for confirmation. He nodded. He was waiting to see where this was going; he had a horrible feeling about this.

'You'll want him, I guarantee it. Otherwise I wouldn't be willing to throw myself in on the deal.'

Satan frowned. 'So, let me get this straight. You're offering me yourself and this character here,' he indicated Stiles. 'Against this soul that I know nothing about as yet, is that right?'

'I'll convert, or whatever it takes, yes.'

This was too good to miss. Barely hesitating Satan put out a hand to shake and Tamar extended hers more slowly. But before they could grasp hands, Eugene dashed Tamar's hand away.

'What are you doing?' she gasped crossly.

Eugene ignored her. 'Take me,' he addressed Satan.

'And why you?'

'Look at me,' commanded Eugene. 'Really look. Compare me to her. I'm no hero. I'm a miserable craven coward.'

Satan looked. Eugene shivered as that piercing gaze stripped him down to his bare naked soul and beyond. 'Hmm.'

Eventually Satan shook his head. 'I don't see …'

'My real name might change your mind.' Eugene told him.

Satan laughed uproariously 'What's in a name?' he demanded. 'I have seen who you really are, you have never done evil, nor do you have the courage to do so. Not like her.'

'You're wrong,' said Eugene quietly. 'In fact, we've met before Lucifer.' Satan started. No one had used his real name to his face for centuries beyond count, and never in that familiar way. 'Who are you then?' he asked with a weak pretence at indifference, although it was clear that his whole being was vibrating with curiosity, and not a little fear. Tamar leaned forward, her eyes intent on Satan's face.

'Let's just say, you are not the only angel of your rank to fall from grace, although I did not fall as far as you. I never suffered from your pride.' As he spoke his face changed – became so bright that it defied the gaze and his eyes burned, until his glance was like a bolt of lightning, yet stern and cool and full of ancient pity.

Satan shied backwards, his hands over his face. 'Ahhh.'

The vision shrank, dimmed and became Eugene again. 'I was punished for my sins, and that punishment I accepted with good grace, content to serve my sentence on earth. I was banished, and my very name was forgotten by all but the very few. Even I forgot who I once was, until now, for the slate was wiped clean and I became only what you see now and no more. Immortal I remained for the nature of a thing cannot be changed except by the will and death frightened me, because of my sins, although I did not remember them. And now it comes, and I am not afraid. Will you take me in her place now?'

'Yes.' He had a greedy look on his face.

'Be careful Lucifer, by your own greed you may yet be undone, and the soul we offer in our place is more to your taste than a thousand fallen angels. Only Judas was more evil by your lights, and yet not by ours, for he was but a man, and men are weak, and we pity them.'

'Show him to me.'

'Seal the deal,' insisted Tamar. She would deal with the fact that Eugene was a former angel later, when she had time for a fit of hysterics – she did not now. 'And I want Jack's soul back *and* his life if you take the other.'

'Agreed,' said Satan after some hesitation. He produced a scroll. 'Standard deal with the Devil form,' he said, 'just need to change the wording a bit.'

The scroll was duly signed – in blood. An affectation which Tamar regarded with barely concealed scorn.

Eugene turned to Tamar after it was done. 'You won't tell the others, will you?' he asked anxiously.

'Tell them what?' she said, her face blank.

'Ah!'

* * *

'What the hell just happened?' Denny was the first to speak, but Tamar hushed him.

'It's not over yet,' she told him. 'At least, I hope …'

The door on the other side of the room opened, not the one Stiles had blown through but the one leading to the garden. Tamar raised her head hopefully.

It was Cindy who came through. 'I thought I'd better …' The words died on her lips when she saw their faces. In the silence, there could be heard an occasional muffled sob from Hecaté.

Cindy went toward her and tentatively put an arm around her. 'Of all the things,' she found herself thinking, 'I never expected to find myself comforting a god, least of all my own god.' It was an uncomfortable feeling. If the gods we pray to are subject to pain and grief – what are they to us?

She raised her head and caught Tamar's eye. 'What happened?' she mouthed. 'Where's Eugene?' Tamar bowed her head, her impression of what exactly had happened was fuzzy, but she was certain that Eugene had offered his soul in exchange for hers and was in Hell now and forever. Satan had managed to cheat her. Why had she allowed him to do it, she could not think, and what was she going to tell Cindy?

Denny put his arm around her. 'It's over,' he told her gently 'Time to tell us what happened.'

* * *

When she had finished her story her eyes went to Cindy pleadingly 'Hate me,' they said. 'Blame me, anything but that terrible pity.' For Cindy looked indeed as if she felt terribly sorry for Tamar.

Then she smiled distantly. 'Who would have thought he had it in him?' she said. 'This is all your fault,' she told Denny.

Tamar was outraged. 'How can you say that? It was *my* fault.'

'No, no, dear,' smiled Cindy, 'I didn't mean it, it was a joke. It was nobody's fault. But Denny knows what I mean, don't you?'

'He was trying to prove something,' said Denny. 'He picked a hell of a time I must say. I don't know if I could have done what he did.' Denny looked quizzically at Tamar, she seemed to have been deliberately vague about the details of Eugene's sacrifice. But now, he deemed, in front of Cindy, was not the time to press her about it.

Hecaté spoke then. 'Perhaps all things have a purpose after all,' she said 'I have never suffered grief before. Perhaps now I shall understand better the grief of others.' She smiled wanly at Cindy. 'You and I understand each other better now, do we not? As could never have been had I not also lost my Jack.'

Cindy wept.

Denny fingered the Athame with a grim look on his face. He looked at Tamar, but she shook her head slowly. 'Perhaps I'm selfish,' she said. 'But I don't want to lose you too. I don't want to feel like that.' She indicated the weeping Cindy and Hecaté. 'Besides ... it – it's not like that, you can't just ...' she broke off suddenly and gave a cry of surprise. Denny spun. Cindy and Hecaté followed his gaze and stared open mouthed.

'What's up?' said Stiles. 'You all look like you've seen a ghost.'

'Well, you at least, shouldn't be surprised,' he said, meaning Tamar. He nodded at Eugene coming up behind him from the garden.

'I have a message for you,' Eugene said. '"A deal's a deal," he said, "but it will have to be paid for." I promised to tell you, but I wouldn't worry about it. He's all brag and bounce that one. Besides, if I'm any judge he's got his hands full now.'

Tamar stared at him for a second filled with wonder as she remembered, briefly, all that had happened.

Eugene put his fingers to his lips with a conspiratorial smile and then she forgot again. Then he turned to Cindy, who looked slightly ashamed.

'I – I ...' she began. But he hushed her. 'It doesn't matter now.' He said with the air of one who had given the final word on the subject, although this was doubtful. However, it hushed her for now.

Stiles managing to break free of Hecaté's fervent attentions for a second looked around the room perplexedly, the others broke into a jabber of explanation none of which he followed. But, as it turned out, it wasn't Askphrit's fate that interested him. 'Where's that little bastard Peirce gone?' he asked when he could get a word in.

'Peirce?' said Denny, wheeling sharply, and fixing Stiles with a glare, 'He was here?'

'Yes.'

'Not when I arrived.'

'And there's no need to look at me like that'

'Sorry.' Denny adjusted his face.'

'Tamar sighed 'Don't tell me, we've got to go and hunt up that little weasel now, haven't we done enough? I would have thought we'd earned a bit of a rest.'

'Leave him to me,' said Stiles, purloining Tamar's favourite phrase of old. 'I made him a promise that I'd like to deliver in person.'

'Fine,' said Tamar, 'but we've got to find him first.'

'You're not serious?' hissed Denny. 'He's a good bloke in a fight and all, but Peirce, well, he's, well not to put too fine a point on it, if you'll excuse the pun, heartless. How's he going to kill him?'

'Don't underestimate Jack' she said, 'He's got – ingenuity.'

'Okay, so how are we going to find him?'

'He'll come to us,' she grinned. 'That's quantum.'

It happened so fast that it was over before anyone had time to react. Peirce grabbed Tamar by the hair, and his fangs were in her neck as they rose together off the ground and out of the window and away. They were staggered by the swiftness of it. Denny let out an inarticulate cry and ran forward to the window. But it was too late they were gone.

~ Chapter Twenty Four ~

TAMAR LAY ON the floor of the ancient bell tower, an old hiding place of Peirce's. Nobody ever thought to look for a vampire in a church even a disused one that had long since been used by nothing but the bats and crows. It hurt a little, the remnants of holiness in the place but not too bad, particularly up here, and it was worth it. He felt totally secure watching Tamar dying on the dusty floorboards, with a gloating expression on his face. Soon she would begin to stir, and then she would be his forever. He preened a little, for the first time in centuries he wished he could use a mirror.

Still he was a handsome devil, he knew that, and she would think so too, without her soul, she would soon forget that mortal and be like himself, bound to nothing but her own lusts, of which he intended to be one.

He was so wrapped up in these pleasant thoughts that he did not notice the figure of Tamar rising up behind him like an avenging angel.

* * *

Denny sat on the floor staring vacantly ahead. Then he closed his eyes and frowned.

Stiles came up behind him. 'Come on mate,' he said, placing a wary hand on Denny's shoulder. 'Now's not the time to despair.'

'I'm not,' said Denny shortly.

Stiles stepped back and looked at the others, shrugging.

Suddenly Denny stood up in one smooth motion that Stiles would have given his eyeteeth to be able to do, and announced. 'Got him!' Then he vanished in a small whirlwind.

* * *

When Denny arrived in the tower, Tamar dropped to the floor like a stone and lay still.

Peirce was a little put out (he had not wanted interruptions) but not really worried. What could happen? It was too late for anything but revenge, and Pierce knew he could not be killed by mortal hands.

'Oh, it's you,' he said languidly. 'How on earth did you find me?'

Denny pushed him aside and ran to Tamar.

'I wouldn't if I were you,' Peirce told him. 'She'll be awake in a minute, and she'll be very, very hungry.' Denny stepped back and gave Peirce a horrified glance.

'Why?' he croaked, looking back at Tamar's inert form.

Peirce studied his long, thin, white fingers for a moment before answering. 'Because I want her,' he said, simply. 'I should have thought that was obvious. Once before, you know, I wanted someone, as much as I now want her, but back then I was different, I had only just been made, and she was a woman I had loved as a mortal. Do you know, I can't remember what that felt like now, so long ago, so long. Anyway, I let her go, I couldn't do it. A decision I have since regretted. What place is there in my world for pity? I am a vampire. What I want, I take. After many lonely years, I swore that never should I stay my hand again if I should find another woman such as she was. I never thought I would.' He shrugged. 'But I did, and now she's mine.'

'She wasn't yours to take.'

'Yours?'

'Nor mine, you had no right.'

'So, kill me then. Ah but you can't, what a pity, if you could, you might still save her. But one so versed in his vampire lore would know that wouldn't he?' Kill me before the dawn, and you'll get her back, just as she was. But I'm taunting you, how very uncivilised of me.' Denny charged, blinded by rage. Peirce stepped lightly out of the way, like a bullfighter taunting a maddened bull, right into Tamar's waiting arms.

'Maybe *he* can't kill you,' she hissed as she snapped his head back sharply, 'but *I* can.' And she sank her fangs into his neck and drained him, spitting out the old dead blood before it could poison her. Peirce crumbled to dust before he even had a chance to make a mess of her shirt.

Denny took a step toward her, but she held her hands out in a gesture of denial. 'No, don't come near me, I can smell your blood from here, and I'm hungry. So hungry I could die all over again. I can hear your heartbeat. It's driving me crazy, please stay back. It didn't work. I'm still a vampire.'

Denny shook his head. 'Not yet,' he said. 'We won't know until the dawn, that's when the transformation occurs.'

'I don't understand.'

'Your sire is dead,' Denny explained, 'and it happened before the dawn, which is when the transformation occurs, which means at dawn you will revert to human form instead of becoming a vampire, as is usual. Although you would only be a half vampire until you made your first kill. If your sire dies before you make your first kill, again, you revert to humanity. But once you make that kill, nothing can save you.'

'*He* was my first kill,' said Tamar dully, pointing to the pile of dust and ashes at her feet, a by now, familiar sight. 'What does that mean, am I saved or not?'

'Only the dawn will tell,' said Denny. 'This has never happened before, that I know of.' He gave a short laugh, devoid of amusement. 'Trust you for that.'

'Then I'll wait for the dawn,' she said. 'If it takes my soul with it, it will also take my body.' She glanced at his stricken face. 'It's the only way. Try to understand, I can't be a vampire. I can't live that way. I don't want there to be even one second when I don't know what it is to love you. It wouldn't be right.'

Denny bowed his head.

'Now, please go.'

He vanished. And Tamar went outside to sit on the ancient gravestones and await the dawn.

'Bloody Hell,' she thought glancing at her watch, five hours to go, 'I wish I'd brought a good book.'

* * *

The clock ticked interminably as Denny sat miserably on his bed waiting, waiting, waiting for the dawn, which seemed to have made its mind up to take itself off to Mexico for a sabbatical and not come back until the weather improved. He had not felt this helpless in a long time. Not since before she came.

When he had returned, he had answered the questioning looks with a terse. 'Too late.' Only adding, when pressed by Stiles, 'Peirce is dead,' before sloping off upstairs.

He realised now, as he thought about it, that he had left them with the impression that he was the one who had disposed of Peirce, still he supposed it did not really matter. Nothing mattered anymore. He resisted the temptation to lift out his books, to pore over them in hopes of finding an answer which he knew they did not contain. It was as he had said. Only the dawn could tell. And before that he had to face the apparently unending night.

Strange thoughts assailed him.

'What if the sun never came up again? A thought he had not had since childhood, when the nights had seemed so long as he listened to his drunken father rant at his mother and the walls of his life seemed to close in around him. Those nights had been long, but not like this. 'God, was a night ever so long?' He felt like that other Denny, the small Denny who had always been so afraid, like the teenage Denny who had always felt so inadequate. But he was not the same; he would never be the same, because of her. *Please let her be all right*. And what if she's not? He forced himself to face it because he would have to go on, whether he wanted to or not, because of what she had shown him about himself. That he was not a coward or useless, because he could do things that others could not, not because of the Athame, which was just a toy – a tool. But because he *would* do them; and others would not. She had called him a hero. He baulked at the term, but he knew what she meant by it. And one day, he would die doing what he did. Right now, there was some comfort in the thought.

His thoughts turned to vengeance, but there was no comfort there. Pierce was dead, or destroyed, as you prefer. And Askphrit was in Hell, who else was there to blame? Only himself, and he was suffering enough. 'God, was a night ever this long?'

* * *

Downstairs the others were sat in a silent circle of grief. They held hands, none of them felt the slightest inclination to move or speak. Where was there to go? What was there to say? Somehow, despite his defeat, in releasing Pierce, Askphrit had won. Suddenly Hell did not seem nearly punishment enough, even to Stiles, who had had a taste of its horror.

Not one of them felt any urge to intrude on Denny's sorrow, not that they did not care, but if he wanted to be alone, let him. He had earned it. And because they did not know to consciously wait for the dawn, for them at least, it crept up on them unawares and all too fast.

* * *

About an hour after dawn, Denny slowly descended the stairs. The living room, where the others had congregated, was still dark. When the sunlight had first begun to fill the room, like an unwelcome intruder on their grief Cindy had risen and pulled the heavy curtains across. This was no time for dancing sunbeams; it had felt like an insult. Denny wandered in and automatically pulled the curtains open. He was heavy eyed and walked like a man asleep. The sunlight smote him like a slap in the face. It was true then; the long awaited dawn had finally come, and had brought with it no Tamar. It was over.

There was a knock at the front door, and it was Eugene who went to answer it. Seconds later he was yelling. 'Denny come quick.'

Galvanized, but not daring to hope – Tamar had no use for doors, at least not in her own house – Denny ran to the door to be confronted with an elderly man, who stood twisting his cap around in his hands. 'She's in the car,' he said. 'She asked to be brought here, 'though I reckon she needs a hospital, if you ask me, but she was so insistent like. But I've never seen owt like it. If I didn't know better, I'd say she didn't have a skerrick of blood left in her, but o' course, she'd be dead, if that were the case. Now – oh there you are sir.' He turned to Denny, who was carrying his precious burden back to the house, and was about to repeat everything he had just said, but Denny hurried past him into the house. The man touched his cap, having replaced it on his head and made to leave.

Eugene grabbed his wrist. 'Thank you,' he said. 'Never fear, you did the right thing – here.' He fumbled in his pocket, but he found it empty. Stiles, who had been hot on Denny's heels, produced his wallet, but the old man was insulted. 'Put that away,' he growled, as if Stiles had opened his flies unexpectedly in a convent school. 'I dint do it for that. What kind of a worl' would it be eh, if'n you can't help your fellow creatures without wantin' a reward?'

Denny had reappeared at the door, to tell them that it looked as if Tamar would be okay. He had left her holding the Athame, and he heard this speech. He smiled; perhaps there were more heroes in the world than he had thought.

'She's going to be okay,' he told the man. 'Thanks to you.'

The old man's face creased into a smile. 'Ah,' said he. 'That's all the reward I wanted. I'll be on my way now sir, if that's all right.' He quite naturally addressed his remarks to Denny as if the others were not even there, Denny had this effect nowadays, he tended to fill the foreground of people's minds.

'Of course,' said Denny. 'I'm sure you must be busy,' he winked at the old man, and they looked at each other as if recognising something of themselves in the other – they understood each other. The old man turned to go. 'Wait,' Denny called. The old man turned inquiringly. 'Could I have your name? I'm sure she'll want to thank you herself, when she's fully recovered.'

'I'm Arthur Charpentier,' said the old man, surprisingly. 'I'm always around, not hard to find.'

Denny grinned. 'Rescuing kittens stuck in trees?' he asked. 'Saving drowning children?'

The old man grinned back. 'Ah, you're a card you are,' he said. 'I reckon you know the score all right. Well, be seein' you.' And he trotted back to his car.

'Yes,' muttered Denny. 'I have a feeling we will.'

* * *

Tamar lay asleep in the vast over decorated, gilded four poster bed that she had chosen when they had gone over the house together. Denny hated the bed, more so at the moment because it was so large and so piled up with overstuffed bedding of every description, even having a large bolster, that Tamar looked fearfully tiny and frail lying in it by herself. Denny had been sat with her since she had come home and he would stay here until she was better.

Downstairs, Stiles had found a TV set and was introducing Eugene to the delights of televised snooker. Cindy and Hecaté were in the kitchen, making themselves useful and showing every sign of being firmly ensconced for the foreseeable future. Stiles and Eugene did not know it yet, but it would be their turn in the kitchen tomorrow.

Denny knew they were still there. They would not leave again, he knew. Although nothing had been said, and probably nothing would ever be said, this would be their home also from now on. Perhaps it was for the best, and the place was certainly big enough. Each couple could take a wing each and never have to see any of the others for weeks at a time if they did not want to.

Tamar stirred and opened her eyes. 'Hi.'

'Hello you,' Denny smiled the smile of a reprieved man. 'Feeling better?'

'Yes, lots.' She sat up.

'You look better,' he observed, and she did, but not the same, his worried eyes noted. She grinned, reading his thought.

She would never be the same, she knew. Her other brushes with death had not affected her in the same way as this one. This time, something inside had broken. Never again would she condemn weakness in others, she had been shown the inner weakness of her own soul, and it had taught her compassion, her pride was humbled permanently. Denny saw the change but did not know what it meant. He was not sure that he liked it.

'What I don't understand is how on earth you made it home in that condition,' he said. 'You were in Ireland you know.'

'Was I? I don't really remember much after the dawn came and I was so relieved to still be here. Then I realised that I was completely exsanguinated. I can laugh about it now, but I tell you, I never felt so stupid, not to have realised that if I did become human again, having no blood left in my body might be a bit of a problem.'

'I should have thought of it, myself,' said Denny. 'I can't believe I didn't.'

'Yes, you're supposed to be the clever one.'

'So, how did you get back here?'

'I honestly don't remember. I collapsed outside the churchyard, and I have an impression of a man bending over me ...'

'An old man – flat cap?'

'Yes, how did you know?'

'Hmm.'

'I have an idea that I asked him to take me home, but I couldn't swear to it, I think I passed out. Then I woke up here. Denny, what's the matter?'

Denny shook himself. 'No, nothing.' He changed the subject. 'I wonder where Pierce ended up. Do you think he's in Hell too?'

'I don't know. Probably though, from what he told of us of his past history, he was almost certainly a Christian before he was turned.'

'Oh, who cares, so long as he doesn't come back here.' She didn't want to talk about him, he saw. He changed the subject again. 'You're making a bad habit of this,' he told her. 'Almost dying on me, I mean.'

She smiled at him, and there was something in her smile now, that would never be absent again, Denny wondered what it was. That part of her mind was closed to him, for now.

'This will almost certainly be the last time,' she said. She cocked her head at him. 'Although, never say never eh?'

Denny started. She was right – Askphrit was stuck in hell, Pierce was gone. It was over. What would they do with themselves now?

She picked up the train of his thought. 'Back to ordinary heroing eh?' she said.

'That's not even a word,' he told her.

'Certainly it is. Webster's dictionary defines it as 'Acts of bravery that ordinary people do, because they can. Whether they want to or not.'

'Or something like that.' Denny agreed.

* * *

When he went downstairs, Denny noticed a glow from the living room; he wandered in and saw that the computer was still on. He leaned over and touched the icon on the screen, it flashed up for a moment, before the screen went dark.

'Close file.'

~ Epilogue ~

ASKPHRIT SURVEYED his new surroundings. He was surprisingly – no, *amazingly* calm. So, it wasn't the Ritz, but his time in prison had been worse. Here, he had his own room, hot and cold running devils – mostly hot. No, not too bad at all.

And Satan seemed an okay sort of creature. He seemed inclined to treat Askphrit more as a sort of favourite than anything else.

He was jaded, Askphrit decided, he had been in this job too long. He did not seem to get any pleasure out of it any more. Security was lax and the torments done by rote – a mere matter of form, with little enthusiasm. Some of the devils, he discovered, resented this, and the fact that there was no chance, any longer, for promotion for the inventive and enthusiastic devil. There had been no promotions in hell for an eternity, he was told. He moved among the employees and inmates of hell alike like a campaigning politician. And he found out more about Hell than Satan ever knew.

He also employed a fiercely resentful Pierce as an extra pair of eyes and ears.

Askphrit had not been surprised to see Pierce arrive shortly after himself. 'Thought they'd get you, without me to keep an eye on you.' Was the extent of what he had to say about it. He did not bother to ask how it had happened. And he did not tell Peirce what had happened to him. That was the past, and the thing to do now was assess the future.

It was Askphrit's nature to look at every place from the point of view of its strategic usefulness. This place, he decided, had possibilities.

COMING SOON

IT'S THE END OF THE WORLD....

Don't believe me? Heard it all before?

No seriously, it's the end of the world ... or it should be.

But someone dropped the ball and now ...

Well, the end of the world might have to be postponed ... indefinitely.

Pandora's Box has gone missing, and without the release of the hopes of man the world cannot end.

So with the world stuck in a war that's going nowhere and the four horsemen of the apocalypse waiting around cooling their heels, the clerks in mainframe are in a panic and are scouring the world for it.

Of course, no one *wants* the world to end. Least of all Tamar and co but can they find Pandora's Box before the clerks in mainframe do?

And she might have known that Askphrit would be at the bottom of it all somehow.

About the Author

Nicola Rhodes often can't remember where she lives so she lives inside her own head most of the time, where even if you do get lost, it's still okay.

She has met many interesting people inside her own head and eventually decided to introduce the rest of the world to them, in the hopes that they would stop bothering her and let her sleep.

She has been doing this for ten years now but they still won't leave her alone.

You have her full permission to read whatever you wish into this work of fiction. As she says herself:

"Just because I wrote this book, doesn't mean I know anything about it."

SCI'ON – The Shadow Worlds

Whenever a decision is taken that is of significance to the world, the world divides and two alternate futures are created.

In the beginning, there was only one world. That world we name SCI 'ON. All other worlds that sprang from it we name the Shadow Worlds.

Some believe SCI 'ON is the only real world and that all others are mere reflections; hence the name. Others believe that all the alternate worlds are equally real and important – however they may have come into being.

Whatever the case, one thing is certain. If SCI 'ON itself – the cradle of creation – were to be destroyed, all other worlds would cease to exist. For SCI 'ON is the mainspring and without it, the shadow worlds would have no point of origin.

*

Johnny Hammond is not your ordinary computer nerd. He has the makings of a hero.

When a mysterious man shows him the way to SCI 'ON Johnny becomes obsessed. And only he can find a way to get there through the myriad of shadow worlds that stand in his way.

But someone does not want him to get there.

*

From earliest childhood, Ryan and Kai have been best friends. The fact that they come from separate universes is not allowed to stand in their way.

As they grow up, they realise that this ability to travel between the worlds is no mere coincidence, as their ultimate destiny unfolds.

www.ingramcontent.com/pod-product-compliance
Lightning Source LLC
Chambersburg PA
CBHW050416260626
47156CB00003B/1038